IN THE PATH
OF THE FANTASY WAVE

As he scrambled to his feet, Brother Paul saw the Animation curtain extending visibly toward them, seeming to accelerate. The faerie city was sprouting suburbs, and a broad, tree-lined avenue was unrolling head-on. Time was disappearing like the final dregs of a draining tub . . .

Now the nova-bugs clustered around a new horror. Paul saw with dismay that it was the creature he had first encountered on this planet, the Breaker!

It was bounding toward him, using its tail as a pushing leg . . .

VISION OF TAROT
The second adventure on
the miracle planet TAROT
PIERS ANTHONY

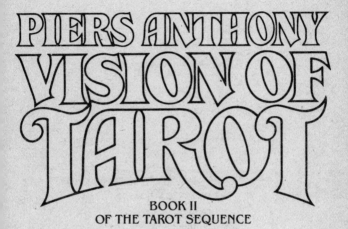

PIERS ANTHONY
VISION OF TAROT

BOOK II
OF THE TAROT SEQUENCE

BERKLEY BOOKS, NEW YORK

VISION OF TAROT

A Berkley Book / published by arrangement with
the author

PRINTING HISTORY
Berkley edition / January 1980
Fifth printing / June 1983
Sixth printing / April 1984
Seventh printing / October 1984
Eighth printing / July 1985
Ninth printing / December 1985

ISBN: 0-425-08097-8

A BERKLEY BOOK ® TM 757,375
Berkley Books are published by The Berkley Publishing Group,
200 Madison Avenue, New York, New York 10016.
The name "BERKLEY" and the stylized "B" with design
are trademarks belonging to Berkley Publishing Corporation.
PRINTED IN THE UNITED STATES OF AMERICA

**Dedicated to
the Holy Order of Vision**

Acknowledgments

Author's Note:

This is the second volume of the three-part, quarter-million word novel of Tarot. Though this segment is unified around the religious and social theme, it is not a complete story in itself, and it is hoped the reader will be interested enough to read the first and third volumes. The first is *God of Tarot*, concerning the nature of the challenge; the third is Faith of Tarot, concerning the nature of Hell. Some reprise of the first volume may be helpful for those who have not seen it:

Brother Paul is a novice in the Holy Order of Vision, a liberal religious sect dedicated to the improvement of the state of man. His superior in the Order, the Reverend Mother Mary, sends him on a mission to Planet Tarot to determine whether the Deity manifesting there is or is not God. Brother Paul discovers numerous schismatic sects on the planet, often at odds; yet the rigors of colony life require all people to cooperate closely or perish. They must identify the true God. Brother Paul becomes the guest of the Reverend Siltz of the Second Church Communist, whose son has taken up with a Scientologist: a local scandal. Brother Paul encounters Amaranth, an extraordinarily pretty and forward worshiper of Abraxas, the snake-footed god. Brother Paul experiments with the notorious Animation effect, controlling it by means of tarot cards, but gets trapped in full-scale visions relating to his own base nature and past experiences that led to his conversion to the religious life. He realizes that his own soul may be likened to compost: the raw stuff of transition from death to renewal.

The present volume commences with Brother Paul's emergence from that play-like vision.

VISION OF TAROT
TABLE OF CONTENTS

1

Discipline: 9

. . . *he found himself reflecting—not for the first time—on the peculiarities of adults. They took laxatives, liquor, or sleeping pills to drive away their terrors so that sleep would come, and their terrors were so tame and domestic: the job, the money, what the teacher will think if I can't get Jennie nicer clothes, does my wife still love me, who are my friends. They were pallid compared to the fears every child lies cheek and jowl with in his dark bed, with no one to confess to in hope of perfect understanding but another child. There is no group therapy or psychiatry or community social services for the child who must cope with the thing under the bed or in the cellar every night, the thing which leers and capers and threatens just beyond the point where vision will reach. The*

same lonely battle must be fought night after night
and the only cure is the eventual ossification of the
imaginary faculties, and this is called adulthood.
    —Stephen King: *'Salem's Lot*, New York:
Doubleday and Company, 1975.

The landscape of Planet Tarot formed about them.
They stood in a kind of scrub forest. A few large trunks
rose from the underbrush, but these were dead and
charred. Some fire must have swept through the area a
decade past, destroying most of the large trees and all of
the small ones, forcing the forest to start over. This was
not necessarily an evil thing; after many years of
fighting forest fires back on Earth, the authorities had
realized that forest fires were part of nature's cycle,
literally clearing out the deadwood to make place for
fresh growth. The big stumps, here, might resemble
buildings in the half light, and the forest was like a city
here was the raw material of the Animation just past.
    Brother Paul looked behind him. They were actually
in a hollow beside the clifflike face of a rocky ridge.
Here was even more direct raw material; a moment ago
it had seemed like a brick wall, and his companion—
    Brother Paul turned to the man. "I am not certain I
know you," he said. *Not in this world, anyway.*
    His companion was a colonist he had not encountered
in the village, a tall, thin, handsome young man,
bronzed and healthy. "I am Lee, Church of Jesus Christ
Latter Day Saints," he said. "I am one of the Watchers."
    "Ah—Mormon," Brother Paul said. "At one time I
mistook you for—" He broke off, not wanting to mention the Fed narc. "But that's irrelevant."
    "Let's move out before the rent in the Animation fills
in," Lee said. "We would not want to be trapped
again." He led the way, walking briskly. But in a
moment he added: "What we experienced appears to be
a hitherto unknown aspect of Animation. I was once
called a member of your sect, though I really can not
claim to know anything about your religion. I gather

this was a reinactment of the experience that brought you into that Order."

"Yes," Brother Paul agreed, surprised. "I was partially blind for several days, because, they said, I had stared into the sun too long. I think it was more subtle than that; my namesake the Apostle Paul was similarly blind after his conversion. Perhaps the drug and my general condition complicated it. The Holy Order of Vision took care of me, and treated me with the memory drug and kindness, phasing down the dosage of the one and phasing up the dosage of the other until I was stable again. I never did recover all my memories. But by then I knew my destiny. I have never regretted that decision."

Lee smiled, grasping the concept. "As the Apostle Paul joined the Christians he had persecuted—"

"So I joined the Order I had wronged," Brother Paul agreed. "In the process I became a Christian in the truest sense. I regret exceedingly that Sister Beth had to die in order to facilitate my conversion—"

"I am sure you have filled her place admirably," Lee said. "We can not know the meaning of God's every act. We only know that there *is* meaning. Why did God allow the Apostle Paul to stone Stephen? Had I been there, I would surely have deemed Stephen a better spokesman for Christianity than a lame epileptic Pharisee Jew." He smiled. "Which shows how little I would have known. Only God is omniscient."

"Amen," Brother Paul agreed, discovering new insight. "The Apostle Paul made Christianity what it is, to a considerable extent. He opened it up to the gentiles. That seemingly minor though controversial change made all the difference."

"It did indeed," Lee agreed. "Perhaps you also will benefit your sect and the world as the Apostle your namesake did."

"A ludicrous dream," Brother Paul said. "Only God knows what an imperfect vessel I am. How much of my Animation did you share?" Brother Paul found that he liked this man, and hoped the horrors of his personal

Animations had not been shown to him. Some secrets were best kept secret.

"Just fragments of it, I think. A game called Tarot Accordian—I do not use cards for entertainment, but I do not pass judgment." He paused. "Do all these episodes represent past experiences in your life or are some allegorical?"

"Some are real; some are sheer fantasy," Brother Paul said, embarrassed. If Lee had seen any of the nightmare visions, he was evidently too discreet to admit it.

"I inquire," Lee said with a certain diffidence, "because something very strange happened to me, and I wonder whether you might explain it. I felt—it was as though another personality impinged on me. An alien consciousness, not inimical, not unpleasant, but rather an exceedingly well informed mind from a distant sphere using my body and perceptions—"

"Antares!" Brother Paul exclaimed.

Lee looked at him, startled. "How did you know?"

"I—cannot explain. But I met a creature from Sphere Antares. He said he might visit me here, or at least I wanted him to—" Brother Paul spread his hands. "A foolish expectation; I apologize."

"Foolish, perhaps. Yet it is an experience I seem to have shared. I don't profess to understand it, but I do not regret it; the alien has a cosmopolitan view I rather envy." He pointed ahead. "Look—there are the Watchers."

And there they were: Pastor Runford, Mrs. Ellend, and the Swami. "But where are the others?" Brother Paul asked. "The ones drawn *into* the Animations, as you were? We can't leave them. . . ."

"No, we can't," Lee agreed as they came up to the Watchers. "Watchers, did you perceive the nature of the Animations we have experienced?"

Pastor Runford shook his head. "We did not."

Brother Paul was relieved. "We have—seen things too complex to discuss at the moment. Several people remain. We need to get them out before—"

Pastor Runford shook his head again, more emphatically. "We can not enter the Animation area. The young woman you call Amaranth went in to warn you about the storm, and—"

"I understand," Brother Paul said. "I'll go back and find them."

"I, too," the Swami said. "We had to retreat during the storm, but for the moment the effect seems to have abated."

Lee was already on the way. The three spread out, searching the landscape that had been a metropolis moments ago—and might be again if the Animation effect returned. Speed was essential.

They found Therion first. He was sitting beneath a tree, looking tired. "That was some scene you folks cooked up," he called.

"I did not arrange it," Lee protested. "I merely played roles assigned to me by the playwright. Some were diabolical—therefore I assumed they originated with you." He did not smile.

"I gather you two do not get along well," Brother Paul said.

"Few of us get along well with rival sects," Lee admitted. "That is the problem of this colony. It is the same all over Planet Tarot; our village is typical. Everywhere we co-exist with ill-concealed distemper. This man is a devotee of the nefarious Horned God—whom I would call Satan."

"A Devil-worshiper!" Brother Paul exclaimed. "That explains a lot!"

"The Horned God was great before any of your contemporary upstarts appeared," Therion maintained, walking with them. "You call him Satan—but that is your ignorant vanity. He is a God—and perhaps the true God of Tarot."

"Sacrilege!" Lee cried. "The Prince of Evil!"

"Listen, Mormon—your own sect is none too savory!" Therion snapped. "A whole religion based on a plagiarized fairy tale—"

Lee whirled on him—but Brother Paul interposed himself. "Doesn't your Covenant forbid open criticism of each other's faiths?"

"I never subscribed to that Covenant," Therion said. "Anyway, I don't find fault with *all* this hypocrite's cult-tenets. Take this business of polygamy—that's a pretty lusty notion. A man takes thirty, forty wives, screws them all in turn—*that's* religion!"

"I have no wives," Lee said stiffly.

"Because there aren't enough girl-Mormons on this planet, and none free in this village! But if there were, you'd have them, wouldn't you?"

"The matter is academic," Lee replied.

"But if it were *not*—if you had the chance to wed just as many young, pretty, sexy, healthy women as was physically possible, how many would you take?"

"One," Lee said. "Plural marriage is an option, not a requirement. A single woman, were she the right one, would be worth more than a hundred wrong ones. I will marry the right one."

"You're a hypocrite, all right," Therion said. "I wish I could conjure a hundred wrong women and show you up for—"

Further discussion was cut off by their discovery of Amaranth. She was standing by a streamlet, looking dazed. "Amaranth," Brother Paul said, struck by her beauty, afresh, though of course he had now had opportunity to appreciate her charms unhampered by any clothing. (Or *had* he . . . ?) It had once been said that clothes make the man, but it seemed more aptly said that clothes make the woman. "Come on out before the Animation effect returns."

She looked at him with evident perplexity. "I don't know—don't know my part. Am I still the fortune teller?"

She *was* confused! "No," Brother Paul said. "We are back in the mundane world. You have no role to play."

"She is always playing a role," Therion muttered.

"What's this about roles?" the Swami asked.

Lee answered him. "It was as though we were in a play, each with his script. Each person could ad-lib, but had to stay within the part. We do not know who the playwright was."

The Swami seemed intensely interested, despite his former cautions about Animation. "To whom did the scenes relate?"

"Well, I seemed to be the central character," Brother Paul said. "Perhaps the others had scenes to which they were central in my absence—"

"No," Amaranth said. "I played my roles only for you. Between roles I—seemed not to exist. Maybe I was sleeping. I thought I had died when I jumped from that copter—"

Brother Paul was uneasy. "Perhaps we should not discuss it in the presence of those who were not involved."

"You *must* discuss it," the Swami said, his gaze fixed. "You are searching for the God of Tarot, for the colonists of this planet."

"It seems I got distracted," Brother Paul admitted.

"I agree with Brother Paul," Lee said. "We have experienced a remarkable joint vision whose implications may never be fully understood, just as the meaning of a person's dream may never be clear. We should maintain our separate experiences, like the members of a jury, until we are ready to make a joint report."

"Yes," Therion said.

The Swami looked from one to the other. "The Devil Worshiper and the Righteous Saint agree?"

"And so do I," Amaranth said. "No one not *in* it can understand it."

"An extraordinary unanimity," the Swami commented. "But I may have an insight. Is it not possible that the power of Kundalini—"

"Remember the Covenant," Therion reminded him gently. Yes, it was evident that these people had little patience with each other's philosophies! Therion had said he did not subscribe to the Covenant and had called Lee a hypocrite. It was becoming clear who the actual hypocrite was.

"I have not forgotten it!" the Swami said with understandable irritation. "But this power, however it may be named—call it the magic of Satan if you prefer—may be the controlling force of your visions.

Brother Paul has the strongest psychic presence of your group, so it seems the play orients on him.''

"Aura," Lee said. "He has aura."

"This is uncertain," Brother Paul said. "The reality of all we have experienced in Animation is speculative—"

"No, I think he's right," Amaranth said. "There is something about you—"

"We forget the child," Therion said.

"One of the Watchers is a child?" Brother Paul asked. "There was a child in the Animation, but I assumed she was a creature of imagination." Those Dozens insults. . . .

"There were to be five Watchers," Lee explained. "Two outside, and three inside the Animation, representing poles of belief. The child was the third inside."

"I will search for her!" the Swami said, alarmed.

"We *all* will search, of course," Lee said. "We have wasted time; the Animation may close in at any moment."

They spread out, striding through the valley. Therion was farthest to the left. Then Lee, then Brother Paul, then Amaranth, and the Swami on the right. There was no sign of the child.

Therion and Lee drifted further left as the slope of the land changed; he could hear them exchanging irate remarks about each other's religious practices, faintly. The Swami disappeared behind a ridge. This region was more varied than it had seemed to be before; the mists had tended to regularize the visible features in the distance. Brother Paul and Amaranth were funneled together by a narrowing gully. Here the trees were larger; the fire must have missed this section.

It was dusk, and as the sun slowly lost its contest with the lay of the land the shadows deepened into darkness. Flashing insects appeared. They were not Earthly fireflies, but blue-glowing motes expanding suddenly into little white novas, then fading. In that nova stage they illuminated a cubic meter of space and were a real, if transient, aid to human navigation.

"What are those?" Brother Paul inquired.

"Nova-bugs. No one knows how they do it. Scientists shipped a few back to Earth, when they first surveyed this planet, but the lab experts said it was a mistake: the bugs possessed no means to glow. So—they don't exist, officially. But we like them."

"Isn't that just like an expert!" Brother Paul exclaimed. "He can't explain it, so he denies it." Yet this was true of people generally, not only experts. "Do you catch them and use them for lamps as the people used to do with fireflies?"

"We tried, but they won't glow when prisoned," she said. "They tend to stay away from the village, too. This is an unusually fine display; some nights they don't show at all."

"Smart bugs," Brother Paul said. Obviously if the novas performed when tamed, there would soon be no wild ones left.

"You know," Amaranth said somewhat diffidently, "I was caught in the—the play accidentally. I was only coming to warn you of the approach of the storm when you didn't answer the intercom. Then—"

"I understand. You were not an assigned Watcher. I'm sorry you got trapped."

"That's what I wanted to say, now that I've got you alone. I'm *not* sorry it happened. I got to show off my own Tarot deck in spite of the Covenant, and my fortunetelling skills—"

"I believe you have omitted some material between those two," Brother Paul said dryly. "I must apologize for—"

"No, *don't* apologize! I wasn't fooling when I said there's something about you, aura or whatever. Was it during the Animation that I said that? Anyway, I meant it. I have to study you to learn how you tamed the Breaker, but that's become more of an excuse than—well, you're quite a guy, in and out of Animation."

"I should hate to think that *all* those scenes were under my control," Brother Paul said. "Some were all right—"

"Like Sister Beth," she agreed. "I am not of your religion, but after that I wonder whether—"

"But others—well, that one in the castle." He was forcing himself to clarify the worst. "Did I rape you?" As though it were a casual matter!

"You never touched me," she assured him. "More's the pity. You can't rape a willing woman."

Never touched her. . . . That was worse yet. "Still, if it was my will that dictated your participation—"

"I improvised some. It was my role to tempt you, and I tried, I really tried, but Therion kept getting in the way. I like to dress and undress. I like men—well, not men like that stuffed shirt Lee or the fake Swami, but men with guts and drives and—"

"Fake Swami?"

"He's not Indian. I mean not Indian Indian. He's American Indian. So all this talk about Kundalini—"

"His origin doesn't matter," Brother Paul said, conscious again of his own mixed ancestry. "If he sincerely believes in his religion—and I'm sure he does—"

"He's still a fake," she said.

"He's *not* a fake! He showed me the force he has—"

"How did we get on this subject?" she inquired, turning to him. "Let's kiss, and see where we can go from there."

Brother Paul was taken aback. Freed from the limits of her Animation roles, she was fully as forward. "Are you always this direct?"

"Well, yes. Haven't you noticed the way I dress? I've got the physical assets, and I want it known before I get old and saggy and lose my chance in life. But I don't turn on to many men like this. I'll admit there aren't many eligible men in this village, maybe not on this planet. Most are like that old bore Siltz, dull and married and guarding his son's virginity like an angry crocodile." Suddenly it was clear to Brother Paul what her real irritation with Siltz was: his withholding of an eligible young male from the matrimonial market. There were evidently a number of such families here so that young men and women could not find each other. "The religious factor complicates it so terribly—but even so, you're special. There's something about you—maybe it *is* the aura the Swami talks about. The way you handled the Breaker! I mean to seduce you, if it's not against your religion, and maybe you'll like it well enough to want more. Once I have you hooked I'll see about landing you permanently. *Is* trial sex against your religion? I can be more subtle if it is absolutely necessary.''

"Well, the Holy Order of Vision does not specifically prohibit—it's regarded as part of our private lives. But there *is* a certain expectation—well, as Sister Beth said—''

Amaranth sighed. "She *was* a nice girl. Not like me. Was there really such a woman in your past?''

"There really was," Brother Paul agreed. "She was not as pretty as you, but the guilt of her death changed my life. I wish that change had been possible without such a sacrifice—but I always come back to the fact that I can not pretend to comprehend the will of God.''

"That's what the Jehovah's Witnesses say when someone chides them about the end of the world not arriving on schedule. 'Don't second-guess Jehovah!' I think it's a copout. *My* religion is I.A.O., and no priestess of Abraxis is afraid of serpents, literal or figurative, *or* the opinion of a sexist God. So if you ever change your mind, I do give samples.''

There was something at once horrifying and refreshing about her candor. It helped to know exactly where one stood. "Maybe Abraxas will turn out to be the God of Tarot," Brother Paul said. This conversation made him nervous, because Amaranth was simply too attractive, in Animation and in life. More trying was that she had seen him in his elemental being, as a lust-laden male, as a fringe-legal gambler, as a drug addict. She had smelled the shit. She had seen the mask stripped from what he once had been, now hidden behind the facade of a gentle religion—*and she did not condemn him.* Was there another woman in the human sphere who, perceiving his psychic nakedness, the filth of his essence, would not recoil? He had no present intention of indulging her offer—yet he obviously had not felt that way in Animation! Which was his true mind?

There was a scream—an extraordinary, unearthly, nape-prickling effort reverberating around the landscape. Some wild animal—or worse.

"Bigfoot!" Amaranth exclaimed. Then, in dawning horror: "The child!"

Both of them broke into a run toward the sound. The terrain was rougher here, as if to balk them now that they were in more of a hurry. There was a thick undergrowth on the slope—tall weeds, small trees, dense bushes, and root-like projections whose affinities he did not know. Nettles caught at his trousers and made tiny gouges in his skin. He dodged to avoid a small glowing cloud at knee height, then discovered it was only the flowering portion of a forest weed. One foot dropped into a hollow, sending him stumbling headlong—until he fetched up against a horizontal branch he had not seen in the dark.

"No—around this way," Amaranth gasped. "I know this area—some. I've come here with the Breaker, when the Animation retreated. I'm healthy—but I can't run like you."

Naturally not. Few men could run like him, and no women he knew of. This was a problem. She knew the land, but could not keep up. He had power to spare, but was wrecking himself in this unfamiliar dark. They both had to slow down.

There was another scream, worse than the first. "Great God Abraxis!" Amaranth cried. "Save the child—"

Brother Paul lurched ahead, electrified by alarm—and caromed off a dead tree. Bark tore away in his face, the sawdust momentarily blinding him, making his eyes smart fiercely. He *couldn't* accelerate; he'd never get there.

"Go up that gully," Amaranth gasped, creditably close behind. She *was* a good runner—for a woman. "But watch for a rock at the ridge—"

Brother Paul stepped close to her, reached his left arm about her waist, and hauled her up on his hip. He plunged on up the slope, carrying her. "There's the

rock!'' she said. He saw nothing, but climbed out of the
gully. "Now the ridge—it drops a yard—we'll have to
jump—"

He slowed, confused. "Oh—a meter." He found the
ridge, let her down, and they both jumped into the black
shadow. It could have been a bottomless crevasse, like
those on the volcano, as far as his sight was able to tell;
without her assurance he would not have dared risk it.
But his feet struck firm ground.

"Short steep slope, then a level place," she said.
"Then another hill."

At the foot of the ridge he put his arm about her
again, for she was still panting. "I can go some . . . but
God, you've got power!" she cried. "It's not all
physical. . . . Just take some weight off my legs—here."
She adjusted his arm to fit higher about her torso, under
the arms. When he took her weight, she drew close to
his side, close and very soft. But he had to keep moving.

They crested the next hill—to confront a vision. On
the plateau ahead the nova-bugs scintillated in their
myriads, their brief explosions like an intermittent
galaxy. To the left was a faerie city, with tall turrets and
flying buttresses and minarets glowing inherently: obviously an Animation conjured by some one. That
meant the Animation effect was returning, sweeping in
from whatever source it had, like malaria through the
body. Soon it would engulf them. To the right, the
direction of safety from Animation, stood a monster.

The creature was about three meters tall, burly and
hairy. It had the claws of a bear and the gross snout of a
boar. Its feet were human, but disproportionately large.

"Where is the child?" Brother Paul asked.

"Somewhere else," Amaranth said, turning to look.
That brought her left breast under his hand. She was
still breathing hard. "Those were Bigfoot's screams, not
hers; I was afraid it was—"

Now a reaction that had been held in abeyance finally
registered. "Bigfoot! You mean there really *is* a
Bigfoot, not just noise and footprints? A tangible,
visible—?" He dropped his arm.

"There," she said. "It hangs out near Animations."

Meanwhile the curtain of Animation was sweeping forward. The faerie city was beautiful, but horrifying in its implication as it expanded toward them. They could enter it merely by standing still—but how would they exit from it?

"I think the child is either safe—or beyond our help," Brother Paul said. "The former, I hope. I don't see any blood on Bigfoot's paws. We'd better save ourselves—and hope the others are doing likewise. Can you run on the level well enough?"

"I'd better!"

They started across the plateau. But Bigfoot spied them. With another horrendous scream it charged to intercept them. In moments it had placed itself in their path, menacingly. The nova-bugs were concentrated in its vicinity, illuminating it almost steadily.

"I'll try to distract it," Brother Paul said. "You move on by."

"But it'll kill you! Bigfoot's terrible!"

"If you don't move, the Animation will catch you," Brother Paul snapped, advancing on the monster. He was not at all sure he could handle it, but he had to try. The thing was not going to let them pass unchallenged, and there was no room to escape without getting caught by the Animation.

Amaranth looked after him with dismay. Then she put two fingers into her mouth and emitted a piercing whistle.

Bigfoot reacted instantly. It charged her. Brother Paul launched himself between them, catching the side of the monster with his shoulder. It was like ramming a boulder. Bigfoot swung about, swiping at him with a paw, and Brother Paul was hurled aside. This thing was agile as well as massive!

As he scrambled to his feet, shaken but unhurt, Brother Paul saw the Animation curtain extending visibly toward them, seeming to accelerate. The faerie city was sprouting suburbs, and a broad, tree-lined avenue was unrolling head-on. Time was disappearing fast. Yet Bigfoot still cut Amaranth off. If only she hadn't attracted its attention by that foolish whistle!

Now the nova-bugs clustered about a new subject. Apparently they were attacted to anything that moved. Brother Paul saw with dismay that it was the creature he had first encountered on this planet: the Breaker. Worse yet!

The Breaker bounded rapidly toward them, its tail propelling it like a fifth leg. But it had not come to renew the fray with Brother Paul. It launched itself straight at Bigfoot. But Bigfoot was wary of the Breaker, circling about, never staying still for the attack. Evidently these two were natural enemies, but the Breaker seemed to have the advantage.

Then, abruptly, Bigfoot whirled and charged directly into the Animation city, so near. It ran right up the avenue, as though entering a picture. The Breaker did not pursue. Every creature of this planet knew better than to enter Animation voluntarily! Except Bigfoot.

The Breaker now oriented on Brother Paul. Unfinished business? He braced to meet it. *He* was not about to follow Bigfoot into Animation! Now that he knew the Breaker's mode of attack, he should be able to foil it.

But there was no need. Amaranth ran across and set her hand on the Breaker's back, and the creature was passive. "This is *my* Breaker," she explained. "I whistled for him to come help us. I wasn't sure he'd hear, or that he'd come, or what he might do—but I couldn't let you face the monster alone."

She had tamed the predator, all right! "Your strength is greater than mine," Brother Paul said. Then, seeing the city almost upon them: "Now let's run!"

They ran, the Breaker bounding beside Amaranth. The Animation curtain was moving more slowly; soon they left it behind. Now, perversely, Brother Paul grew more curious about what he might have found had he entered that city: an Arabian Nights' fantasy? And he realized that Amaranth and the Breaker had, coincidentally (or was there such a thing as coincidence, when Animation was involved?), just enacted another Tarot card: the one variously termed Strength, Fortitude, Discipline, or Lust, wherein a fair young lady pacified a powerful lion. Was there more than casual meaning in these occurrences?

Lee and Therion had made it out. There was no sign of either the Swami or the child. "Maybe they found another route?" Mrs. Ellend suggested hopefully.

"Pray that it be so," Pastor Runford agreed.

One thing was sure: Brother Paul would never again underrate the potentials of Animation! This was no laboratory curiosity; it was a ravening force.

The party made its way to the village, and Brother Paul returned to Reverend Siltz's home. "There will be a meeting tomorrow," Pastor Runford said as they separated. "There you will make your report. Please do not discuss the matter with others prior to that occasion."

Brother Paul would have been happy never to discuss it with anyone ever. In fact, he would have felt considerably more at ease had he never entered Animation.

Reverend Siltz was at home alone, eating a cold supper. "I hoped you would return safely, and feared you would not," he said. "You must be hungry."

"Yes. I haven't eaten in two days."

Siltz glanced at him, surprised. "When the occasion is proper, I hope to learn of your experience. I understand time can be strange, in Animation."

"The rest of the planet can be strange, too. We encountered Bigfoot—and were saved by the Breaker. I believe I can tell you about that much, since it happened outside of Animation, if you are interested."

Siltz was interested. He was fairly affable. "We shall have to extend our guarding radius. Normally the Breaker will not approach the Animation area, so it is safe to travel there alone, provided one does not actually enter Animation. We did not realize we were subjecting the Watchers to this threat."

"The Breaker did not come on his own. Amaranth whistled for him—and he came to help her. Your colony's decision to try to tame the Breaker instead of eliminating him seems to be paying dividends already."

"So it would seem. She has made far more progress

than we realized. Perhaps we shall tame this planet yet!" Siltz turned up the wood-oil lamp and gave Brother Paul a chunk of wooden bread. "I regret there is no better food since the communal kitchen is closed at this hour. But this is nutritious."

"You know," Brother Paul observed, his gaze passing from the lamp to the unlit wood stove, "with woodheat so critical in winter, I'm surprised you do not use it more efficiently."

Siltz stiffened slightly. "We use it as efficiently as we know. The Tree of Life is exactly that to us: life. Without it we die. What magnitude of improvement did you have in mind?"

"About four hundred per cent," Brother Paul said.

Siltz scowled. "I am in a good mood tonight, but I do not appreciate this humor. We utilize the most efficient stoves available from Earth, and we use the wood, sparingly. Even so, we fear the winter. Each year some villagers miscalculate, or are unfortunate, and we discover them frozen when the snow subsides. To improve on our efficiency five-fold—this is an impossible dream."

"I'm serious," Brother Paul said. It was good to get into this thoroughly mundane subject after the horrors of Animation! "Maybe my recent experience shook loose a memory. You should be able to quintuple your effective heating, or at least extend your wood as much longer as you need. It is a matter of philosophy."

"Philosophy! I am a religious man, Brother, but the burning of wood is very much a material thing, however it may warm the spirit. Such an increase would transform life on this entire planet. If you are not joking: what philosophy can make wood produce more calories per liter?"

"Oh, the wood may burn less efficiently. I was speaking of its usefulness to you, in extending your winter's survival. You are presently wasting most of your heat."

"Wasting it! No one wastes the wood of the Tree of Life!"

"Let me explain. In the Orient, on Earth, there are

regions of extreme climate. Very hot in summer, savage in winter. The Asiatic people developed racial characteristics favoring these conditions: fatty tissue buffering face and body, a smaller nose, yellowed skin, and specially protected eyes. But still the winter was harsh, especially when over-population denuded the resources of the land. Wood and other fuel for heating became scarce, so they learned to use it efficiently. They realized that it was pointless to heat space when it was only the human body that required it. So—''

"One must heat the space of the house in order to heat the body," Siltz said. "We can not simply inject wood calories into our veins!"

"So they designed low, flat stoves, set into the floor, that consumed the fuel slowly, emitting only a little heat at a time," Brother Paul continued. "The family members would lie against the surface of that stove all night, absorbing the heat directly, with very little waste. The room temperature might be below freezing, but the people were warm. And so they avoided the inevitable heat loss incurred, by warming a full house, and extended their fuel supply—''

"I begin to comprehend!" Siltz exclaimed. "Heat the *body*, not the house! Like those electric socks, when I was a lad on Earth. By day we exercise; we do not need the stove, even in winter. It is at night, when we are still, that we freeze. But no one would freeze on an operating stove, getting slowly cooked by it! It would require major reconstruction of our stoves, but it would extend our most valuable asset and save lives. And in the summer, with less wood to haul, we could grow more crops, make more things." He looked at Brother Paul, nodding. "I did not approve your mission here, Brother; but you may have done a remarkable service for our planet this night."

"Not the one I anticipated," Brother Paul said wryly. "But I'm glad if—''

There was an abrupt pounding on the door. "Reverend Siltz, I will talk to you!" a female voice cried.

Siltz's affability vanished. "I am not available!" he called.

"Oh yes you are!" she said, pushing open the door. "I demand to know—"

She broke off, seeing Brother Paul. She was a slip of a girl with dark hair flaring out like an old style afro though her skin was utterly fair, and she fairly radiated indignation. She was not beautiful, but well-structured, and her emotion made her attractively dynamic.

"My house guest, Brother Paul of the Holy Order of Vision," Reverend Siltz said with ironic formality. "Jeanette, of the Church of Scientology."

"The investigator from Planet Earth?"

"Your son's—?" Brother Paul spoke at the same time as the girl.

"The same," Reverend Siltz agreed, answering both. "Now, since we may not discuss religion, and I do not choose to discuss private affairs—"

"Well, *I* choose to discuss both!" Jeanette flared. "What did you do with him?"

Siltz did not answer.

"I am not leaving this house until you tell me where you sent Ivan!" she exclaimed. "I love him—and he loves me!"

The man remained silent. "This does not seem to be an opportune moment to discuss your concern," Brother Paul said to the girl. "You see, you place Reverend Siltz in the position of violating either his hospitality or his commitment to avoid discussing religion in my presence. I am not supposed to be influenced by—"

Jeanette turned on Brother Paul. "Well, maybe someone *should* speak Church to you! How do you expect to do anything for this colony if you don't know anything about it?"

Siltz looked surprised. "She has a point."

"She may, at that," Brother Paul agreed. "But as long as this Covenant of yours is in force, it behooves us to honor it."

"I will bring up the matter at the meeting

tomorrow," Siltz said. "One does not have to agree with a given mission to prefer that it be done properly rather than bungled."

"I'm bringing up my matter *tonight*," Jeanette exclaimed. Exclamation seemed to be her natural mode of expression. "You sent Ivan somewhere so he wouldn't be with me. You'll never get away with it! I have every right—"

"You have no right!" Siltz roared. "He is my son, a dedicated Communist! He will marry a good, chaste, Communist Church maid."

Jeanette's eyes blazed. Brother Paul was uncertain whether this was an optical effect of lamplight refraction, or an illusion stemming from her expression, but it was potent. "Do you claim *I* am not chaste?"

It was evident that Siltz realized he had gone too far but he carried on gamely. "Your whole religion is unchaste!" he retorted. "Your O meters, your clouds—"

"That's E meters and clears!" she cried. "Instruments and classifications to facilitate the achievement of perfection in life."

"Instruments and means to separate fools from their money!"

"There *is* no money here on Planet Tarot, and your son is no more fool than you are, being of your blood!"

This reminded Brother Paul uncomfortably of The Dozens. If he didn't break it up, the language might degenerate to that stage. The lady was pressing Siltz hard. "Surely—"

They ignored him. "Scientology remains a foolish cult," Siltz said hotly. "What good could come from the inventions of a science fiction writer turned psychologist and finally Messiah? I believe in the separation of Church and Fiction."

"You believe in the separation of Church from common sense!" she cried. "Do you throw away good wood because it may have been harvested by a crew of another religion?"

Siltz blanched, evidently recalling his recent conversation with Brother Paul. "No, I would not go that far. I seek a superior Communist way to utilize it, however."

"If you think Communism is so much better, why doesn't Ivan agree?"

"My son *does* agree! He's a good Communist!"

"Then why not let him marry me? He might make a convert!"

Siltz burst out laughing. "Never! A female canine like you would surely subvert him. That is why he must remain with his own—"

"Where?" she demanded. "Where is there a maid of your faith for him with half as much to offer as I have?"

Brother Paul made a silent whistle of amazement. This young woman certainly did not sell herself short!

Siltz contemplated her with distaste. "What has a maid like you to offer besides transient sex appeal and an unstable personality?"

She blazed again. "Transient! Unstable!" But then she caught herself. "I will not let you bait me; I will answer your question. My father was one of six brothers and two sisters. My grandparents are still alive and well on Earth. My great-grandfather lived to age 92, working until he died in an automobile accident where he was not at fault. I carry a heredity of strong, long-lived males and fruitful females. With me you would have grandsons to support you in your age, to cut wood for your winters—"

"Enough," Siltz said. "I must admit you have some recommendations. But in what Church would those grandsons be raised?"

She stared at him, abruptly silent.

"What Church?" Siltz repeated.

With an effort, now, she spoke. "I shall not deceive you. The Church of Scientology. They must be Clears."

"Perhaps some compromise—" Brother Paul began.

"No!" she flared. "No compromise! Not in religion!"

"But as you pointed out," Brother Paul said, "common sense—"

"To Hell with common sense! You don't know anything about it!" She spun about and marched out.

"I'm sorry," Brother Paul said to Reverend Siltz. "I should have stayed out of it. I *don't* understand Planet Tarot attitudes. She's a spitfire."

"No," Siltz said thoughtfully. "She is a good girl, better than I thought. She has good heredity, and she refuses to compromise her faith. She neither lies nor crawls, and she is intelligent. Did you observe the way she attacked me without ever actually insulting me? Never in the heat of argument did she forget her objective, which is to sell me, not alienate me. That was very clever management." He paced about the small room, his fingers linked behind his back. "My son is not strong; he can be swayed. He needs a steadfast woman. If there were many good, religious Communists to choose among, I would not compromise. But there are so few! Even the young women of other religions are a poor lot, like that harlot who tames the Breaker. Religion need not make a man a total fool. If I could strike a bargain, maybe for the first two grandsons—"

"You mean the lady is taming the lion after all?" Brother Paul inquired.

Reverend Siltz sighed. "I do not know. She is so small, I thought she was weak. Her Church is so crazy that, I thought she was crazy too. But strength is not necessarily of the body, and discipline stems from the soul." He looked up. "I will bring Ivan home. What follows—will follow."

II

Nature: 10

Thus the frontal lobes may be involved with peculiarly human functions in two different ways. If they control anticipation of the future, they must also be the sites of concern, the locales of worry . . . The price we pay for anticipation of the future is anxiety about it. Foretelling disaster is probably not much fun; Pollyanna was much happier than Cassandra. But the Cassandric components of our nature are necessary for survival. The doctrines for regulating the future that they produced are the origins of ethics, magic, science and legal codes. The benefit of forseeing catastrophe is the ability to take steps to avoid it, sacrificing short-term for long-term benefits. A society that is, as the result of such foresight, materially secure generates the leisure time necessary for social and technological innovation.
—Carl Sagan: *The Dragons of Eden*, New York: Random House, Inc., 1977.

The meeting was held in the morning at the village center, around and on the pile of wood. It appeared to be a complete turnout. Of course, time was not wasted, men and women were working quietly on basket weaving, sewing, carving, and tool sharpening. One old woman was carefully binding metal blades to the ends of poles, fashioning spears; frequently she hefted a spear in one hand, testing its balance. The weapon-maker was certainly a vital member of this community! Brother Paul wondered idly whether she made tridents on alternate days.

Reverend Siltz guided Brother Paul to the top of the pile, which was firmer than it had seemed. The wood had been carefully fitted, reminding him of the meshed stones of the Egyptian pyramids. Fuel storage this might be, but it was no casual matter.

"We have no formal organization, no leader," Reverend Siltz explained on the way up. "We are unable to agree on such things. So we operate by lot and consensus. You will take charge, and make your report, and render your decision. Then perhaps we shall have unity."

"But I have no decision!" Brother Paul protested. "I got all mixed up in Animation—"

"No decision?" Siltz asked. "I assumed—"

Lee and Therion and Amaranth were climbing behind them. "It is not Brother Paul's fault," Lee said. "We Watchers became enmeshed in this Animation, distorting it—and another person was drawn in, one not even scheduled to Watch. Perhaps others, too, that we do not know about. Brother Paul had no chance to work unfettered."

Brother Paul paused in his ascent, thinking of something else. "The child—did she return to the village?"

"No," Therion said gravely.

So she remained in Animation—or lost in the wilderness. If she still lived. Bigfoot had entered Animation in the vicinity where she had been lost. . . .

Suddenly it came home to Brother Paul, from a new direction: *Animation was no game.*

Reverend Siltz reached the top. A hush fell on the throng. "I was chosen by lot to host our visitor from Earth, Brother Paul of the Holy Order of Vision," he announced. "My opinion of this mission is not relevant. Brother Paul is a good man, a sincere man, and he has proffered advice on technical aspects of our colonization that may prove extremely helpful. But certain complications have occurred. I beg your indulgence while I explain.''

The crowd remained quiet, but Brother Paul could tell from the manner several people glanced up at Siltz that the explanation had to be convincing. If they thought the Communist had tried to interfere, or tried to influence Brother Paul's report, there would be trouble.

After a moment, the Reverend continued: ''We had not intended to send Brother Paul into full Animation at once. He was only experimenting in the fringe zone. Two Watchers remained outside: Mrs. Ellend and Pastor Runford.''

''The Christian Science Monitor and the Jehovah's Witness Watcher,'' Therion remarked. No one laughed.

''Three more were placed within the Animation zone,'' Siltz continued. ''A Mormon, a disciple of the Horned God, and a seeker of the Nine Unknown Men. We deemed this to be a sufficient representation for our purpose, this diversity of faiths. All were instructed to remain passive and not to attempt any Animations of their own; they were merely there to observe and to assist Brother Paul should his inexperience lead him into danger. However, he went further into the zone than we anticipated, and then a storm manifested. A volunteer, the priestess of Abraxas, entered the zone to warn Brother Paul of the probable expansion and intensification of the effect—but the storm developed rapidly, and she was herself trapped by the Animation. Thereafter, all the interior Watchers became involved, and the situation was out of control. Fortunately, the storm abated in due course and the effect receded—but one person did not emerge. Since Animation was returning, the search for her had to be aborted. In addition, Bigfoot appeared to be driven off, ironically, by the Breaker. Thus the mission was disastrous, and Brother Paul was unable to complete his quest for the true God of Tarot.''

There was a general sigh. Brother Paul saw the mixed chagrin and relief on these faces, and was ashamed.

These colonists had with evident effort united enough to facilitate his mission, and he had let them down.

"Swami Kundalini was recovered from the fringe area during the night, but remains in shock," Reverend Siltz continued. "The child he sought—must be presumed lost."

"We should never have assigned a child!" a voice cried.

Reverend Siltz ignored this. "Now I shall ask Brother Paul of Vision to make his report, to the extent he chooses, buttressed by the reports of the two surviving Watchers and the inadvertent participant. Then we must decide what to do."

Brother Paul noted how delicately this gruff man phrased himself on this occasion. Siltz had established a broad option for Brother Paul to speak only on what points and to what extent he wished, had skirted the question of the fate of the child, and had shown none of his private opinion of Amaranth. The Communist Reverend was a fairly skilled public speaker. And politician.

Now Siltz turned to Brother Paul. "We have only two rules for this meeting. We do not discuss the comparative merits of religions, and the speaker holds the floor until he yields it to another of his choice. Those who wish to take the floor after you will indicate this by raising their hands, and you will choose from among them. I now yield to you." And he made his way down the pile.

Some floor! "I can only tell you in a general way what happened inside the Animation," Brother Paul said. "And why I think it failed. I would prefer not to go into detail; it became uncomfortably personal." For a moment he thought he smelled feces. There were scattered smiles. Many of these people knew what Animation was like, though probably they had not had as solid a taste of it as he had. "It seems that Animation, when several people participate, is a kind of play, whose elements are drawn from the minds of the participants. When there is one person, it may be a constant feedback of his own hopes and fears, exaggerating them until he is destroyed. When there are several people, as in this case, all contribute, and to a certain extent this mitigates the feedback and prevents unhealthy intensification of a single theme. But the result is an unpredictable presentation, as the wills of the players overlap. The events of Animation have their own reality; when one person sees a thing, all others see it exactly as he does, even though it may have no objective reality—or the reality it possesses is rather different from what it is perceived to be." He paused. "I fear this is unclear. I mean that if one person perceives a burnt tree trunk as a building, others will perceive it similarly, and they can touch it or verify it with any other sense. It is a real building, for the duration of the Animation."

Brother Paul looked about and saw that they did understand. They were not, after all, newcomers to this concept. "When two people fight in Animation, the blows are solid, though they may perceive each other as strangers or even as monsters. And when a man and a woman make love—" He shrugged. "I did things like these. I am not proud of my performance. Some of my scenes were completely fantastic; others were reviews of events in my past life that I had forgotten or suppressed. I did not intend to—to do or remember these things. I turned out to be a weaker rede than I knew." Rede was not quite the word he wanted, but perfect phrasing did not always come when summoned. "I can only offer in explanation my theory of Animation precession: that the human mind is an immensely complex thing of psychic mass and inertia, weighted and freighted by a lifetime of experience. When pressure is put on it, it does not yield directly to the force, but shifts in an unexpected direction. I sought to find God; instead I found—shame. I do not know, or care to know, what I would have found if I had sought shame." He smiled, briefly. "Thus, I have no evidence whether the God of Tarot exists or which God He might be. I am sure my experience does not refute God, but neither does it confirm Him. I am sorry."

Brother Paul looked about, hoping to find someone

seeking the floor. Lee caught his eye. "I yield the floor to the Watcher, Lee, of the Church of Jesus Christ of Latter Day Saints."

"Thank you, Brother Paul," Lee said. He stepped to the peak of wood, a handsome young man in the morning sunlight. "What Brother Paul has told you is true. But I wish to amend it somewhat. There was a play, and we were actors within it. But the rest of us neither controlled it nor contributed substantially to it. The play was governed by the will of one person, and we assumed the roles that person dictated. That person was Brother Paul. I believe that a phenomenon called *aura* accounts for this control—"

"Covenant!" someone called from the crowd.

"I am not speaking religion," Lee said, frowning down at the interrupter. "I am speaking of a practical psychic force that—"

"That is the heart of a dozen religions!" another person cried.

"Then I can not speak," Lee said with resignation. He looked about. "Who wants the floor?"

"I do!" a female cried. It was fiery little Jeanette, the lady suitor to Siltz's son.

"I yield to you, Scientologist," Lee said gracefully.

"I move we suspend the Covenant," Jeanette cried. "Brother Paul did not get anywhere because he was not allowed to know anything of our real nature. All he has seen is the polite play we put on for him, pretending everything is fine—so he found a *play* in Animation instead of God. Let him see us as we are now—a feuding rabble of religions!"

There was an outcry of protest, but Jeanette would not be daunted. "I move we suspend the Covenant!" she repeated. "Do I have a second?"

Now there was silence. "She has the floor until her motion is seconded or withdrawn," Lee murmured in Brother Paul's ear. "She can really tie up this meeting, if she doesn't care about what people think of her—and she doesn't. She's out to have her way, regardless."

"What's wrong with her motion?" Brother Paul

inquired. "I suspect she's right. I *do* need to understand this colony better—as it truly is."

"There would be chaos," Lee said, and behind him Therion and Amaranth murmured agreement.

"Bless it, I deserve a vote on my motion!" Jeanette cried. "We can't remain hog-tied for failure. Give me a second!"

"I so second," a man said at last. Heads turned. There was a general gasp of amazement. The seconder was the Reverend Siltz.

Jeanette stared at him. "Communist, you jest."

"I have very little humor," Siltz responded stiffly.

"Never thought I'd see the day!" Therion remarked. "The old crocodile supporting his worst rival for the hand of his son."

"I think that the rivalry has been overstated," Brother Paul said. "The Reverend Siltz is at heart a Humanist; the welfare of man is more important to him than a particular concept of God. Jeanette would make his son a good wife, and he is becoming aware of that. She has only to prove herself."

"This is a scatterbrained way to do it," Therion muttered.

Jeanette hesitated; then her face firmed. "I yield to the Reverend Communist for seconding."

"Now the Second conducts the debate and vote," Lee said. "Siltz is a good organizer; he'll dispose of it quickly."

"I seconded the motion of the Scientologist because I believe it has merit," Siltz said "I have had the opportunity to talk with our visitor from Planet Earth on non-Covenantal matters, and find him to be a sincere and sensible man. I am sure he is the same in the realm of religion; we know the reputation of his Order. Our visitor failed us because we failed him. It is too late to correct that mistake—but by similar token there is no longer any harm in letting him know us honestly. Hearing no objection, I shall conduct the vote without debate."

"By the Horns of Heaven!" Therion swore. "He's

supporting her! But that's all she'll ever get from him. The vote, not the son.''

The villagers, similarly amazed, offered no objection. ''Those in favor of the motion will signify by so saying,'' Siltz continued.

There was a mild chorus of favor.

''Those opposed.''

There was silence. ''He is persuasive,'' Amaranth whispered.

''The motion carries,'' Siltz said. ''We are now free to express ourselves without restraint. But I caution speakers to be brief and to adhere somewhat to the subject of Brother Paul's visit, or nothing will be accomplished.'' He looked about. ''I yield the floor to Pastor Runford.''

''Thank you, Reverend,'' the Jehovah's Witness said. ''As many of you know, I opposed the experiment Brother Paul represents, and Watched it only to be certain it was honestly attempted, knowing failure was inevitable. Because the end of the universe is imminent, it is pointless to seek Jehovah by artificial means. He will make Himself known in his own fashion, very soon. As is said in the Bible: ''He shall judge between the nations and shall decide for many peoples; and they shall beat their swords into plowshares and their spears into pruning hooks. Nations shall not lift up sword against nation, neither shall they learn war any more.'' Therefore, we should not seek Him in the horrible apparitions of Animation, but must prepare ourselves to meet Him in our hearts, our souls. Man has devolved since Adam, each generation being successively more evil than the last until even the patience of Jehovah Himself is exhausted. All will be destroyed except those 144,000 who—''

''So you're opposed!'' someone yelled. ''Let someone else talk!''

''The genie's really out of the bottle!'' Therion said with enthusiasm.

''This is the problem,'' Lee murmured. ''Suspension of the Covenant opened Pandora's Box. Soon the *real* nuts will crack open.''

Brother Paul shook his head in silent wonder. There seemed to be *no* religious tolerance here! To each sect, all other sects were erring cults, and their adherents nuts.

"I retain the floor," Runford said firmly. "You the majority failed because you attempted an abomination! You courted Animation, which is like a harlot bearing gifts, and of her the Scripture has said: 'And I caught sight of a woman sitting upon a scarlet-colored wild beast that was full of blasphemous names and that had seven heads and ten horns. And the woman was arrayed in purple and scarlet, and was adorned with gold and precious stones and pearls and had in her hand a golden cup that was full of disgusting things and the unclean things of her fornication. And upon her forehead was written a name, a mystery: "Babylon the Great, the mother of harlots and of the disgusting things of the earth." ' "

"Bravo, witless Witness!" Therion cried. "That is our demoniac Key of Tarot, titled Lust, misread by others as Strength or Fortitude or even Discipline. You alone have called it out correctly in all its splendor. Blessed be that harlot!"

"You're an absolute beast," Amaranth exclaimed under her breath, half-admiringly.

"You are surely damned!" Runford cried at Therion, his whole body shaking with anger. "You shall be trodden in the wine press outside the city, and blood will flow as high as the bridles of the horses. Great will be your terror at Armageddon. Your flesh will rot away while you stand upon your feet; your very eyes will rot in their sockets, and your tongue in your mouth. Worms will swarm over your body—"

"Please, Pastor Runford," Mrs. Ellend said gently. "Truth is the still, small voice of scientific thought. Heaven represents harmony, and divine Science interprets the principle of heavenly harmony. In *Revelation* we are told: 'And there appeared a great wonder in heaven; a woman clothed with the sun, and the moon under her foot, and upon her head a crown of twelve stars.' We must always seek to ward off

Malicious Animal Magnetism, called MAM. The great miracle, to human sense, is divine Love. The goal can never be reached while we hate our neighbor of whatever faith—"

"What's wrong with *profane* Love, ma'am?" Therion demanded. He was evidently a born heckler, as perhaps was fitting for a child of Satan. Brother Paul, though genuinely interested in the views of the others, wished he would shut up. He had encountered Jehovah's Witnesses on Earth and found them to be honest and dedicated people, strongly reminiscent of the earliest Christians. He had also read some of the writings of Mary Baker Eddy, founder of the Christian Scientists, and been impressed with the sensible nature of her remarks. In any event, Brother Paul did not believe in ridicule as an instrument of religious opposition; in religious debates, as in other types, facts and informed opinions were proper ammunition.

"Who has the floor?" a young man inquired amid the babble of reactions.

"You do, Quaker," Runford snapped.

"Then allow me to tell thee how I view the problem," the Quaker said. 'When George Fox was a young man nineteen years of age in the year 1643, he was upon business at a fair when he met his cousin who was a professor of religion—what we might call today a minister—in the company of another minister. They asked George to share a jug of beer with them, and since he was thirsty and liked the company of those who sought after the Lord, he agreed. When they had drunk a glass apiece, the two ministers began to drink healths, calling for more and agreeing between themselves that he who would not drink should pay for the drinks of all the others. George Fox was grieved that people who made a profession of religion should act this way, rivaling each other in inebriation at the expense of the more restrained, though this was perhaps typical of societies of that time and since. Disturbed, he laid a groat on the table, saying 'If it be so, I'll leave you.' He was sleepless that night, praying to God for the answer, and God commanded him to forsake that life and be as a stranger to all. So he went, steadfast though Satan tempted him, and in time he founded the Society of Friends, also called Quakers because we were said to quake before the Lord. But our guiding principle is not quaking, rather it is the knowledge which in every person is the inner light that enables him to communicate directly with God, so that he requires no minister or priest or other intercessory to forward his private faith, and no ritual or other service. God is with us all, always; we have but to turn our attention inward in silence."

The young man paused, looking at Brother Paul. "Now I would not presume to lecture to thee, friend, or to comment on thy private life. I only ask thee to consider whether Truth is more likely to come out of Animation than out of a bottle."

Brother Paul, impressed by the Quaker's soft-spoken eloquence, had no ready answer. Maybe this Animation project had been ill-advised. The Quaker had not too subtly likened Animation to alcohol, and perhaps to all mind-affecting drugs; as such it was certainly suspect. If a divine spark of God were in every person, why *should* anyone have to search in Animation?

"I would respond to that, Friend," a woman said.

"Speak, Universalist, and welcome," the Quaker said.

"Thank you, Friend. I have an anecdote of the man who was a cornerstone of our faith, John Murray. Made desolate while a young man not yet thirty by the death of his lovely wife, and uncertain of her personal faith because of his changing perception of the nature of God, John sought only the solace of isolation. He set sail in 1770 for America. The captain of the ship intended to land at New York City, but contrary winds blew them aground at a little bay on the Jersey coast. John was put in charge of a sloop onto which they loaded enough of the cargo to enable the larger ship to float free of the sand bar at high tide, but before the sloop could follow, the wind shifted, trapping it in the bay. John Murray was unable to proceed, and there was no food aboard, so he went ashore to purchase some. Walking through the coastal forest he came upon a good-sized church, all by itself in dense woods. Amazed, he inquired at the next house and learned that an illiterate farmer had built the church at his own expense in thanks to God for his successes. The Baptists had petitioned to use that church, but the man told them 'If you can prove to me that God Almighty is a Baptist, you may have it.' He said the same to other denominations, for he wanted all people to be equally welcome there. Now he only waited for a preacher of like views to come—and he said God had told him John Murray was that man. John, chagrined, declined, protesting that he was no preacher, having neither credentials nor inclination. He intended only to proceed north to New York to turn the sloop over to the Captain as soon as the wind was favorable. 'The wind,' the man informed him, 'will never change, sir, until you have delivered to us in that meeting house a message from God.' John struggled against this notion, unwilling to bow to such manifest coincidence, wishing only to buy the necessary supplies for the sailors of the sloop. The man supplied him generously, refusing payment, while persisting in his suit. And as the days of the week passed and Sunday approached, the wind did not change. At last, on Saturday afternoon, John yielded, but prepared no text for the morrow: if God really wanted him to preach here, God would provide the words. On Sunday morning people came from twenty miles away, filling the church, and John Murray stood before them and preached the message of the Universal Redemption: that every human being shall find Salvation, and no one will be condemned to eternal suffering. And with that sermon, that bordered on heresy in that day but moved his congregation profoundly, John Murray found his destiny. When he finished it, the wind shifted, and he took the sloop to New York. But he returned immediately, and that church became his own, his home in the New World, and he preached that message for the rest of his life. Others persecuted him, seeking to suppress his view, for they believed that only a select minority would achieve Salvation—but he was instrumental in fighting the case of religious freedom through the courts and safeguarding it—that very freedom that was to make America great. The wind had guided him, despite himself, to his destiny—and that destiny was significant for mankind."

The Universalist looked at Brother Paul. "Now I would not presume any more than my esteemed colleague to urge any particular course of action upon you," she said. "But it would seem that the qualities of Animation are as yet unknown, and therefore cannot be labeled good or evil. Likewise, the purpose of God may be at times obscure in detail, so that no person can be assured in advance of the correct course. Are you certain it is proper to depart *this* shore without ascertaining the status of the effect, though you may have personal reservations? Which way does the wind blow in your life?"

Brother Paul felt suddenly cold. "You mean—go back into Animation?"

"No!" Pastor Runford cried. "Heed not the blandishments of Satan's council! One man in shock, a child lost, the mission failed—as it was Jehovah's will that it fail! Animation is the curse of evil!"

The lost child. How would she ever find her way out of that jungle of images? How would he ever live with himself if she did not?

"But we agreed!" someone exclaimed. After a moment's concentration Brother Paul recognized him as Malcolm of the Nation of Islam, suddenly converted from a reasonable man to a fiery partisan. "Allah decreed—"

Anonymous voices clamored, with few distinguishable:

"It is finished!"

"The Bible says—"

"The hell with the Bible!"

"According to the Koran—"

"Shove your Koran—"

The meeting dissolved into a fury of shouts. Brother Paul understood now what the Covenant had done. These fanatic cultists of all religions were unable to unify about a single principle unless strict procedural rules were followed, and even then the peace was troubled. Everything would fall apart unless someone took charge. Yet whoever did would face extraordinary rancor. It had to be someone who had nothing to lose here, who was not dependent on the grace of incompatible religious, who was prepared to plow ahead regardless of the resentment of others, simply because the wind had brought him to this shore and the message of the wind needed to be heeded.

Brother Paul got a grip on himself. Then he took a deep breath, braced himself, and let out an ear-splitting martial-arts Kiai yell: "SHADDAP!"

There was a startled silence. In that momentary calm, Brother Paul pre-empted the floor. "There are few things I'd abhor more than returning to Animation," he said. "But I did come here to do a job, and it is a job that still needs doing. For your local socio-political situation, and perhaps for mankind. If there *is* a single God of Tarot, a Deity of Animation, it is my duty to make every attempt to locate and define Him."

He paused, mentally taking hold of the problem while noting the scowls of those who were unalterably opposed to this quest. "I think what is needed is a survey of religions, made within the context of Animation. Some might be closer to the True God than others—assuming there is a God to be found in Animation. So if I go into Animation with that specific object, keeping my mind open to whatever may develop without pre-judgment, and am wary of the diversions of precession—" He paused again, thinking of something else. "The Watchers—if they are willing to come in again, this time for the disciplined, formal quest—"

Pastor Runford objected. He had recovered control of himself and seemed calm. "Do you not realize that very few people ever emerge from a second deep Animation? You are placing your sanity and your life in jeopardy."

"The sanity and life of that lost child are already in jeopardy," Brother Paul pointed out. "So is the welfare of this entire colony. You need to be united to survive the—"

"Family quarrels are the worst kind," Mrs. Ellend said. "We must apply scientific criteria to the problem."

"That is what I have in mind," Brother Paul said. "I trust I have learned from my egregious mistakes and will now be able to proceed properly. Perhaps I will fail again, and I confess the prospect of re-entering Animation fills me with dread. I do not understand the nature of the effect, or of my own mind, or of God—in fact, the nature of Nature is a mystery to me. Yet I must at least try, hoping that the guiding hand of whatever God there may be will manifest for me, as it did for George Fox, and for John Murray, and for each and every one of the people who have found Him in other circumstances."

"You have courage," Pastor Runford said. "I find myself forced to agree with the Reverend Siltz: though I disapprove your mission, I must approve of your dedication. I will therefore stand Watch at the fringe, as I did before."

"So will I," Mrs. Ellend said.

"I appreciate your support most deeply," Brother Paul said. He turned to the people behind him. "And you, who risk so much, Lee and Therion. And you, Amaranth—you were accidental, but maybe that too was a product of the wind. If I could have the support of the three of you in that nightmare—"

Lee nodded. "I share your misgivings—and your rationale. It will not be easy, but it must be done. At least we must search for the child."

Therion and Amaranth nodded agreement. Brother Paul felt the camaraderie of shared experience as he faced the three, appreciating their acquiescence. This was, in a special sense, his family; they shared his experience. They alone knew what the first Animation had been like. "We only have to decide what is right, even though it may seem unnatural, and do it."

But they all knew that nature would have her way, whatever their definitions might be. For nature was another name for the God of Tarot.

III

Chance: 11

The Wheel of Fortune card of Tarot appears to be an iconographical transformation of a more complex and subtle ancient symbol. That is, the original meaning of the spoked wheel was forgotten, and a new meaning applied. This sort of error is common in Tarot and has led to great diversity of interpretations. The original in this case would seem to be some variant of the Wheel of Becoming, also called the Wheel of Life and Death, as represented in Buddhist mythology but probably predating Buddhism. The source religion of Western Asia is unknown, but certain similar themes run through Buddhism, Brahmanism and Hinduism of India, and Mithraism, Zoroastrianism and Judaism of Asia Minor, suggesting that there was once a common body of information. The Wheel of Becoming may also have manifested in Babylon as the horoscope of astrology.

In the middle of this Wheel of Life are animals symbolizing the three roots of evil: lust, hatred, and ignorance. Five spokes divide its main area into the realms of hells, animals, spirits, gods, and men. Around its rim is the circle of causation, shown by twelve little pictures representing concepts too subtle to be described simply. Rendered approximately, they are: Ignorance, Formation of Life, Individual Awareness, Personality, 'Thought' as the sixth sense, Contact, Sensation,

Desire, Sex, Marriage, Birth, and Death. A number of
these concepts and pictures can be equated to those of
the Tarot, such as the brutish man Ignorance to Tarot's
Fool, the man for Thought to the Hierophant (teacher),
the lovers' embrace of Contact to Tarot's Lovers, and
Death to Death. Most contemporary Tarot decks have
no equivalents to the Wheel's concepts of Sensation,
Desire, Sex, Marriage or Birth—which suggests that
these may have been lost in the translation of forms.
Perhaps in due course they will be restored, possibly by
the addition of new cards to the Tarot deck. Meanwhile,
Tarot's Wheel loosely represents the concept of Chance.

Near a river stood a huge handsome tree whose thick
foliage extended irregularly outward and cast a deep
shade. It seemed to be a fig tree.

Brother Paul walked toward it. Could this be the Tree
of Life? That would be as sure a route as any to the God
of Tarot. His companions had disappeared, but he
knew they would reappear when summoned for their
roles.

Beneath the tree sat a man who might have been in his
mid-thirties. It was hard to tell, because he seemed small
and old before his time. He was emaciated. His hair and
beard had been shave, and he was garbed in rags. He did
not avert his eyes as Brother Paul approached.

"May I join you?" Brother Paul inquired.

The little man made a gesture of accommodation.
"Be welcome, traveler. There are figs here enough to
sustain a multitude, and water is in the river."

Brother Paul sat down beside him and crossed his
legs. He picked up a fig when the man did so and
chewed its somewhat tough flesh slowly. "You are an
ascetic? I do not mean to intrude on your privacy if you
prefer to be alone."

"I tried asceticism until I very nearly wasted away,"
the man said. "I gained no worthwhile insights. I
decided it was useless to continue starving and torturing
myself. Then I discovered that when I ate and drank,
and became stronger, my thoughts became clearer. I
realized that the teaching which says that a man must

starve himself in order to gain wisdom must be wrong.
It is the healthy man who is best able to perceive the
world and contemplate religious truth." He glanced at
Brother Paul. "By this token, you must be a very per-
ceptive man, for you are the healthiest I have encountered. May I inquire your name?"

"I am Brother Paul of—a distant culture. And you?"

"I am Siddhattha Gotama, once a prince, now a
beggar-monk."

Siddhattha Gotama—the man known to history as
the Buhhda, the Awakened One, the Enlightened. The
founder of one of the greatest religions of all time,
Buddhism. He had indeed been a prince and had
renounced his crown voluntarily to seek revelation.

"I—am honored to meet you," Brother Paul said
humbly. Though he regarded himself as Christian, he
had deep respect for Buddhism. "I too am a seeker of
truth. I have not yet found it."

"I have looked for seven years for enlightenment,"
Siddhattha said. "Often I have been sorely tempted to
desist from begging and return to my wife and son.
Always I remind myself that I could never be happy
again in the palace, so long as I knew others existed in
hardship and misery. Yet I seem to draw no closer to
any insight how to enable others to be happy."

This, then, was before the Buddha had attained his
revelation. "Have you inquired of teachers, of wise
men?"

Siddhattha smiled ruefully. "I visited the great
teacher Alara. 'Teach me the wisdom of the world!' I
begged him. He said to me 'Study the Vedas, the Holy
Scriptures. There is all wisdom.' But I had already
studied the Vedas and found no enlightenment. So I
wandered on until I encountered another great teacher,
Udaka, and I asked him. He told me 'Study the Vedas!'
Yet I knew that in them was no explanation why the
Brahman makes people suffer illness and age and death.
I am also doubtful that one can attain wisdom by
hurting himself or sitting on sharp nails."

"In my culture," Brother Paul agreed, we are told
much the same. 'Read the Bible.' Yet human warfare

and misery continue, even among those who profess to hold the Bible most dear. I suspect we shall not find the ultimate truths in any book. Yet life is often a difficult tutor."

"That is true," Siddhattha agreed reminiscently. "When I was a prince, I went out hunting. I saw a man, all skin and bones, writhing in pain on the ground. 'Why?' I asked. 'All people are liable to illness,' I was informed. But in my sheltered life I had not been exposed to this, and it made me very sad. Next day I met a man so old his back was curved like a drawn bow, and his head was nodding, and his hands trembled like palm leaves in the wind so that even with the aid of two canes he could hardly walk. 'Why?' I asked. 'He is old; all people grow old,' I was told. Again I was saddened, for I had known only youth. Next day I saw a funeral procession, with the widow and orphans following behind the corpse. 'Why?' 'Death comes to all alike.' This horrified me, for I had never contemplated the reality of death in man. I knew so little of life and of people; I had spent my life in foolish pleasures. Why was I so well off, while others suffered? I understood now that I was the exception and that the great majority of people in the world were ill and poor. This did not seem right. Yet even as I contemplated this, my lovely wife was giving a party with many pretty girls singing and dancing, and that music only heightened my confusion. When my family observed this, it was assumed that the entertainment was not sufficient, and so the girls were made to perform with such vigor and endurance that they dropped from exhaustion. How their loveliness had changed! Next day I went to the market place, and there among the merchants I saw an old monk dressed in coarse yellow robes, begging for food. Though he was old and sick and poor, he seemed calm and happy. Then I decided to be like him."

"I think you found much enlightenment at that moment," Brother Paul said. "Maybe the ultimate truth can be found only in one's own heart." That was the Quaker belief, he recalled.

Siddhattha turned to him. "That is a most intriguing

thought! I wonder what I might find, if I simply sit here under this Bo Tree until I have plumbed in my own soul this truth.''

The Bo Tree! Now Brother Paul remembered: it was called the Tree of Wisdom, for it was where the Buddha had spent his Sacred Night and attained his crucial Enlightenment. "I had better leave you alone, then.''

"Oh, no, friend! Stay here with me and search out your own truth," Siddhattha encouraged him.

Well, why not? This might be the most direct route to his answer. The God that Buddha found—that had to be a major contender for the office of God of Tarot.

Dusk was rising. The sun descended. But they were not allowed to meditate in peace. A group of people approached the Tree, and it was obvious that they intended mischief. Three were young and quite pretty women; the rest were motley ruffians of assorted appearance.

Brother Paul jumped to his feet, about to warn off the intruders, but Siddhattha stopped him. "These are the cohorts of Mara, the Evil One, who seeks to dissuade us from our pursuit. For seven years he has followed me. But he cannot harm us physically so long as we remain under this Tree. Do not try to fight him; that is what he wants. It is futile to oppose evil with evil.''

Could this be true? Brother Paul backed off, yielding to the Buddha's judgment. Mara the Evil One—the Buddhist Devil. This was to be no ordinary encounter!

Sure enough, the crowd stopped just beyond the spread of the Tree. But now there came an elephant, overwhelmingly tall, its measured tread shaking the earth, and riding it was a large, somewhat paunchy man bearing a sneer of pure malice. This, surely, was the Evil One.

"Come out, cowards!" Mara bawled.

Siddhattha remained seated. "The Evil One has eight armies," he explained to Brother Paul. "They are called Discontent, Hunger, Desire, Sloth, Cowardice, Doubt, and Hypocrisy. Few can conquer such minions; but whoever is victorious obtains joy.''

Brother Paul wrinkled his brow. "I believe that's only seven armies. Not that those aren't sufficient!''

Siddhattha's brow wrinkled in turn. "I always forget one or two. Evils are not my specialty." Surely the understatement of the millennium!

Now the three women came forward. They were seductively garbed and moved their torsos in a manner calculated to enhance their sexual appeal. "Come meet my daughters," Mara cried. "They are experts in the pleasing of men." And, acting as one, the three beckoned enticingly.

Brother Paul felt the allure. Somehow the Animation had produced a triple image of Amaranth, and she was good at this type of role.

"Now I remember Mara's other army!" Siddhattha exclaimed happily. "Lust!" But he seemed to be pleased only by the intellectual aspect; these lush bodies did not tempt him.

The women turned about and left with a final triple flirt of the hips. It was obvious they had failed. Siddhattha would not be corrupted by sex. And why should he be? He had a wife and son at home, along with a crown, and probably a full harem, if he ever felt the need.

Now armed men came forward, dressed in animal skins, gesticulating wildly, screaming. They resembled demons. The sun was now down, but the moonlight illuminated them with preternatural clarity. Siddhattha was not alarmed. "Mara personifies the triple thirst for existence, pleasure, and power. The satisfaction of selfishness is Hell, and those who pursue selfishness are demons." And the demon-men could not touch him.

"A most apt summary," Brother Paul agreed. He liked this man and found nothing objectionable in his philosophy. But how was he to be certain whether the Buddhist God was or was not the God of Tarot?

"You and I can sit here and reflect on the Ten Perfections," Siddhattha said.

The demon soldiers retreated. Mara was furious. "I tried to be gentle with you, " he cried, "but you would not have it. Now taste the wrath of my magic."

No more Mr. Nice Guy, Brother Paul thought, almost smiling.

Mara raised one hand. Immediately a whirlwind blew, forming an ominous black funnel that swept in to encompass the entire Bo Tree. But in the center was the calm, and not a leaf stirred. Brother Paul looked out at the whirling wall of dust in amazement and with not a little apprehension, but Siddhattha ignored it. "It is only air," he murmured to Brother Paul.

The whirlwind vanished. "Well, try water, then!" Mara screamed. A terrible storm formed, and rain pelted down, causing instant flooding all about the area. But not a drop penetrated the foliage of the Bo Tree, and Siddhattha sat serene and dry. Instead, Mara's elephant trumpeted and splashed its feet in the water like a skittish woman, upset.

"Earth!" Mara cried. And the storm converted to a barrage of rocks, sand, and mud. Yet again these things had no effect on the seated man, who had not changed his position since Brother Paul appeared in the scene. The few stones that penetrated the Bo Tree fell to the ground like harmless flowers. Those that struck the elephant, in contrast, made havoc; the poor creature danced cumbersomely about, trying to protect itself.

Mara was livid. "Fire!" he cried. And live coals came down, setting fire to the grass and brush outside the Bo Tree and hissing into the river. Siddhattha was not afraid, and so he was inviolate.

"You have conquered the attack of the four elements," Brother Paul said. "You have beaten the Evil One."

"No, the battle has just begun. Now he will lay siege to my spirit."

Mara gestured, and the bright moonlight went out, making the world black. But a glow arose from the Bo Tree, restoring visibility there. From the darkness beyond, Mara bawled: "Siddhattha, arise from that seat! It is not yours, but mine!"

The seated man only shook his head in mild negation.

"I am the Prince of the World!" Mara said. "I hold the Wheel of Life and Death!" Light returned, revealing him standing just beyond the Tree, clutching a huge wheel with five spokes so that only his head, feet and hands showed around its rim. His body, oddly, did not show behind it at all; the center was filled with moving images.

"The Wheel of Becoming," Siddhattha agreed. "The hand of death is on every one who is born. Yet I shall not die, O Evil One, until my mission in life has been accomplished."

"And what is that mission, O Ignorant One?" Mara demanded with a sneer.

"To spread the Truth," Siddhattha replied simply.

"*What* Truth?"

Siddhattha, who had been doing so well before, was unable to answer. Brother Paul saw this as another variation of the Dozens, with the Buddha turning away insults by soft replies. But now he was in trouble.

Mara advanced, bearing his Wheel forward. It was an impressive and sinister thing, its various aspects turning in opposite directions, confusing the eye. "If you cannot answer, O Shriveled Ascetic, the victory is mine!" The role-player was Therion, of course, and he was enjoying this.

Siddhattha looked at Brother Paul beside him. "Friend, I fear I have lost the battle, for the Truth has not yet come to me, and Mara must have his answer." There were tears in the man's eyes.

"But the Evil One will bring only evil upon the world!" Brother Paul said, as though that could help. "He controls the Wheel of Becoming, and he is the Prince of the World. Only your good can stop him!" He put his hand on Siddhattha's frail shoulder.

With that contact, something happened. "I feel—the spirit of God," Siddhattha said wonderingly. "Are you a messenger from—?"

"No, no!" Brother Paul said hastily. It had been the contact of auras the man had felt. "I am only another Seeker."

Still the thing grew. What had been quiescent in Siddhattha all his life was now awakening. He was becoming conscious of his aura—and it was an extremely powerful one. "The spirit of God—is in me," he said, certainty coalescing. "And now—I have found the key to Wisdom, the First Law of Life! It was within me all the time, awaiting this moment."

Siddhattha stood. He was not tall, but his new enhancement gave him stature. "Listen, Mara, and be damned: FROM GOOD MUST COME GOOD, AND FROM EVIL MUST COME EVIL."

Brother Paul was troubled by this statement. From what he remembered of symbolic logic, a false hypothesis that led to a true conclusion was regarded as valid. That suggested that it was possible for Good to come from Evil. Obviously this man did not subscribe to that notion.

Mara gave a cry of pure anguish. He staggered back, seeking his elephant—but when he touched it, the beast collapsed. All his minions scrambled away from the Bo Tree in a rout.

Brother Paul stood watching, amazed. And realized that Siddhattha was now the Buddha, the Awakened One. And that, symbolic logic or not, the God of this man—could indeed be the God of Tarot.

But to be sure, he would have to survey the other great religions of the world and eliminate them from consideration. Maybe the Eightfold Path was the correct one, but that could not be certain yet.

"My business here is done," he said to the Buddha. "I hope we shall meet again." The Bo Tree faded out.

Brother Paul stood in a landscape whose sky contained three suns: a full-sized one and two little ones. The vegetation, however, was Earthlike to a degree: what looked like arctic fir was adjacent to tropic palm. The air was breathable though slightly intoxicating. Gravity was less than he was used to, but the terrain was so rough that he was sure the amount of energy he would have to expend to travel anywhere would counterbalance this.

In fact, he stood on a slanting ledge above a bubbling lava flow. A waft of fumes came up, and he hastily stepped back. His foot slipped in snow, and he half-fell into the ice of a stalled avalanche. A meter back from the boiling rock the deep freeze of winter was encroaching. No wonder the plants were narrowly confined! The spread from hard frost to perpetual warmth was within one to two meters.

But what had this to do with religion? He had intended to check one of the most modern and vigorous of the world's great faiths: Voodoo. It had originated in Black Africa and spread to the Americas with slavery. Christianity had been imposed on the nonwhite population, so these people had compromised by merging their native Gods with the Catholic Saints, creating a dual purpose pantheon that permitted them to satisfy the missionaries while remaining true to their real beliefs. The truth, were it ever admitted, was that there were more voodoo worshipers in Latin America during the 20th Century than legitimate Christians, and the depth of their religious conviction and practice was greater. Brother Paul had flirted with the Caribbean Santeria, or regional Voodoo cult, while on a quest for his black ancestry, and found it both appalling and appealing. The chicken-disemboweling rituals, roach-eating, and mythology of incest revolted his white middle-class taste, but the sincerity of the serious practitioners and the religion's obvious power over the masses satisfied his youthful need to belong. Later, as a Brother of the Holy Order of Vision, he had dealt on a professional level with Santeros, or Witch-Doctors, and found them generally to be as concerned and knowledgeable about the needs of believers as were Catholic priests, medical doctors, or psychiatrists. Folk medicine thrived on in Voodoo. The Holy Order of Vision did not hesitate to refer a troubled person to a reputable witch-doctor when the occasion warranted it. These were true faith-healers of modern times.

But this was an alien world! How had Animation produced this instead of the Voodoo Temple he had sought? Was it Precession again? His idea had been to bracket the religions of the world, to survey the extremes, and then work into the center, eliminating as much as possible. Fairly, of course. But if Precession had struck, there was no telling what he was into.

"Oh." It was a young woman, dressed in a strange

half-uniform. One side was a well-padded shieldlike af-
fair, covering her body from head to heel. The other
side was—nothing. She was, in fact, half-nude.

"I seem to have lost my way," Brother Paul said.

"But where is your sub-fission?" she asked.

"I—fear I do not understand," he said, shifting
about to ease the chill of his left side, too close to the
snow. Suddenly he understood the rationale of her
costume: her right side was insulated against the winter
side of this ledge, while her left was comfortable in the
summer side. Presumably, when she traveled in the
other direction, she reversed sides. Apparently in this
world the air was resistive to the convections of radical
temperature change, so that extremes of climate could
coexist without turbulence. Still, when storms did
develop, they were probably ferocious.

"Where is your sister, your wife?" she asked.

"I have neither sister nor wife."

"I mean your sibling mate, in the eye of Xe Ni Qolz,"
she explained. "How is it you venture out in half?"

This was not becoming any more intelligible! "I have
just arrived from—from another planet. I am an only
child, unmarried."

Her pretty brow furrowed. "I hadn't realized another
ship had arrived. You had better hide before you get us
all in trouble."

"I don't even know where I am or what is wrong!"

She considered him speculatively. "Look, this is
somewhat sudden, but maybe a break for us both. I just
had a fight with my brothub, so I snuck out alone, but
I'm afraid a Nath will spot me. How about filling in
with you?"

Brother Paul could not make sense of this.
"Brothub? Nath? What do these terms mean?"

She stepped forward and took his arm. "No time to
explain," she said. "Look, there's one now!"

He followed her gaze. There, sliding along the edge of
the snowbank was something like a shag rug—but it was
flowing uphill. "That—can it be alive?" he whispered,
amazed.

"Just fake it," she whispered back. "Let me do the talking."

He seemed to have no alternative.

The rug slid up to them and paused two meters away. Brother Paul saw that it moved by shooting out myriad tiny burrs on threads, then hauled itself forward by winching them in. Truly alien locomotion! "Pull-hook, Sol," the thing said. It spoke strangely in a kind of staccato. Brother Paul conjectured that it was tapping the ground with hundreds of miniature hammers in such a manner as to create a human-sounding pattern of sonics.

"The same to you, Nath," the girl replied.

"What entity-pair are you?" Nath inquired.

"I—we—" She faltered, not knowing Brother Paul's name.

"I am Brother Paul," he filled in. "Of the Holy—"

"And I am Sister Ruby," she interjected. Then she turned to Brother Paul and flung herself into his arms, pressing one winterized and one summerized breast against his torso and planting a passionate kiss on his lips.

"It is good to perceive such sibling love," Nath said. "May the Wheel turn well for your regeneration." Then the creature heaved itself smoothly up over the snow and on around them.

"Xe Ba Va Ra enhance you, Nath," Ruby called after it.

"All right, now," Brother Paul said. He had identified her, of course: Amaranth in a new part. As sexy as ever. But now he wondered who had played the part of Buddha in the prior scene. The man had been too small to be either Lee or Amaranth. "Will you explain what—"

"Yes, yes, everything," she said. "Come with me to the Temple of Tarot, and I'll explain on the way." She walked down the ledge-path, weaving smoothly around the foliage, and he had to follow. He couldn't remain here; it was impossible to be comfortable in this arctic tropic.

"First," he said as he caught up, momentarily distracted by the way his expelled breath fogged on the frigid side and by her bare buttock flexing on the hot side, "What world is this?"

"We're a human colony in the Hyades cluster," she said. "We were founded three hundred years ago by mattermission, but then it turned out we were actually inside Sphere Nath, so we were subject to their government. Since our supply line had broken down and the Naths were well established, this really was better. All we had to do was obey their laws and honor their customs, and they treated us just as well as Sol would have. Better, maybe. That's part of the Intersphere Covenant, you see. I don't think Sol ever established diplomatic relations with Nath, but at the fringes of the Spheres it is Galactic custom to work these things out—"

"Wait, wait!" Brother Paul cried. "You mean to say human beings are being governed by alien creatures that look like—that rug?"

"Yes, of course. The Naths are really rather nice. We had some trouble at first, but once the Wheel of Tarot was established everything was fine. Now we worship our Saints, and they don't know the difference."

"The Wheel of Tarot," he repeated. "Would that be related to the Wheel of Life and Death, or the Wheel of Becoming?"

"Yes, it is also called that. It—"

"With five spokes? Each section representing—"

"Yes, the Naths call these sections Energy, Gas, Liquid, Solid, and Plasma. You know, the five states of matter, each one phasing into the other, completing the circle. Each with its representative Deity, that we call—"

"You worship alien Gods?" he asked, dismayed.

She paused momentarily in the path. "Look, Brother—if we didn't honor their religion, their missionaries would be push-hooked, and then their government might decide not to expend good resources maintaining an alien squatter-colony. We *need* Nath equipment and material and knowhow and communications, and if we don't get them we'll—well, can you imagine scrounging a living from this terrain, alone?" She gestured up and down the slope, taking in the lava and ice. "So we follow their religion. They don't demand that of us, but we really have to."

As the Blacks and Reds of Latin America had to follow Christianity, overtly. Now it was coming clear. "So you merged your Saints with their Spirits, so that they would believe you were honoring *their* religion?"

"That's correct. It was easy, in four sections of the Wheel. Their God of Gas, Xe Kwi Stofr, is our Saint Christopher, and—"

"I don't quite see the connection. Gas would equate to the element of Air, which is the Tarot suit of Swords, generally associated with intellect or science or trouble, while St. Christopher—"

The path debouched into a small valley sheltered under an overhanging cliff. Here there was a building in the shape of a roofed wheel, complete with five sections. Massive dikes diverted the lava flow, causing it to pass on either side of the Wheel, burning back the ice. A fringe of trees of diverse species surrounded the island Wheel. Evidently this was a permanent lava flow—truly alien to Earthly experience and enough to interrupt anyone's chain of thought. A narrow bridge, fashioned of wedges of stone, passed over one of the lava streams to the island. The whole thing would have been difficult for human beings to assemble without the machines of an advanced technology—and the colonists obviously lacked those. So it had to be the beneficial handiwork of the alien civilization: the Naths.

Actually, it made sense that there be more sapient aliens in space than just the protoplasmic entities of Antares. He had no reason to be surprised. Man would inevitably encounter these aliens, and it was best that mechanisms for peaceful interaction exist.

"Let me tell you about St. Christopher," Ruby said. "He was a huge man who chose to work for the most powerful king on Earth. When he saw that the strongest

king feared the Devil, Christopher went to work for the
Devil. But then the Devil flinched at the Cross, so
Christopher sought the one who was associated—"

"Yes, of course," Brother Paul said. "That was
Jesus—"

"Don't say that name!" she cried, cutting him off.
"The Naths know our origin-religion, and if they
thought we were backsliding—"

Brother Paul nodded. "So the Sword of Tarot
becomes the Cross that St. Christopher sought. And the
Wand suit becomes—"

"Saint Barbara, locked in the tower because she
would not marry a rich pagan," she said. "The bolt of
lightning that avenged her martyrdom becomes the symbol of energy of the Nath Nature Spirit Xe Ba Va Ra.
And the suit of Coins stands for Nath's Solid, the Spirit
of Trade, Xe Jun Olm Nar, whom we call Saint John
the Almoner, so generous in his alms. Their Spirit of
Art, Xe Gul Yia Na, is our Saint Juliana, who tied up
the Devil. The only real problem is—"

"You seem to have it worked out pretty well," he
said. "I'm surprised that the mere exchange of names
persuades the Naths you are converts to their religion."
Yet that same device had been effective for the Voodoo
adherents in Christian countries. When a man kneeled
before a statue of St. Barbara, spoke her name rev-
erently, and left an offering, who could say for sure
whether it was the Catholic Saint he prayed to in his
heart or Xango, the Voodoo God of lightning? Who
could say which entity answered that prayer? Did it
really matter?

"The Naths do not separate religion and morality,"
she said. "They believe that if we profess belief in their
spirits, we must necessarily follow their cultural code.
So they do not inquire too closely, so long as we do not
violate it in any obvious manner. Still—"

"The Naths seem like good creatures," he said. Now
they were crossing the bridge. He flinched away from
the hot fumes rising from it. "I hardly begrudge you
your original religion, for it is my own, though perhaps
I indulge in an earlier variant of Chris—of that faith."

"Three hundred years earlier," she said.

"Oh? How would you know that?" He had expected some kind of objection from the role-player, who was not a Christian. She must be seething!

"That's how long it takes a freezer-ship to reach here from Sol at half-light speed or less. So you are a man of twenty or twenty first century Earth, thawed out after a sleep that seemed to you just a moment."

Freezer-ship? Suspended animation for three centuries? Well, it was a natural conclusion for a native girl. But how would Amaranth have known of such things, assuming they were valid details of future history? There were nuances to these Animations that seemed to defy rational explanation.

"At any rate," he continued as she showed him into a section marked with a picture of jolly Santa Claus in his fat red suit and spreading white beard, "I don't really see that such subterfuge is necessary here. Why not simply inform the Naths that you worship similar Gods to theirs, though they go by different names? I'm sure the aliens would understand."

"They would," she agreed. "They do. In four aspects of the Wheel. But in the fifth—"

"That would be the suit of—" He broke off, startled. "Wait! We already *have* four suits! A five-sectioned wheel can not be matched to—"

"We are now in the Re-Fissioning aspect of the Wheel, the problematical one," she said, stripping away her one-sided snow suit. Now she was naked, and though no more of her showed than would have appeared in a mirror reflection of her nude half, she seemed much barer than before. "Governed by the state of Liquid, or the Spirit of Faith, the key to this whole compromise. Xe Ni Qolz, whom we call—"

"Saint Nicholas!" he exclaimed, making the connection to the artwork of this chamber. "Old Santa Claus!"

"Yes, the Saint for the Children. Father Christmas." She took his hand and led him to a broad couch. It was amazing how an inconsequential act of disrobing assumed quite consequential implications. Before, he had oriented on her clothed half; now— "The Naths do not spy on us, precisely, but the walls are translucent to their perception. They don't use sound, exactly; it's more like infrasonics. So the Nath governor is aware of everything that goes on here."

"Well, we have nothing to hide," he said uncomfortably. Certainly *she* was hiding nothing, physically. She was very free with her body, as he remembered from a prior Animation—except that he could not be sure it *was* her body that he—

He stifled that thought. At any rate, he had every intention of leaving her alone this time. All he wanted was information.

"We have one thing to hide," she said. "The one thing we could not do to accommodate Nath, as colonists." She began to remove his clothing.

"Hey, stop!" he protested.

She leaned over and kissed him. "Don't make a commotion. Just relax and enjoy it. Remember, we told the Nath we were siblings. They have very good communications. They will be instantly aware if we do not act the part."

"I am a Brother of the Holy Order of Vision," he said, determined not to let his survey of religions go the same way as his first Animation sequence. She might be determined to give one of her samples; he was determined not to take it. "That's a kind of title, indicating my status. It hardly means I am your biologic brother—and in any event, this is no sisterly approach you are making to me."

"Shut up and listen," she said, continuing to work on his clothing despite his resistance. "The Naths expect us to maintain proper sexual morality; that is how they know we are true converts. To violate their standards—" She spread her hands appealingly. "We just couldn't survive as a colony without Nath support. You've seen what this planet is like—and this is just the habitable portion! I think the close proximity of so many neighboring stars evokes crustal unrest, causing continuous volcanic action—not that I object to volcanoes, but—"

"All *right*," he said. He knew she liked volcanoes in symbol and reality, just as she liked serpents. "You need Nath support; I believe that. But I think it is fine that the Naths insist on sexual morality. So do I! But you—"

"The Naths do not reproduce quite the way we do," she said. "Each Nath is bipart; it has a male section and a female section. The one we talked to was actually a married couple."

"I see. When Naths tie the knot, they really do tie it! But surely they can appreciate that human beings, uh, merge that closely only for procreative purpose. They can't expect us to go about tied together physically—"

"They understand. But they do expect married couples to stay reasonably close together and to merge often. So we display much more continuous affection than you may have been accustomed to back on Earth. We don't really mind. It does seem to make for more successful unions."

"For married couples, that's fine. But you and I are, if we accept your description to the Nath, brother and sister. So—"

"Oh be quiet," she said. "I had to tell the Nath that because single people just don't *go* about. Half an entity can't make it on its own, by the Nath rationale. The whole colony would have been in trouble, not just you and me. You can't believe how sensitive they are about this one thing. *It is their religion*, damn it! I was a fool to go out there alone, and you should have stayed aboard your ship until you got a proper briefing and escort."

"Sorry," he murmured apologetically. "If you'll just stop undressing me, I'll listen better."

"Well, maybe we can fake it for a while," she agreed reluctantly. She pushed him down on the couch and stretched out beside him in a most provocative manner. "When the Naths want to reproduce, they fission. They split apart into their male and female halves. That's one of the two times in their lives they *aren't* locked together. Then each half regenerates—do Earthworms still do that?"

"They do," Brother Paul assured her.

"Except that a male Nath-half can't regenerate the opposite sex, or vice versa. So male regenerates male tissue, and female regenerates female tissue—am I embarrassing you?"

"You are talking about alien reproduction," he reminded her. "Why should I be embarrassed?" He *was* embarrassed, but by her body and actions, not her discussion.

"That's right, you're fresh from Earth. The local pornography doesn't bother you, yet. Anyway, a unisex composite is inherently unstable."

"I should think so," Brother Paul agreed. "It would be like homosexuality, lesbianism—"

"Except it is a necessary part of their reproduction," she said. "The unisex sets quickly re-fission. Then there are four sub-Naths, and two females. Actually, male-original and male-regenerate, and the same for the females. Then they recombine, forming—"

"I see," Brother Paul said. "But that's really like a human family. The parent-couple produces two children, a boy and a girl. Nath mechanism differs in detail, but—"

"That detail is a hell of a difference," she said. "Some of the fragments have to go out and merge with other family fragments, to keep the genetic pool circulating—"

"Yes, of course. That's why human beings are exogamous, marrying outside their immediate family. Otherwise the species would quickly splinter into dissimilar species. There has to be interbreeding among the members of—"

"But it is not the children, the regenerates, that are exogamous," Ruby said. "They are too new to handle it properly. So it is the old individuals who split up, and re-merge elsewhere. They—"

"They have to divorce after procreating?" Brother Paul asked, startled. "That's not my idea of a stable marriage! Who takes care of the children?"

"The children take care of themselves with general

help from the larger Nath community. They merge into a Nath couple, and—"

Brother Paul was shocked. "But that's incest!"

"Now you begin to understand the problem," she said. "By their standards and their religion, it is immoral for siblings *not* to mate with each other and for parents *not* to separate and remarry other divorcees. So if we want Nath support for our human enclave—"

"We have to commit incest and break up families," Brother Paul finished. "At last I get your drift. As a colony, you are torn between your economic needs for survival, and your human sexual morality, with a dual-aspect religion papering over the dichotomy. Yet if you explained this basic difference to the Naths—"

"Our ancestors tried," she said. "The Nath missionaries explained *their* position to us. They said we had been living, as a species, in intolerable sin, and they could not support it. It was their duty to lead us into the light despite ourselves. Naths are very accommodating creatures, but on this point they are inflexible."

"Just like missionaries," Brother Paul said with a sigh. "But how do you get around it?"

"The Nath biologists probably know, but the missionaries don't know or profess not to know, that human couples do not generally produce twins, and more seldom are there male-female twins. So when we have babies we meet here in the Children's aspect of the wheel and surreptitiously exchange them, making up exogamous pairs that we then raise as siblings. All humans look more or less alike to Naths, so they don't catch on. They can track a particular family if they choose, as they may have done with us two, but when there is a crowd of us they don't bother. Thus our children grow up and reproduce without damage to the human genetic pool. Then, with Nath blessing, they divorce and seek partners of their choice."

Brother Paul shook his head. "I appreciate the necessity, but I am appalled at the means!"

"Now we'd better mate," she said. "They will get suspicious if we stall any longer or if we leave without doing it. If they decide to make a general investigation, they could discover the truth, and that would wipe us all out. The colony cannot afford even the suggestion of suspicion!''

''But casual sex—''

''Casual, hell! This is serious.''

''Politically or economically motivated—this is against *my* religion!'' he protested.

''You don't have the *right* to come here from Earth with your irrelevant standards and place our survival as a colony in peril,'' she said.

Shocked, Brother Paul realized she was correct. This psudo-religion of the Hyades colony of the future was valid on its own terms, alien as they might be. He could not accept it—but he also could not condemn it.

Yet if he could not eliminate *this* type of religion from consideration, how could he eliminate *any* religion? All were valid on their own terms. He could continue his survey for the rest of his life and never be able to choose between them. He was no closer to his answer than before.

Who was the God of Tarot? He needed some more direct means of finding out.

But first he had to dispose of the matter at hand. These Animations were to a certain extent under his control, despite the constant pressure of precession. Presumably he could turn them off when he wished. But if he did that, quitting the game as he tired of it—of what validity would be any answer he might eventually obtain through these Animations? He suspected he really had to play the game through by its own rules to protect its relevance. Which meant that he had to resolve the dilemma here before leaving. How could he protect both his own integrity and the welfare of this Hyades colony?

Ah—he had it. ''Ruby, you should be making love to your brother-husband, your brothub, not me. You aren't really mad at him, are you?''

She frowned prettily, loath to answer directly. ''He's not here, and the Naths—''

"He is here. *I* am the one who is not here. There is no freezer-ship from Earth. I am a ghost."

She laughed. "Oh, come *on*! That isn't in the script!"

"It is *now*."

"All right. I'll play along. I've always been curious about how a ghost made love."

"In a moment I shall assume my true form: that of your beloved brothub, who shall turn out to have been with you all the time. Are you ready?"

"This can't—"

"Now." And Brother Paul made an effort of will, hoping Precession would not abort it, and faded out of the picture.

As the scene disappeared, he wondered: who played the part of her brothub?

IV

Time: 12

The Sphinx, crouching a little distance away from the foot of the Great Pyramid, is carved out of the granite plateau itself; there is no break between its base and the original rock. Its height, about 75 feet, gives some idea of the enormous labour it must have entailed to free it of unwanted stone and to level the base. Its total length is 150 feet; its height from breast to chin is 50 feet and from the chin to the top of the head 25 feet; the circumference of the head, taken round the temples, is 80 feet, the face being 14 feet wide and the head 30 feet long. The layers of granite from which it has been carved divide its face into horizontal bands in a curious way; its mouth is formed partly by the space between two of the layers of stone. A hole several feet deep has been drilled in the head: this was probably used for the placing of ornaments, such as the priestly tiara or the royal crown.

This carved rock, reddish in colour, has a tremendous effect as it stands overlooking the desert sands. It is a phantom that seems keenly attentive; one would almost say that it listens and looks. Its great ear seems to hear all the sounds of the past; its eyes, turned towards the east, seem to look towards the misty future; its gaze has a depth

*and fixity that fascinates the spectator. In this
figure, half statue and half mountain, can be seen
a peculiar majesty, a great serenity and even a certain gentleness.*
—Paul Christian: *The History and Practice of
Magic*, New York: Citadel, 1969.

Brother Paul stood in front of the Sphinx. The stone
creature was impressive in the light of the full moon, the
more so because its nose was intact: this was evidently
before Napoleon's gunners had shot it off.

What an animal it was, crouching there like a living
thing! Brother Paul felt a prickle at the back of his neck.
This was an Animation; could he be sure this monster
was *not* alive?

But it was absolutely still. No breathing, no heart-
beat, no motion of eyes. Inanimate, after all. Fortunately.

Still, he would test it, just to be *sure*. "The sexual
urge of the camel is stronger by far than one thinks," he
said aloud, quoting the poem from a memory that
predated his entry into the Holy Order of Vision. "One
day on a trek through the desert, he rudely assaulted the
Sphinx."

He paused, listening, watching, No reaction. Was the
monster truly inanimate or merely waiting? "Now the
posterior orifice of the Sphinx is washed by the sands of
the Nile—which accounts for the hump in the camel,
and the Sphinx's inscrutable smile."

Still nothing. No doubt about it: if the thing stood
still for that verse, it was dead.

He contemplated the parts of it. A woman's head,
suggesting human intelligence, aspiration, and strategy.
A bull's body, signifying the tireless strength necessary
to pursue human fortune. Lion's legs, indicating the
courage and force also needed, that is to say the human
will. And eagle's wings, veiling that intelligence,
strength, and courage until there came the time to fly.
Thus the Sphinx as a whole was the symbol of the concealed intelligence, strength, and will possessed by the
Masters of Time.

Famous Greeks had come here to study at the feet of the Masters: Thales, Pythagoras, Plato, and others. Thales had been the first to embrace water as the primary substance in the universe, explaining change as well as stability. Pythagoras, known for his doctrine of the transmigration of souls and the Pythagorean Theorum. Plato, primarily known for his Dialogues, presenting his mentor Socrates and the thesis that Knowledge is Good, Ignorance Evil. Giants of philosophy, all of them. Now it was Brother Paul's turn to meet the Masters those famous Greeks had met—if he dared.

Time to proceed. Brother Paul walked to the front of the Sphinx. There between its extended forelegs was the outline of a door into its chest. The door was made of bronze, weathered to match the stone of the statue. He walked up to it, took a breath, and put one hand forth to touch it.

Nothing happened. The metal was neutral, neither cool nor hot, and it was solid. He felt around the edges to find a handle or niche, but there was none. He could not open it.

He sighed silently. He lifted a knuckle and rapped, once. There was no response. Did he really want to enter this structure? He rapped again, and then a third time. Theoretically, the ancient Masters had possessed all knowledge and could answer his question—if they chose to. But first he would have to undergo their rite of passage. That, according to whispered legends, could be hazardous to health. Yet he continued knocking, half hoping no one would answer. Then, at the fifth rap, the door silently opened.

Two hooded persons stood inside, their faces invisible. One, by his bulk and manner, seemed male; the other was shorter and slighter, seeming female. "We are Thesmothetes, guardians of the Rites," the male said. "Who are you that knocks at the Door of the Occult Sanctuary?"

Brother Paul controlled his nervousness. "I am a humble seeker of truth. I wish to know the identity of the True God of Tarot."

Within the shroud there seemed to be a frown. "Do you understand, Postulant, that you must give yourself over entirely to our discretion?" the Thesmothete asked. "That you must follow our advice as if it were an order, asking no questions?"

Brother Paul swallowed. "I understand, Thesmothete."

The man stood aside. "Enter, Postulant."

Brother Paul stepped inside. The female touched the wall; a small spring depressed, releasing a hidden mechanism. The door closed silently—and the interior was completely dark.

A small hand took his. This was surely the silent Thesmothete, the lady. She guided him forward, into the bowels of the Sphinx. To the place of digestion? *The sexual urge of the camel . . .* no, don't even *think* that! By a slight pressure on his fingers the female made him pause. He felt her form lower a few centimeters, and realized she had stepped down. He put forward a foot cautiously and found the step.

It was a spiral staircase. Brother Paul was a compulsive counter; he had tried to break himself of the habit in recent years, but during stress the desire sometimes returned irresistibly. He had to know how many there were of whatever he encountered, however inconsequential. He counted thirty steps before the passage leveled out.

Here there was another door—bronze, no doubt—to be opened silently, passed through, and closed. Obviously the Thesmothetes had this labyrinth memorized, so they could find their way unerringly. The air was cooler in the new passage, but not musty. This suggested that it was well vented, for he was in a time millennia before the day of air conditioning.

His footfalls echoed, giving him the impression of a large, circular chamber. He thought of a story he had read once, Poe's "The Pit and the Pendulum," and his nervousness increased. But of course his guides were beside him and knew their way; they would not let this party fall into any oubliette, with or without pendulum.

Suddenly both Thesmothetes halted, the male's arm

barring Brother Paul's forward progress. "We stand at
the brink of a precipice," the man said. "One more stop
will hurl you to the bottom."

Just so. Had Brother Paul made his way here alone,
in this gloom he could have fallen into it. He should
have brought a light—but then they would not have admitted him. "I will wait," he said. He was about to ask
the purpose of this march to the brink, but remembered
his promise to ask no questions.

However, his question was answered. "This abyss,"
the male said, "surrounds the Temple of Mysteries and
protects it against the temerity and curiosity of the
profane. We have arrived a little too soon; our brethren
have not yet lowered the drawbridge by which the
initiates communicate with the sacred place. We shall
wait for their arrival. But if you value your life, do not
move until we tell you."

Did the Thesmothete protest too much? Maybe there
was an abyss and maybe there wasn't—but Brother
Paul could not afford to proceed on the assumption that
there was no threat. Not after the things he had experienced in other Animations. They had so arranged it,
this time, that his control over specific visions had been
nullified. He was at the mercy of these anonymous
people and had been from the moment he entered the
Sphinx. Yet he had come here voluntarily; he was on the
threshhold of the unknown, and if the answer were
here—

Suddenly there was light, blinding after the darkness.
Two grotesque monsters stood before him, each in
white linen robes, one with a gold belt and a lion's head,
the other with a silver belt and bull's head. Even as his
eyes adjusted and took them in, a trap door opened between them. From this rose a grisly specter brandishing
a scythe. It was most reminiscent of the skeletal figure
of Death in the Tarot. With a horrendous roar it swept
the scythe at Brother Paul's head.

His first instinct was to tumble back, out of range of
the weapon. His second was to duck under the blade
and grapple with the specter. But his third overrode the
first two: he stood frozen.

The scythe's blade swished so close over his head that it might have parted his hair. Indeed, a small lock of it tumbled across his face. "Woe to him who disturbs the peace of the dead!" the monster screamed, whirling entirely around and sweeping the scythe at Brother Paul a second time. But again he judged the path of the blade, and again he did not flinch. This was a scare tactic, not a serious attack; a test of his courage that his judo training had prepared him for.

Four more times the scythe came at him, and each time he stood firm. But on the seventh stroke the creature shifted its balance; this time it was going for his neck!

Brother Paul gambled: he stood firm. They surely had not arranged this elaborate presentation merely to execute an unresisting man. And as the blade touched him—the monster vanished. It dropped down its hole, and the trap door closed. This, too, had been a bluff; the threat had no substance.

Now the lion and the bull removed their masks. Brother Paul saw their faces for the first time: Therion and Amaranth.

"Congratulations," Therion told him. "You felt the chill of murderous steel, and you did not flinch; you looked at the horror of horrors and did not faint. Well, done! In your own country you could be a hero." He frowned. "But amongst us, there are virtues higher than courage. What do you take to be the meaning of our costumes?"

Brother Paul had already worked that out. "You are the lion, one of the aspects of the Sphinx, with the golden belt, representing the astrological Leo and the Sun. She, masked as the bull, is another aspect of the Sphinx, Taurus, and the Moon. The Sun and Moon together are supposed to exert the most direct influence on the lives of earthly beings. Yet man does not live by Sun and Moon alone; there is always the savage influence of Time, bringing the chance of untimely death—"

"You are most impressively apt," Therion said. "Yet we have a value superior even to this intelligence. That is

humility—voluntary humility, triumphing over the
vanity of pride. Are you capable of such a victory over
yourself?''

So the physical test was over. Good! Brother Paul
was ready for the moral one. "I am willing to find out."

"Very well," Therion said. "Are you ready to crawl
flat on the ground, right to the innermost sanctuary
where our brethren wait to give you the knowledge and
power you seek in exchange for your humility?''

Why this follow-up challenge? He really was not
seeking power. Still, he seemed to have no choice but to
accept. "I am."

"Then take this lamp," Therion said. "It is the image
of God's face that follows us when we walk hidden from
the sight of men. Go without fear; you have only yourself to be afraid of henceforth.''

Brother Paul, thinking of his experience of the Seven
Cups, did not find this reassuring. What other horrors
lurked—in himself? He accepted the lamp and looked
about. The chamber was formed of blocks of granite
shaped into a dome; there was no entrance or exit. But
again he remembered his stricture and made no inquiry.

After a moment, Amaranth touched another hidden
spring in the wall. An iron plate slid aside; it was coated
with granite to resemble a full block when in place.
Behind it opened a corridor, an arcade, narrow and so
low it was impossible to crawl through it on hands and
knees. "Let this path be for you the image of the tomb
in which all men must find their eventual rest," Therion
intoned. "Yet they awake, freed from the darkness of
material things, in the life of the spirit. You have
vanquished the specter of Death; now you can triumph
over the horrors of the tomb in the Test of Solitude.''
And both Thesmothetes extended their right hands
toward the opening.

Now Brother Paul hesitated. Why were they sending
him *alone*, now? What sort of horrors did they consider
so awesome? That constricted hole—if it got any
smaller, once he was in, he would be unable either to
squeeze through or to turn about. He would have to
retreat, feet first, as though in the throes of a breech

birth—and surely the entrance-exit panel would be closed and locked.

The two Thesmothetes remained as they were, fingers pointing to the hole. They neither reproached him for his weakness nor encouraged him to carry on with the test. What would they do if he balked, now?

Actually, he knew. He had read of a test like this once; the memory was faint, elusive, and only returned as it was refreshed by this present experience. The postulant who lost his nerve was not excluded or even reproached. He was merely led out of the sacred place. The law of Magism dictated that he would never again be tested; his weakness had been judged. So—if he wanted his answer, it was now or never. The law of Animation was as inflexible in its fashion as the law of the ancient Egyptian mystics. He had not yet encountered the same vision twice; the vagaries of the dynamics of this situation were too great to permit him to rerun any scene.

Brother Paul was not unduly claustrophobic, but he didn't like this at all. He was not the most slender of men; a passage sufficient for a 150 centimeter tall Egyptian or Greek might not suffice for him. If he got wedged in amidst these thousands of tons of stone—

Still the two Thesmothetes waited, pointing, as still as statues. Brother Paul offered up a silent prayer to whatever God governed this demesne—Thoth, perhaps?—and got down to enter the dread aperture.

Amaranth got down beside him. "God be between you and harm in all the empty places you must go," she murmured and gave him a quick sidewise swipe of a kiss on the lips. Then Brother Paul pushed the lamp forward and crawled into the hole.

The tube sloped gently downwards. Its circumference was of polished granite, absolutely smooth as though drilled by a giant worm. There *was* room for him, barely. By a combination of elbow-drawings and knee-hitchings, augmented by toe-flexes, he moved himself forward until his full length was within the tunnel.

A terrible clang deafened him momentarily as the bronze door fell back into place. As from a distance, a

reverberating voice came: "Here perish all fools who
covet knowledge and power!" It was followed immediately by an echo: "power...power...power...
power...power...power...power!"   Seven   distinct
echoes, hammering themselves into his brain. The effect
was foolishly terrifying; sonics could have a fundamental influence on a man's emotion, bypassing his
reason. Brother Paul knew that—yet still felt the
frigtening impact.

Had the Magi condemned him to death after all? That
still did not make sense; they could have barred him
from the Sphinx at the outset. If they intended to bury
him alive, why had they given him this good lamp?

Gradually the irrational fear subsided. There had to
be an exit to this tube; all he had to do was keep moving.
Yet it went on and on! Brother Paul had a fair sense of
orientation, perhaps a function of his compulsive
counting. It informed him that he could no longer be
within or beneath the Sphinx! This interminable tunnel
was proceeding under the surface of the plateau itself—toward the Great Pyramid! Furthermore, it was
still descending, deeper and deeper into the rock. What
would he do if his guttering lamp went out?

Still it continued. His elbows and knees were sore,
perhaps bleeding, but he could not stop. Nervousness
prevented him even from resting. He passed the lamp
from one hand to the other, finding different ways to
crawl . . . and crawl.

At last the tunnel expanded. What a relief! He got up
on his hands and knees for a space, then proceeded at a
stooping walk. But the floor still sloped down;
the added space was gained by the floor's retreat from
the level ceiling. He was not being allowed nearer the
surface.

Abruptly the floor terminated. The wan light of the
lamp showed a vast crater, a cone plunging deep into the
rock, its slides slick and hard. An iron ladder picked up
where the tunnel left off, leading down into that gloomy
cavity. There was no other route; only by getting on the
ladder could he proceed forward, or rather downward.

He now had ample room to turn about, but was sure a retreat up the tunnel would not be wise.

He started down the ladder, nervously testing each rung before putting full weight upon it. All were sturdy. And of course he counted: ten, twenty, thirty, on.

There were exactly one hundred rungs. But the ladder did not lead to another level or sloping passage. It terminated in a circular hole. Brother Paul had no object to drop experimentally into it, but he was sure this was an oubliette: a fatally deep dungeon with no exit. He could not trust himself to that!

Yet there was nowhere else to go! What now?

"God be between me and harm in all the empty places I must go," he repeated, staring down into the dread void. And added mentally: *And may there be avenues of escape from those empty places!*

Brother Paul studied his situation. There *had* to be an alternative; this setup was too elaborate to be a mere death trap. He had to believe that! All he had to do was figure out its rationale. The ladder went down and stopped; there was no question of a hidden continuance because the final rung was in the dank air over the pit. Still, he could look.

He climbed down, then poked both legs through the bottom rung, hooking his knees over it. He bounced twice, with increasing vigor, testing its solidity; it would hold his weight. He leaned back, slowly, holding the lamp carefully upright as his angle changed, letting his torso swing around until he hung upside down by his knees. His head projected through the hole, and his lamp illuminated the chamber below.

It was a featureless well, plunging straight down beyond the reach of his lamp. The walls looked slimy, and there was no second ladder below the one he was on. This was a one-way avenue . . . probably filled with water at the nether terminus. Maybe that fluid would break his fall—but he did not care to risk it. Not yet.

He had been more or less given to understand that he had nothing to fear but himself. Now it occurred to him that this was subject to alarming interpretation. If he

decided to drop into the oubliette, and that was an
error, would he have killed himself? All he had to do
was make the correct decision—without adequate information.

Well, he had no need to remain on this ladder! He
caught the rung with his left hand, held the lamp steady
with his right, and drew himself up until he could ex-
tricate his feet. Then he started back up the hundred
rungs.

About twenty rungs up—twenty two, technically—he
spied a crevice in the cone. A flaw, invisible from above
because the upper wall overhung it slightly. Was this
natural or artificial?

He had grown wary of chance here. He leaned as far
over as was convenient, holding the lamp extended to
the left. This gap was broad enough for a man to
squeeze through—and there were steps inside! Here was
his alternate route!

He balanced carefully and swung himself into the
crevice. The steps were slippery but solid. They advanced deeper into the wall; the crevice was becoming a
new tunnel, at places so narrow he had to proceed
sidewise, but it was definitely going somewhere. It
coiled into a spiral. At the count of thirty, the steps
ended at a small platform, and the way forward was
barred by a bronze grating.

Was this a service access, intended for the use of the
Thesmothetes, that he had spied accidentally? If so, it
would be a dead end for him since the grating was
locked and unattended. Yet it did not seem extraneous.
Twenty two steps up on the ladder from the bottom,
matching the number of Major Arcana of the Tarot, appearing only when the Postulant was returning from his
fruitless quest to the oubliette. Surely no coincidence!
But what, then, was the significance of thirty alternate
steps, here? These passages seemed to have a motif of
thirties and hundreds, and that did not equate to any
Tarot deck he knew of. So if there were a numeric
rationale here, he had not yet fathomed it.

Brother Paul peered through the grating. Ahead was
a long gallery, lined on each side by statuettes of

sphinxes: fifteen on each side. Thirty in all. Between statues, the walls were covered with mysterious frescoes. At this angle, he could not quite make out their nature, but there was a haunting familiarity about them. Fifteen lamps rested in tripods set in a row down the center of the hall, and each lamp was in the shape of a sphinx.

A Magus walked slowly down the hall toward him. No—it was the female Thesmothete, Amaranth, garbed in the manner of a priestess. Her face was veiled and her gown covered her body completely, but he recognized her provocative walk, that pushed out hip and breast in subtle but quite feminine rhythm.

"Son of Earth," she said, smiling, "you have escaped the pit by discovering the path of wisdom. Few aspirants to the Mysteries have passed this test; most have perished." So that explained what happened to those who entrusted themselves to the oubliette!

"The Goddess Isis is your protector," she continued. Brother Paul remembered the Egyptian Isis, said to be the Goddess of Love. "She will lead you safely to the sanctuary where virtue receives its crown." Virtue supervised by the Goddess of Sex? The geese were being put in the charge of the fox! "I must warn you that other perils are in store, but I shall aid you by explaining these sacred symbols which will clothe your mind with invulnerable power." No question: Amaranth was now Isis. This was her kind of role.

Isis opened the gate by releasing another secret spring. She took Brother Paul by the hand and led him down the gallery. She moved slowly, almost languourously, but even so this was far too rapid for him to properly assimilate the portraits they passed. All the wisdom of the ancients spread out here—and he had to zoom past it like an ignorant tourist!

But perhaps that was the point. He was only looking, not buying. If he chose to remain here indefinitely, if he qualified by passing all their tests, *then* he could linger over each symbol for as long as he liked. Years, if necessary.

"First we review the aspects of Nature," Isis murmured. "Here is the Crocodile." She gestured with her

free hand toward the nearest picture, just before the
first sphinx. It depicted an Egyptian peasant walking by
a river, two bags slung over his shoulder, while a crocodile paced him in the water. "It symbolizes Folly."

The Zero Key of the Tarot! So Tarot *was* at the root
of this! Now he had an excellent frame of reference,
enhancing his understanding.

"The Magus," she said, indicating the representation
across the hall. "Representing Skill." It was an Egyptian magician, very like the European one except for
costume.

"Veiled Isis," she said, going right on to the next.
"Memory—among other things." And the veiled figure
portrayed was—her. He did not need to guess at the
identity of those "other things" she was thinking of. He
remembered Amaranth in her landscape dress, her
breasts living volcanoes. Amaranth as naked Temptation in the Vision of the Seven Cups. As Sister Beth of
the Holy Order of Vision, whom he had tried to seduce.
What was her true role this time?

What else but Temptation again! A temptation he
was sure he had to resist here, if the terrible weight of
the Pyramid were not to crush him.

But she had already moved on to the next picture—and it was blank. "The Ghost," she said. "The
Unknown or Unidentified; the Infinite; the Nothingness."

What? *This* was no Tarot card! He stopped by it,
about to inquire—but caught himself. No questions!
His thoughts about her sexual temptation had almost
distracted him into a different trap. He would just have
to accept the fact, for now, that this was not Tarot. Not
precisely. It was—an unknown.

"Isis Unveiled," she said, abruptly throwing off her
veil. Now she was Woman in her full splendor, her face
absolutely lovely in the lamplight. She played variations
on a single theme, but she certainly had the equipment
for that! "Action."

Action. She still held his hand, and now she was
drawing him in close, raising her lips. So eminently
kissable.

He moved his hand, carrying hers along, guiding it and her toward the next exhibit. His action—was to pursue the lesson further.

She yielded gracefully. She had a thousand little ploys; the failure of one was of little account. If this had been another test, he had passed it—probably.

"Now we review the aspects of Faith," Isis continued. "Here is the Sovereign, symbol of Power." She moved on. "And the Master of the Arcana, representing Intuition. And here are the Two Paths, showing Choice."

Brother Paul moved along with her, nodding. These were very like the Tarot, but not identical. That card of the Unknown. . . .

But now she paused. She made a convoluted shrug and her robe fell away. Now Isis stood in a short skirt and halter, as scenic as ever. "Also known as The Ordeal," she said, moving in close again.

The ordeal of rejecting her? That seemed the only safe course, much as he might have liked to try her constantly proferred sample and be done with it. Celibacy and rejection of sex were all very well for the unhealthy recluse, but Brother Paul was a thoroughly healthy and social man. However. He advanced to the next picutre.

Immediately she followed. "The Chariot of Osiris, signifying Precession," she said.

Precession! He almost challenged that, but again caught himself. He had expected her to give the interpretation as Victory. Each time the Tarot connections became slightly firm, something broke them up again!

She moved on. "Desire—Emotion," she said of the next. Well, that might equate to the Thoth Tarot version of Strength, titled Lust.

But then she showed the next: "The Tamed Lion—Discipline." *That* one had to be Strength! But then what—? "Also called the Enchantress, Strength, Spiritual Power, and Fortitude," she continued. And the picture was of the woman calming the lion. Yet—

"Here is the Family of Man—Nature," she said. He didn't recognize that one in Tarot either. "And here is

the Wheel, symbolizing Chance. And the Sphinx, alter-
nately known as the Veiled Lamp, which unveiled is
Time." Now that was all mixed up! The Hermit card
was Time, while the Sphinx bestrode the Wheel of Fortune. But she went on talking, preventing him from getting his thoughts organized. "Chronos, who was once
Chief of the Gods."

Brother Paul had another realization: he had been encountering aspects of these images all along, since his
arrival on Planet Tarot. Maybe since his first assign-
ment to this mission! Was this his own fate being sum-
marized? If so, he was about to glimpse his future!

Isis gave him no time to consider the ramifications of
that. "Here are the aspects of Trade. The first is Past,
suggesting Reflection; the next is Future, symbolizing
Will."

Brother Paul peered at the pictures, but could not
grasp them in the time he had. Surely both of these were
merely aspects of Time! Did they show his own past and
future? Reflection he could understand; he was much
given to it himself. But how did Will relate? He thought
he saw an airplane, and a bottle of wine, and a
document, and trees, and a child, but somehow neither
picture would come together meaningfully. If only he
had more time to study—

"Here is Themis, Goddess of Law, signifying
Honor." Strange; Brother Paul remembered Themis as
a Roman Goddess, rather than Egyptian. But perhaps it
only showed that this sequence of images derived from
multiple sources and was not limited to any single
mythology. Rome had existed in the period of Egypt's
greatness; archaeology had verified the presence of
Rome a thousand years before the legendary date of its
founding by the wolf-suckled brothers, Romulus and
Remus.

"The Martyr—Sacrifice," Isis continued. This
seemed to be the card he knew as the Hanged Man,
suspended by one foot from a gibbet. Was *that* in his
future? He was driving himself crazy with these
speculations!

"The Scythe—Change," she said. He knew this one

as Death or Transformation. "Imagination—Vision." That one he could not place at all, though there was something irrelevantly familiar about the illustration. A field, with a tower to one side, and a gully at the other—

"The Alchemist, signifying Transfer." Transfer! That was the term the alien Antares had employed for the transposition of auras from one host to another—

"And the aspects of Magic, that some call Science," she continued inexorably. What torture, to be treated to these tantalyzing glimpses of half-familiar revelations! Surely it all did fit a larger pattern, if only he could—

"Here is Typhon, known as Fate, signifying Violence." It was the Devil. "The House of God —revelation." He knew it as the Lightning-Struck Tower, though that was probably an iconographical transformation. A familiar card—yet he felt a premonitory dread. He was of course searching for the House of God—but this cruel edifice seemed more Satanic than Angelic. Some interpretations indicated this card was actually the House of the Devil, signifying Ruin.

Meanwhile, Isis was blithely removing her remaining apparel. Revelation—naturally she would take it not only literally, but physically! He wished this tour were over; he was maintaining a firm countenance, but she was making it very difficult. What happened to a Postulate who yielded to the obvious suggestion and put his lustful hands (lustful *hands*? Ah, the eupherhism!) on the priestess?

"The Star of the Magi," she continued, and now she looked very much like the nude girl in that picture. "Hope and Fear."

Exactly.

"Twilight—Deception." Yes, another familiar card that he knew as the Moon. Deception was surely the key concept here! In revealing her entire body, she deceived him about her intentions. As did all women . . . .

"And the Blazing Light, suggesting Triumph." Well, he hoped so! But trumph for whom?

"And the aspects of Art," she said. Nude art? He wondered how many people would be interested in art if it were not thoroughly peopled with naked young women. To his mind, a nude young man was as artistically beautiful as a woman; but it was sex, not esthetics, that made the difference. Women did not dash out to buy portraits of nude men as avidly as man bought nude women, so the definition of Art became—

"Here is Thought, that we interpret as Reason." The picture was—well, it looked like a field of stars. "The Awakening of the Dead, meaning Decision." The picture resembled the Judgment card he knew. His own moment of Judgment might be upon him all too soon! "The Savant, meaning Wisdom."

Naked, she advanced to the last picture and spun about, showing herself to advantage. "The Crown of the Magi—Completion," she said. She stepped close, caught his head in her hands, and drew it down for a quick kiss. Then she opened the door at the end of the gallery and stood aside.

Beyond that door was a long, narrow vault. At its end were the leaping flames of a blazing furnace.

"Son of Earth," Isis said, "Death itself only frightens the imperfect. If you are afraid, you have no business here. Look at me: once I too passed through these flames as if they were a garden of roses."

Brother Paul looked at her. Suddenly she was much more tempting. If he put his hands on her, stroked one or two of those perfect fruits—would she acquiesce? Or would sudden disaster befall him? Would the touch of her flesh be worth the penalty?

He looked again at the flames. The teaching he had just received, hurried and elliptical as it was, would be useless to a man about to die. There had to be a way through! He stood, as it were, at the fork in the road, the Two Paths, also known as the Ordeal. The choice between Love and Fire. Had he learned enough to make it through?

Actually, there *was* a way to overcome fire or at least hot coals. South Pacific natives heated rock to red heat and walked barefooted over it, and there was no fakery involved. The secret was a special effect that could be noted with droplets of water dancing on a hot frying

pan: the heat evaporated just enough water to form a
layer of steam, and the droplet floated on that steam,
insulated from the much higher heat of the pan. Thus
the droplets could take many seconds to dwindle, instead of puffing entirely into vapor almost instantly, as
happened on surfaces heated more moderately.
Similarly, the natural moisture of the native's feet
became that layer of steam, enabling them to walk the
coals without being burned. So if he could find an area
where the flames were low enough to expose the hot
coals, he might be able to cross. If he had the nerve.

Abruptly he faced forward and stepped into the new
chamber. Again the door clanged shut behind him,
forever closing off what might have been. He was alone
again, unable to retreat. Did God stand between him
and the flame?

But as he approached the furnace, he discovered that
it was largely illusory. Wood was arranged on iron
grills, and lamps were so placed that their light
suggested open flame. A path wound between these
mock-ups, on through a vaulted passageway. He moved
forward with renewed confidence. God *was* here!

The path ended abruptly at a stagnant pool. Who
might guess what lurked beneath that slimy surface?
Brother Paul turned about, so as to retrace his route and
look for an alternate—and a cascade of oil descended
from sluices in the ceiling. There was a spark, ignition,
and the oil became a curtain of flame. The pretend furnace had become a real one!

He had to plunge back through that flame—or go forward through the water. Or wait, hoping one threat or
the other would abate. But that was not the way of this
series of challenges; he had to show his mettle by
conquering the hurdles, rather than by avoiding them.
Somehow.

The water seemed the better bet. Brother Paul
removed his robe, wadded it tightly, and held it in his
right hand along with his lamp. Then he stepped
cautiously into the pool.

There was a slippery slope beneath that urged him on
faster than he cared to go. Each step brought him

deeper. Knees, thighs, waist; the water was chill, which was encouraging because it meant reptiles were less likely to inhabit it. Chest, shoulders, chin; now he held the lamp over his head. Any deeper and he would have to swim—but then he would risk dousing the light, for he could not safely carry it high and level while swimming.

Now he could see that he had indeed reached the middle of the pool. With luck—or the foresight of those who had designed this test—the deepest part. Had someone measured his height, so they could fill the water to the appropriate level? Now it should grow shallower—

It did. With relief he advanced up the slope. This had been basically a test of his fortitude and not a complex one. A choice between fire and water. In fact all these tests were rather basic and physical; a modern-day examination would have been considerably more sophisticated. He had overestimated the subtlety of the—

His foot plunged into a gap in the underwater flooring. He lunged forward, slapping the water with his left hand and windmilling with his right to recover his lost balance. He made it; his questing toes found the side of the gap. A mere pothole! But his glowing lamp toppled off the bunched garment and plunged into the water. He made a desperate grab for it with his left hand, but missed—and in any event, it had been extinguished. He might re-light it by taking it back to the curtain of flame—if its oil had not been hopelessly diluted by the water, and if he could get it close enough to that fire without burning himself, and if—

He looked back. The curtain of flame had died out. Only the sitting lamps remained. So even if he had his lamp and it were operative, he could not light it.

He stopped. Idiot! All he had to do was pick up one of the other lamps. But there was a little light to see by, and maybe there were other traps awaiting the man who tried to backtrack. Best to accept the consequence of his error and go on without the light. His overconfidence had been responsible for his spill—a lesson in itself. Only himself to fear!

He climbed out of the water. At the far edge à flight of steps led to a platform surrounded on three sides by a spacious arcade. On the far wall was a brass door, set behind a narrow, twisted column sculpted in the shape of a lion's jaws. The teeth held a metal ring. That was as much detail as he could make out in the dim light.

He stopped before the door. The air was chill, and he was shivering. Once he got dry, he could don his robe again and be more comfortable. But now, one by one, the distant lamps went out; the reflection of the last one came across the water, then faded. He was in complete darkness again.

If he had tried to go back, to pick up one of those sitting lamps—would he have gotten there in time? If they were all short of fuel, none of them would have done him much good anyway, and he could have been trapped in the water in darkness. It would have been easy to wander astray, into much deeper water, where creatures might lurk. . . .

A voice sounded in the gloom. "Son of Earth, to stop is to perish. Behind you is death; before you, salvation."

Brother Paul was not yet dry; he decided to take the voice at its word and proceed without dressing. He extended his hand, finding the carved door. That ring in the lion's mouth—was it a handle? Or a trap? If he pulled at it, would the door open or would those teeth clamp on his hand?

Well, he could circumvent this one! He shook out his cloak, drew it lengthwise into a kind of cord, and carefully threaded it through the loop. Then he held one end in each hand and gave a sharp yank.

A trap door opened beneath his feet. He dropped—and came up short, hanging on to the robe-rope. Again he had underestimated the trap! He could not afford to judge too many more such items!

Well, on with it. He pulled himself up on his makeshift rope. "Easier for a rope to pass through the eye of a needle . . ." he muttered, thinking of the centuries of confusion caused by a simple mistranslation in the Bible, wherein the term "camel's hair rope" had been rendered as "camel." Then he swung his feet up and walked himself onto the main platform. Had he not been in good condition, this would have been a difficult or impossible maneuver. He gained his balance on the main floor and removed the robe from the ring. Good thing that ring had been well anchored!

Then he heard the trapdoor closing. Now the brass door opened, spilling light into the hall. Therion the Thesmothete stood there, carrying a bright torch. "Come, Postulant."

Brother Paul followed him through a series of galleries set off by locked doors. At each door Therion murmured a password and gave a secret signal, and it opened.

During one of these pauses, Brother Paul slipped back into his robe. Now he felt more confident. At last the test was over!

They came finally to a crypt that Brother Paul's directional sense informed him had been hollowed out of the Great Pyramid itself. This was a chamber never discovered by the archaeologists! The walls were polished stone, covered by symbolic paintings. At each corner stood a bronze statue: a man, a bull, a lion, and an eagle. Hanging from the high ceiling was an elaborate lamp. Brother Paul observed that the beams of light between the statues and from the lamp together formed the outline of a pyramid: five corners counting the apex.

In the center was a huge round silver table, and on this table stood two cups, two swords, two coins, scepters, and lamps. The four symbols of the Tarot suits, plus the lamps necessary to see the rest in this sunless chamber.

Therion turned to him. "Son of Earth, I have only to give the sign and you will be plunged alive into subterranean depths to eat the bread of remorse and drink the waters of anguish until the end of your days. But we are not vindictive; all we ask of you is your solemn oath that you will never reveal to anyone the least detail of what you have seen or heard this night, and you shall go free. Will you give this oath?''

Reasonable enough. A secret society would not remain secret long if it did not institute such a precaution. But Brother Paul's mission required that he express his knowledge outside. ''I will not,'' he said.

Therion stared at him incredulously. ''That was intended to be a rhetorical question, Postulant. There is only one answer.''

''Not for me.'' Had he gone through all this—for nothing?

''Beware, Postulant! Defiance is punished by death!'' And a menacing roaring sounded as the overhead lamp was extinguished. The chamber was now lighted only by tremulously flickering candles set behind the statues.

''My information cannot benefit anyone, if it is sworn to secrecy,'' Brother Paul said, unmoved.

Therion pointed to the cups on the silver table. ''Then you must undertake this trial,'' he cried. ''One goblet contains a violent poison; the other is harmless. Choose one, without reflection, and drink it down.''

Brother Paul stepped up to the table, picked up the right cup, and drank its contents down.

Therion smiled. ''I tried,'' he said. ''Both drinks were—safe.''

As Brother Paul had figured. A test of pure chance would have been pointless; courage, not life or luck, was the issue here.

''Worthy zealot,'' Therion said, ''You have passed all tests. Now you are ready to share the wisdom of the ancients. Magic is composed of two elements, knowledge and strength. Without knowledge, no strength can be complete; without some sort of strength, no one can attain knowledge. Learn how to suffer, that you may become impassive; learn how to die, to become immortal; learn restraint, to attain your desire: these are the first three secrets the Magus must learn to become a priest of Truth. He must study with us for twelve years to master it, as Moses of the Jews did, and Plato of the Greeks did, and—''

"Twelve years?" Brother Paul demanded.

"To start. After that the *real* education begins."

"I can't wait twelve years!" Brother Paul protested. "I can't wait twelve *weeks!* I need my answer now." Before it was time for him to be shuttled back to Earth; the mattermission schedule would not be modified for the convenience of one man.

"This is impossible," Therion said firmly.

"Then I must depart."

Therion gestured, and a panel slid open in the floor before his feet. "There is your exit."

From the pit came the noise of rattling chains and panting struggle and the roar of some great beast. Then there came the scream of a human being in dreadful agony—abruptly cut off.

Brother Paul stepped forward to look into the pit. There was a lion-sized sphinx tearing at a naked human body lying before it.

Brother Paul stepped around the pit, snatched one of the swords from the table, flexed it twice to get its heft, then jumped into the hole. The last things he perceived as he acted were Therion's gape of incredulity and Amaranth's scream from somewhere in the distance. Then his feet struck the back of the vicious sphinx. He swung his sword down—and the Animation exploded into nothingness.

V

Reflection: 13

The contradiction between politics and morality, never far below the surface in so-called normal times, reasserts itself with particular vehemence in times of revolutionary change. Why is it that the revolutionaries sooner or later adopt, and sometimes intensify, the cruelties of the regimes against which they fight? Why is it that revolutionaries begin with camaraderie and end with fratricide? Why do revolutions start by proclaiming the brotherhood of man, the end of lies, deceit, and secrecy, and culminate in tyranny whose victims are overwhelmingly the little people for whom the revolution was proclaimed as the advent of a happier life? To raise these questions is not to deny that revolutions have been among the most significant ways in which modern men—and in many crucial situations modern women—have managed to sweep aside some of the institutional causes of human suffering. But an impartial outlook and the plain facts of revolutionary change compel the raising of these questions as well. In my estimation the essence of the answer rests in this fundamental contradiction between the effectiveness of immoral political methods and the necessity for morality in any social order. Against his opponents, whether they be a competing revolutionary faction or the leaders of the existing government, a revolutionary cannot be scrupulous about the means that he uses, if he is serious about his objectives and not merely an oratorical promoter of edifying illusions. If he refrains from using unscrupulous means, the enemy may use them first and destroy the revolution itself.

—Barrington Moore, Jr. *Reflections on the Causes of Human Misery*, Boston: Beacon Press, 1972.

Brother Paul walked through the forest, seeking the others. He was momentarily intrigued by the scenery, noting its five levels: grass grew on the ground, giving way at the edge of the path to small leafy plants or vines, which in turn gave way to tall weeds like miniature meter-tall trees. Then head-high bushes, and finally the much taller trees.

He still did not know what he would say to the colonists; he had seen much and experienced much, but still lacked a proper basis on which to judge. God was in all of these or none; how could he know? The matter was so highly subjective that he doubted any objective verdict was possible. Yet he was obliged to make his appearance—after he rounded up the others, before the rift in Animation closed up again.

The region seemed unfamiliar. Had he come this way before? He must have wandered considerably during his visions; certainly he had walked much and crawled more. Yet he still had to be within a few kilometers of his starting point and somewhere within Northole, or he would have walked right out of the Animation. As perhaps he had done.

Maybe his best course was to orient on the sun and march in a straight line. He would surely intersect a local path that would lead him to the village or other habitation. This was a standard mechanism of the type to be found in intelligence tests; it was therefore suspect, but should do for the time being.

Abruptly the forest opened out onto a broad, flat clearing. He started across it, then halted as he discovered concrete. This was a modern highway!

No—it proceeded nowhere. The pavement ended abruptly about a hundred and fifty meters to his left. A dead end, yet an oddly well-kept road. No weeds overgrew it. What could be its purpose, here on Planet Tarot?

Curious, he followed it to his right. Wisps of mist obscured the way ahead, but within a kilometer a building loomed.

He stared, amazed. That was an airport control tower. This was a runway! Yet there were no airplanes on this primitive world. This made no sense.

How had the colonists mustered the resources to construct such a massively modern facility? It might be within their technological capacity, since theoretically all the knowledge of Earth was available to every colony planet, but the sheer labor would be ruinous! These people hardly had fuel enough to heat their homes or resources enough to do more than palisade their villages against natural threats. And if they had resources that had been concealed from him (and why should they deceive him?), to expend them on something as useless as this, in a world where the automobile did not yet exist, let alone aircraft—something was crazy!

A mock-up! That would be it—a grandiose imitation, a shell, a monument to what might be in the planet's future. On what a scale, though!

Intrigued, Brother Paul marched up to the terminal. The thing was huge, girt by ribbons of asphalt, parking lots, access ramps and satellite sub-terminals. Everything was in place. The cars and planes looked completely authentic, so much like Earth of a decade ago that the nostalgia was almost painful. The shrubbery was well-kept, and there was an attractive fountain with the water splaying in artistic patterns.

People were going in and out, just exactly as though on Earth, each appropriately garbed for the occasion, each preoccupied with his own concern. Brother Paul joined the throng at the main entrance, trusting that his presence would not interfere with the show. His Holy Order of Vision habit was in style anywhere. He was curious to see whether the interior was as well appointed as the exterior.

It was. Phenomenally long escalators conveyed people to the operating floors. Loudspeakers bellowed unintelligibly. Short lines formed at ticket desks. Buzzers sounded as people moved toward marked departure gates carrying too much metal. This restoration was absolutely perfect; no detail seemed to have been omitted!

A hand tugged at his. "Come on, Daddy—we'll miss our flight!"

Startled, Brother Paul looked down to discover a young girl hanging on to his hand. She was eight or nine years old, blue-eyed, with two long fair braids. "Daddy, *hurry!*" she cried urgently.

"Young lady, there seems to be a confusion of identities," he said, resisting the pull.

She persisted. "You said it leaves at nine-fifty, and it's nine-forty now, and we haven't even found the gate!"

"I'm not even married," Brother Paul protested, as much to himself as her. Where was her family? He didn't want to lead this child astray.

"Oh, Daddy, come on!" And she fairly dragged him on.

He had either to yield somewhat or to risk an embarrassing scene with a strange child. He suffered himself to be hauled along. "But I don't have a ticket," he said irrelevantly, hoping this would distract her. A ticket for what?

"You let me carry the tickets, remember?" And she relinquished his hand long enough to rummage in her little patchwork handbag. She brought out two envelopes girt with baggage tags and validations, looking very official. "See?"

He was beginning to regret the nicety of detail in this exhibit! He took the ticket folders and examined them. The first envelope was made out to Miss Carolyn Cenji. That was a shock, for he hardly ever used his surname and had thought most colonists were not aware of it. He shifted to the second envelope—and it said Father Paul Cenji. The immediate destination was Boston.

He set aside the riddle of the names for the moment. There was a Boston on Planet Tarot? Yes, it was certainly possible; some hamlet named after the Earth original, used on tickets for verisimilitude. Cute. Still, that did not justify all *this*!

"Flight 24C for Boston boarding at Gate 15," the loudspeaker blared with sudden, atypical clarity.

Brother Paul smiled. Old, old pun! 24C—two four cee—to foresee. This whole elaborate display was an exercise in that foresight, the aspiration of a backward planet looking firmly toward the future. Or perhaps looking into the recent past, nostalgically, when technology and power were cheap; why else were they employing the name of an Earth city? Strange how difficult it could be to distinguish future from past in certain situations. *Was* there much difference between them?

"That's *it*!" Carolyn cried with little-girl excitement. *"Hurry!"*

Still trying to figure out how his name had gotten on the ticket—let alone that of a nonexistent daughter! —Brother Paul suffered himself once more to be drawn along toward Gate 15. There had to be some mistake—but which mistake *was* it? His presence here on Planet Tarot was no secret, but it had hardly been the occasion for widespread publicity. An important person might have been treated to such a personalized tour of the exhibit, but he was not—

They joined the line at the security access. Should he inquire of one of the other people? Or would that violate the spirit of this charade?

Maybe the child's real father would be at the Gate—it was the obvious place—and this confusion of identities or whatever could be straightened out. He did have other business and had already allowed himself to be diverted too long. Perhaps he had been tempted by the mock airport because he didn't really want to face another community meeting with another null report. But he would not permit that to overwhelm him.

Now they were hustling through the metal detector—no buzz!—and up to the Gate. The attendant checked the tickets with perfect officiousness. "Very good, Father," he said. "Go right on in."

Father? But of course that was on the ticket; it hadn't quite registered before. "I am Brother Paul, and I fear there has been a—"

"Right. Nonsmokers to the front. Families with children board first." The man was already looking to the next.

"Daddy, we're holding up the line!"

Could her father have boarded already? It seemed unlikely without the ticket. But since the plane was only another mock-up, such details hardly mattered. The man *could* have boarded. A coincidence of names, but a distinction in title and marital status. Though how the girl could be confused about her own—

The boarding tube debouched into the airplane. Brother Paul sighted down the narrow aisle, searching for heads in the triple seats to either side. There was no one in cleric habit.

"This one," Carolyn said. "In front of the wing, so we can see out."

"I can't stay on the plane!" Brother Paul protested. "I only stopped by the terminal to see what—"

"Please fasten your seatbelts," the stewardess said.

"Wait! I have to get off—" But the boarding tube had already separated, and the plane door was closed. He was trapped.

Well, it wasn't as if the plane were actually going anywhere. He had wandered into a most elaborate setting and ritual, but that was all. He sat down in the seat beside her and fastened the seat belt. He did not want to appear to be a complete spoilsport.

The airplane began to taxi forward.

Brother Paul lurched up—and got nowhere. The seat belt bound him securely. He grabbed the buckle convulsively, got it loose, stood up, looked about—and paused again.

If he jumped off now, as the mock-up trundled realistically around the concrete runway, the little girl

would be left to endure her "flight" alone. Half the fun
of it would be gone for her. He certainly would never
desert a child on a real flight; why should he do it now?
His cruelty would be much the same, figuratively.

He settled back into his seat and rebuckled. His other
appointment would simply have to wait a little longer.
No doubt the Watchers, discovering him absent, would
check the edges of the Animation area and locate him
here in due course. Since the child's real parents were
not present, Brother Paul would have to keep an eye on
her until they turned up. As Jesus Christ Himself had
said about the least of children—

The plane turned, orienting on the main runway, the
one Brother Paul had originally spied. The machine accelerated. The vegetation outside shot by. This was no
gentle push; the passengers were pressed back into their
couches. It seemed like two hundred kilometers per
hour. Fascinated, Carolyn peered out of the slanted
window. Brother Paul squinted past her head, as interested as she, though for a different reason. This was
really quite an effect!

The nose lifted, then the tail. The plane angled up,
still driving relentlessly forward. This was becoming *too*
realistic; how could it stop before the pavement gave
out?

The passing foliage dropped below. Take off!

Take off? Brother Paul stared past the child through
the few waving strands of her hair that had yanked
themselves free of the braids. Already the landscape was
twenty meters below and dropping rapidly, forced
behind by the monstrous thrust of the jets.

Suddenly he caught on. Motion picture film projected
on the window as the structure of the plane was angled.
To make it *seem*, by means of tilt and vision, as though
they were flying. Very clever illusion.

Soon the window image showed clouds, and the plane
leveled out. Champagne was served; Brother Paul
declined his glass. There had been a time when—but he
would never touch any mind-affecting drug again!

The stewardess walked down the aisle, plunking
packaged breakfasts on the little shelves that folded out

from the seats in front. Scrambled eggs, sausage, toast, and fruit juice.

Breakfasts? Was this morning? Well, it could be, after all his time crawling through the labyrinth under the Sphinx. Subjective impressions of the passage of time were suspect once a person had been in Animation.

"Can I have milk?" Carolyn asked.

"*May* you have milk," Brother Paul said absently.

The stewardess smiled and produced a glass of milk. She was a buxom lass, and a chain of thought related the milk to—but he cut that off. Invalid, anyway; many people were not aware that cows did not freshen until bred.

Carolyn had a great time with this "picnic" meal, but Brother Paul was pensive. Why such an elaborate set with real food just like that of a past day on Earth (no wooden soup!), as though this really were a pre-mattermission airplane flight? It was really getting beyond the simple entertainment stage. Why squander the meager resources of Planet Tarot on such an exhibition of nostalgia?

Yet when he thought about it, it began to make more sense. He suffered from some nostalgia himself. It *was* nice to revisit the affluent, technological past, even briefly, even in mock-up. It had been so many years since he had been on a real airplane—and then it had not been as large or elegant as this one. So why not relax and enjoy the show?

They finished their meal—Carolyn left much of hers, he noted distastefully; he did not like waste—and the stewardess cleared away the trays.

Now they were far above the clouds—37,000 feet, the pilot's announcement said, causing Brother Paul to pause in his speculations a moment to translate that into kilometers: about eleven and a quarter—and he could have sworn his ears popped. The flight was level and dull. Some of the other passengers were reading, and others were sleeping, just as though they had made this trip many times before. Even as nostalgia, this was beginning to pall; enough was enough!

"Who was Will Hamlin?" Carolyn asked suddenly.

Startled, Brother Paul glanced at her. "What do you know about Will Hamlin?"

"Nothing," she replied brightly. "That's why I asked, Daddy."

Brother Paul oriented on the question, for the moment setting aside the other confusions of this odd journey. For there had indeed been a Will Hamlin. . . .

Paul had first met Wilfrid G. Hamlin as a brand new freshman college student of eighteen. Paul was going around interviewing instructors, as was the system at this small, unusual institution. He was trying to make up his mind which courses best suited his nascent intellectual needs.

The oddness of this college was really the reason Paul had come. It had no irrelevant entrance requirements, no tests, no grades, and no set curriculum. The students talked with the instructors, each of whom gave a little sales pitch for his particular class, and then selected the courses that seemed most promising. If an insufficient number of students picked a given class, that class was discontinued before it started. Somehow, each semester, it all worked out, though it always seemed impossibly chaotic. The classes themselves were of the discussion variety with no lectures; the instructors merely tried to organize the expressed opinions and bring out the fine points as the classes proceeded. It was all very relaxed: education almost without pain.

Will Hamlin was a small man without distinguishing traits other than a slight stutter. He had a little cubbyhole of an office off the unfinished hallway leading to the Haybarn Theater.

Brother Paul shook his head, remembering. Three years later he had had an adventure of sorts in that hall—but that would hardly interest a child—

"Yes it *would*!" Carolyn insisted. "Tell me, Daddy!"

Um. Well—

One of Paul's classmates, call him Dick, and another friend, call him Guy—though perhaps two other people had actually been involved in this minor escapade —well, the three of them and their three girlfriends, who shall be nameless (no, Carolyn, it is just

a kind of convention: you don't say anything untoward
about girls if you can help it. They are supposed to be
unsullied)—the grandmother (or was it the grand*father*?
Call it the former) of one of these six had taken to making
his own wine, and lo, a sample was on hand here at the
college. Dandelion wine from homegrown weeds—it
really was not very good. So in true collegiate tradition
these bright young people—and they *were* pretty bright,
their actions and scholastics to the contrary not-
withstanding—had decided to improve upon this wine
by distilling it. They rigged up a little still in the science
lab at night (night was the chief period of action; day
was reserved for sleeping and, on occasion, a college
class or two), and after various mishaps in the dark succeeded in deriving the essence: perhaps a cup of 100
proof liqueur. But the bad taste of the original had been
intensified by the distillation; now it was the very quin-
tessence of awfulness. What to do with it? They carried
it through the Haybarn Theater, on the way to the Community Center—but three drops spilled like guilty blood
on the floor of the hall outside Will's office. (That's
right—the college was so informal that all instructors
and administrative personnel right up to the president
were addressed by their first names.) Brother Paul had
lost all memory of the final disposition of Distilled Old
Grandma, but he clearly remembered passing through
that hall the following morning—and catching a good
whiff of Old Grandma. His stomach turned. That
region had been impregnated with the stench, and of
course no one would confess the cause. Poor Will,
whose door opened directly onto it!

"No, I didn't *think* you'd understand," Brother Paul
said. "In retrospect, it really isn't funny. Just an
irrelevant reminiscence—" But Carolyn was stifling a
girlish chuckle. Well, perhaps that *had* been the level of
that episode! A stink in a hall. . . .

Oh, the Haybarn Theater? Well, the whole college
had been converted fourteen years before Paul's
arrival—yes, he was actually older than the
college!—from a New England farm, and the main
building had been the big red gambrel-roofed barn.

Now the rough-hewn rafters showed high above the
theater section; the hay had been removed, but a bird or
two still nested in the upper regions. The office of the
college president was in a silo. Will had not rated a silo.
Which brings us back to that first encounter. Maybe
being educated in a barn causes the mind to become lit-
tered with stray thoughts, running around and getting in
the way like the stray dogs that roamed the campus. But
now we have returned to what we were talking about.
There was hardly room in Will's niche to turn around,
but at least he had a window. On hot days that was a
blessing.

"Dos Passos' *U.S.A.*," Will was saying. Brother
Paul smiled with the force of another reminiscence. He
had thought it was a place. Like Winesburg, Ohio, or
God's Little Acre.

The problem was that each instructor described his
course as though the student already knew what it was
all about. Paul had no idea whether he wished to visit
Dos Passos, U.S.A., or whether he preferred to contemplate the Individual and Society under the tutelage
of another prospective instructor, or perhaps drama or
art or music or any several of a number of other of-
ferings. It was all very confusing.

In the end, Will's course was one of those which Paul
elected to attend. In due course he learned that Dos
Passos, U.S.A., was a monstrous place, three volumes
long and as big as twentieth century America, and well
worth the experience of struggling through its labyrin-
thine and fragmentary bypaths. It was, indeed,
somewhat like life itself.

Paul learned a good deal more, and grew more, than
could be accounted for in horizons of the classroom or
dreampt of in the philosophies of the instructors. The
college campus itself was a kind of Winesburg or Dos
Passos, with devious interactions complimenting the
open ones. The grapevine kept all interested parties
posted on the on-going student, faculty, and student-
faculty liaisons; some interactions were hilarious, some
serious, and some pitiful. Some people thrived in this
melting pot of intellectual and sexual personality; others

were destroyed. A little freedom could be a devastating thing! Paul himself came through it—mainly by luck, he decided in retrospect—more or less whole. But he had learned a certain tolerance and became less inclined to judge a person by some particular aspect of his or her personality such as physical impairment or lesbianism or schizophrenia. During this overall educational experience, much of what Paul was later to become was shaped, though there had been scant evidence of it at the time.

In those years Will became Paul's faculty advisor. The advisor system at this college was closer than what was normal elsewhere; the advisor had quite specific involvement in the student's curriculum and concern with his overall welfare. Paul had by then become a student activist—this too was the normal course—and through him Will had another fairly shrewd insight into some of what was percolating through the deeper recesses of the tangled campus scheme.

The college tried to prepare its community for life in the great outside world by being a more or less faithful microcosm *of* that world. Students ran most of the campus routine, washing the dishes, cleaning the floors, tending the grounds, organizing the fire department, and serving on committees. Periodically, the faculty members were routed out to participate in these chores too, rather than being allowed to molder in their ivory towers (as it were: silos), but it was a thankless attempt. Most routed-out faculty soon drifted back to their normal ruts.

The whole was governed by the Community Meeting, consciously patterned after the Town Meetings of rural New England. Periodically, students, faculty, and administrators got together and thrashed through the agenda, utilizing formal Parliamentary procedure. The assorted committees that ran things in the interims reported to this meeting and were given new directives. Some of these committees tended to develop wills of their own, honoring the adage that power tends to corrupt, and this could lead to trouble. The most notorious was the Executive Committee, called Exec for short, composed of the heads of the other committees together with the president of the college, selected faculty members, and representatives from each student dormitory. At times Exec concealed what it was doing from the larger community in order to prevent its less popular decisions from being reversed by the Community Meeting. "We should be the *head* of the Community, not the *tail*," one Exec member put it. To which an irate community member responded: "Exec's acting like the *asshole* of the Community!"

For example: there was one student in his mid-twenties, a former small businessman called Deacon or "Deac" for short. He organized a Community cooperative store that sold cigarettes, cosmetics, stationery, and sundry other necessaries at reduced prices. The enterprise was doing well, and it served a Community need; therefore, the organizer was cordially disliked by the anti-free-enterprise elements of the Community. They tried to torpedo the co-op in various ways not excluding the rifling of several hundred dollars worth of supplies from the storeroom, but Deac was smarter than they, and the co-op survived. He had a candy machine installed; there was a great outcry against it as being counter to "Community spirit." But one evening the Community Communist, who had protested most vehemently against "commodity fetishism," was observed to sneak in and surreptitiously infiltrate a coin to obtain a box of raisins from the orifice of the evil machine. That was perhaps the co-op's ultimate success.

Deac had a little dog. Dogs were not permitted on campus by Community law. But the college president's beautiful Irish Setter, called Pavlov because he tended to drool, wandered freely around and in the buildings. Pavlov once watered down a terrified student standing in the dining room. So the rule was not enforced. Deac's little canine was fed and housed off campus, but tended to follow the example set by other members of the community, going where the action was. (No one ever saw a dog attending a class, which showed how well the canines understood the situation.) Certain members of

the Executive Committee saw their chance. The owner
was responsible for the pet; the dog had broken the law;
therefore, Deac was expelled from the Community. (No
one suggested the college president should be served in
the same fashion; there were, it seemed, limits.)

There was an immediate outcry. Deac had his enemies
in Exec, but he also had his friends in the Community.
The majority sentiment was clearly in Deac's favor, if
only as a concern for fair play. So Exec maneuvered
cleverly to prevent the issue from being placed on the
agenda. With luck, Deac would be gone before the
Community could formally discuss the matter: a *fait
accompli.*

As it happened, Paul was then the Community
Secretary, and his friend Dick, of Old Grandma repute,
was Chairman of the Community Meeting. They con-
ferred—they were after all roommates, as were their
girlfriends, in a singularly cozy arrangement—and
discovered that the prior agenda was advisory only; it
could be set aside and anything discussed by the simple
decision of the majority. So the notice of the Meeting
was posted with the old agenda, so as not to alert the opposition, and plans were made and circulated.

The Meeting was called to order. The formalities were
undertaken so that the first thing discussed was the Dog
Law. A motion was made: abolish the law. Discussion?
Three people spoke in defense of the law; no one spoke
against it. With amazing suddenness the matter came to
a vote—and the law was terminated by a massive,
hitherto silent, majority. Deac was back on campus
since he could not be expelled for his dog's violation of
a nonexistent law. Too late, the anti-Deac forces that
dominated Exec realized that they'd been had. They had
been outmaneuvered and destroyed by the same
machine tactics they had initiated. Paul wrote up the
whole inside story for the Minutes of the Meeting,
hardly concealing his pride in his own participation.

Later in life, Brother Paul was to find that machine
politics, far from being a local Community aberration
or perversion of the system, were in fact typical of
global politics. It gave him a very special comprehension

of the forces at work in the historical McCarthyism and HUAC or House UnAmerican Activities Committee, itself one of the least American institutions. Power *did* tend to corrupt, in the macrocosm as in the microcosm, and at times desperate measures were required to right the determined wrongness of those supposedly representing the will of the majority. It was a phenomenon Paul never quite understood, the Good Guys acting just like the Bad Guys, but at least he learned to recognize it when he saw it. The college had, indeed, educated him for real life.

However effective this education was, the enrollment of the college was impecuniously small, and the administration decided to expand. They felt more students would come if Community standards were stricter. Certain faculty members felt that sexual morality was entirely too free among the students. (Certain students felt the same way about the faculty, but that was another matter.) So the faculty set curfews on the lounges: no males in female lounges or females in male lounges after ten p.m. each night.

Now this stirred resentment; students regarded the lounges as a Community resource and used them at any hour of the night. (A daytime curfew might not have been so troublesome.) In addition, the lounges were under Community authority; the faculty was a minority within the larger Community and could no more preempt control of the lounges unilaterally than Exec could kick out a dog-owning student on its own. So the new curfew was without legal foundation and was duly ignored.

Until Paul, with five other students, was spied sitting and talking in a female lounge at 10:40 p.m. by the night watchman. Now Paul had not endeared himself to certain elements of the faculty, and this was not merely a matter of helping to overturn the dog law. He had stood up for his student rights on other occasions and generally carried the day. From a shy freshman he had become a self-assured senior. Theoretically, this was the very kind of development the college favored: individualism was character. In practice, this was frowned upon when it manifested as opposition to new faculty curfews for lounges. Paul was summoned before the faculty Social Standards Committee, popularly known as the Vice Squad.

Now Paul had tangled with the Vice Squad before. The precepts of its formation and operation were anathema to him. He happened to be one of two student members of that Squad, part of the window dressing to make it seem like a Community guidance operation. He had been extremely awkward dressing. He had brought to the attention of the college president a private student-faculty liaison involving one of the faculty members of the Squad itself. "How can this Committee be expected to enforce social standards that it does not itself honor?" The encounter was all very polite on the surface, and the president made no specific commitments. But that member of the Squad had been expeditiously removed for reasons never quite clarified. It had not been the first time Paul had locked horns with the president. He had respect for the man and had learned how to prevail without causing unnecessary embarrassment. The president was tough but basically honorable: the ideal administrator. Still, the Squad no longer felt comfortable with Paul.

Another time, the night watchman had caught a student couple in dishabille and in a compromising juxtaposition—but by morning had forgotten the name of the boy involved. The girl was known, but she refused to name her companion, and it was against faculty policy to punish girls for that might create a bad image in the eyes of the parents of prospective future female students. Thus the new law was applied selectively with discrimination practiced for the sake of image. The hypocrisy of this was evident to the students, if not to the faculty. Some girls were temperamentally innocent, but others were otherwise; to assume that the male was necessarily the instigator was at best naive.

At any rate, the entire student body knew via the grapevine who this boy was, and possibly certain faculty members knew it too—but this information was not available to the Squad. The lines of battle were hard-

ening. In a community that had once been united, ugly
currents were manifesting. Like the historical war in
Asia, an originally simple and possibly justifiable idea
had been transformed into self-destructive force. Paul,
when questioned by the Squad, repeated his philosophical aversion to its purpose. "I know who the
boy is—but I shall not tell you." And he smiled, rather
enjoying the situation. Perhaps, he thought in
retrospect, that smile had been a mistake. The Committee was unable to act, and had to drop the matter,
but—

Next time the watchman caught a couple (coupling
was a popular form of education), he took down both
their names. There would be no slipping the noose this
time! By sheer chance, the boy this time was Paul's
friend Dick, and the couple had been using, with Paul's
permission, Paul's own nocturnal hideaway: in the attic
of the Community library, under the eaves. It was set up
over the rafters with a mattress, tapped-wire electricity,
and a bottle of 100-proof vodka (definitely not Old
Grandma!), and was accessible by a rope ladder and
trap door. It was perhaps the finest and most private
love niche on campus. But Paul was not in it, that particular night, and so the turn of fortune had led to the
discovery of his friend instead. Dick had been hauled
before the Vice Squad and suspended from campus for
one week.

There, but for the grace of God. . . .

(Oh, that's just a figure of speech, Carolyn. It
means—well, if you had a piece of candy, and you gave
it to a friend, and she ate it and got sick, how would you
feel?) Actually, he was simplifying the story considerably, saying in a few words what was passing in
voluminous review through his head and editing the
juicier details.

Paul, necessarily silent about his own stake in this
matter, did not take this lying down. There was a policy
in the Community that the victims of theft be reimbursed for their losses from the Community Treasury.
Paul introduced a motion in the Meeting that his
suspended friend be similarly reimbursed for his travel

expenses, owing to the illicit action of the Vice Squad. It was a preposterous notion—but such was the sentiment of the aroused Community at this stage that the motion carried. The money was paid—and the implications were hardly lost upon either faction. The Vice Squad had suffered another black eye, even in its technical victory. But Paul, too, had been privately wounded. He had lost his hideaway and had a friend suffer in lieu of himself. The stakes were rising, and his brushes with disaster were narrowing his options.

During this extended sequence, Paul was in the Community Center when the night watchman entered on his rounds. The watchman was a large, amiable, husky young man hardly older than the students involved. "Here is the man," Paul announced loudly to the room in general, "who performs his job—beyond the call of duty." It was an extremely pointed remark whose import was lost on no one present; only the most diligent search had enabled the watchman to locate the hidden couple, starting from a single footprint in the snow. Yet the watchman had only done his job, however excellently, and was doing his job now. He merely smiled in response to Paul's remark, as it were turning the other cheek, punched the time clock, and departed.

Now it was Paul himself on trial—and the Vice Squad had quite a number of scores to settle. It would be simplistic to suggest that their handling of the case was merely a matter of revenge, yet this was a factor that could not be entirely discounted, for Paul had caused the Committee more embarrassment than had any other person. He symbolized to a certain extent, the opposition to the very legitimacy of the Squad.

There was a preliminary hearing. As with the medieval Inquisition, these things had to be done according to form. Three of the students in the lounge had been females (fully clothed and in their right minds); since it was their lounge, they were left out of it. They would have been left out regardless, as had two prior girls. The first of the three boys said: "I don't agree with the lounge curfew or recognize the authority of this Committee—but since I can not afford the kind of trouble this Committe will make for me if I stand on my rights, I shall not do so. I apologize for breaking the rule, and I shall not break it again. '' This was exactly what the Committee wanted to hear; he had capitulated and acknowledged its power. He was let off without punishment. He finished out the semester and did not return to the college next year. It was a script Paul was later to recognize in totalitarian regimes across the world—but it was not one he was prepared to follow, then or ever.

The second student turned to Paul. "Do we go that route, or do we fight?" Paul knew the other wanted to fight—indeed, he was the one who had remarked on the anal propensities of Exec—but did not want to stand alone. "We fight," Paul declared. And together they let the Vice Squad have it, denouncing the Committee with a thoroughness possible only to bright college males.

In due course they were summoned for the verdicts. The other student entered the room first, emerging with the news that he had been suspended for one week. Paul, more ornery and more careful, brought along a tape recorder. The reaction of the Vice Squad would have been surprising to those who did not know the people involved. The faculty members refused to utter their decision for the recorder. Paul refused to hear it without that protection. So he departed without verdict.

The Community held a massive protest rally over the student's suspension, meeting after hours in the female lounge. Where else? When the night watchman came, some fifty names—well over half the student body— were delivered to him to report to his owners. It was a mark of honor to be on that list. But the Squad termed this a "Demonstration" and ignored it. They didn't want half the Community; they wanted Paul. Tactic and counter-tactic; this stage of the battle was a draw.

The student body then had a formal meeting in a male lounge; the faculty, by pointed invitation, attended. It was polite but hostile; some very fine rhetoric was recorded, blasting the faculty position. To repeated questions of propriety, legality, and ethics, the college president stated flatly: "If the suspension is not honored, I will close the college." He was serious; he spoke in terms of power, not morality. And in the end the students, being more reasonable and vulnerable than he, backed down; they had lost the confrontation. The student left on his week's suspension (more correctly, he hid out for several days, awaiting the decision on Paul), and Paul finally worked out a compromise with the tape-shy Squad: they gave him a written sentence. This turned out to be significant, for when the other student missed an important drama rehearsal owing to his suspension, arousing the ire of the drama coach, the Squad denied that it had actually suspended him for a full week. Paul's written statement gave the lie to that, and he called them on it in the next Community Meeting. Yet the Squad had won this engagement. The action had alienated the entire student body and made a mockery of Community government, but the will of the faculty had prevailed.

In all this fracas the faculty had held firmly to the position maintained by the college president: the lounge curfew was legitimate and so were the suspensions. But privately there were faculty dissentions. A respectable minority had sympathy for the student position. In addition, the college was then in a more acute financial crisis than usual; not all the faculty members had been paid for the past month. They *knew* the college could close! In the face of these ethical and practical stresses during this upheaval, only one faculty member had the courage to speak out. He did so at the student protest meeting in the presence of the college president. In qualified language he supported certain aspects of the student position and denied that the president spoke for *all* the faculty; since the president had made this claim, Will came eloquently close to calling him a liar. Will Hamlin—Paul's counselor.

"And that," Paul concluded as the airplane descended, "was Will Hamlin—the only one with the guts to speak his mind honestly, though it may have imperiled his tenure at the college. At the time, his act of courage was largely obscured by the complexities of the situation; others may not have cared or even noticed.

Standing up for what's right is often a thankless task. But *I* never forgot. Perhaps the later hardening of my own dedication to principle was sparked by that example. In later years I received solicitations for financial support signed by one of the members of that Vice Squad; they were routine printed things, but that signature balked me, and I did not contribute. But this time I heard from Will—and I could not in conscience refuse him. Now he seems to be the only one I knew then, who remains at the college today, twenty years later."

Twenty years later? Brother Paul heard himself say that and wondered—for he had graduated only ten years before. Now the other mystery returned: how had this child happened to ask about a man in Brother Paul's past? It was an unlikely coincidence—yet somehow it did not *seem* coincidental. Almost, he could remember—

"Daddy, my ears hurt!" Carolyn said.

The immediate pre-empted the reflective. "It must be the pressure," he told her. "As the plane descends, the air—" But her little face was screwing up in unfeigned discomfort; it was no time for reasonable discussion. "Try to pop your ears," he said quickly. "Hold your nose and blow. Hard. Harder!"

Finally it worked. Her face relaxed and she smudged away a tear. "I don't like that," she announced.

He could not blame her. He had not felt any discomfort himself, but knew the pressure on the eardrums could be painful, especially to a child who could not understand it.

Now the plane was dropping through the clouds—and there were the streets and buildings of Boston.

Brother Paul knew he was no longer on Planet Tarot. Not in perception, at least; this had to be another Animation. But it was a strange one, following its own course regardless of his personal will. Will? Was that a pun? Was his true will to remember Will Hamlin?

If this were merely another vision—how could he ever, after this, be certain of reality? He had been so sure he was out of the Animations! If he had no way of knowing, as it were, whether he was asleep or awake. . . .

And the child, Carolyn—was she a mere hallucination? The strange thing was that he was coming to remember her, a little—though he was unmarried and had no children. So how could he remember her? The manifestations of Animation might transform the world of his senses, but had not hitherto touched the world of his mind. His firm belief in the sanctity of his basic identity had sustained him throughout this extraordinary adventure; if his private dignity, his concept of self-worth deserted him or was otherwise compromised, he was lost. He did not want anything diddling with his mind!

He concentrated, trying to break out of the Vision. Carolyn turned toward him, her eyes big and blue. "Daddy—are you all right?"

Brother Paul lost his will. If he vacated this Vision—what would become of *her?* He suspected she had no reality apart from his imagination, but somehow he perceived her trapped in a scheme from which the protagonist was gone. Horrible thought! He had to see her safely home—or wherever. *Then* he could vacate. Obeying the rules of the game.

The Boston airport was like any other—of the pre-exodus days. Only the city surrounding it seemed different, shrunken. Yet not like most present cities, for it had electric power, and the skyscrapers showed lights on the upper floors, signifying occupancy. Strange, strange!

The ground rushed up. The wheels bumped. The plane braked, and finally taxied up to the terminal. "Well, we made it," Brother Paul murmured.

They de-planed and found themselves in the main terminal. According to the tickets they had a couple hours to wait before boarding their next plane. "Can we eat at the airport, Daddy?" Carolyn asked hopefully.

Brother Paul checked and discovered he had money in the form of sufficient cash; they could eat. The prices were too high, the food nutritionally inadequate, but the little girl was happy. She didn't care what she ate; she merely wanted *to have eaten* at an airport. Afterwards they walked around nearby Boston, Carolyn finding everything fascinating from glassy buildings to cellar grates. He liked this child; it was easy to share the spirit of her little enthusiasms. She had always been that way, hyperactive, inquisitive, excitable. Right from the time of her birth, he remembered—

Remembered *what*? She was a construct of the present, having no reality apart from this vision, with no past and no future. Wasn't she?

Brother Paul shook his head, watching her trip blithely ahead, busy as a puppy on a fascinating trail. He felt guilty for breaking up the illusion. Why *not* remember—whatever he had been about to remember?

At last they reported to the Air Non Entity terminal for the hop into the unexplored wilds of New England. After the huge jet liner, this little twenty-passenger propeller plane seemed like a toy. But it revved up as though driven by powerfully torqued rubber bands and zoomed up into the sky well enough. Every time it went through a cute little cloud it dipped, alarming Brother Paul and scaring Carolyn. It just didn't seem *safe!*

"Daddy, tell me the story about the little grades that weren't there," Carolyn said brightly as her transient attention wandered from the dip-clouds. Anything that continued longer than five minutes lost its appeal for a child this age, it seemed.

But the little grades: how had she known about that? He must have told her before, and now she was showing the other side of the coin of short attention: she liked to have familiar things repeated, always with the same details.

Well, it was pointless to rivet their attention on the clouds zooming by so perilously close outside or to concentrate on the incipient queasiness of motion sickness. So he closed his eyes to the all-too-suggestive vomit bags tucked conveniently in the pouch of the seat-back ahead, and told (again?) about the nonexistent grades. Carolyn was already learning to detest grades, and she liked to hear about his more sophisticated objections to the System. Gradually he fell into the scene himself, reliving it, though the words he spoke to her were once again simplified for her comprehension.

The college used no grades. That was one of its initial attractions: the freedom from the oppressive pressure of examinations, of number or letter scores, and from all their attendent evils. Paul had not liked competing scholastically in high school against those who cheated; this had soured the whole system for him. For though he did not cheat, his position in his class was affected by those who were less scrupulous. Thus he had graduated below those whom he knew he had outperformed. Furthermore, even with honest performance by participants, testing was imperfect, and he suffered thereby. He learned slowly but well, and retained his knowledge longer than the average, sometimes improving on it after the tests were past. Others forgot the material as soon as the tests were done. Yet their grades reflected not what they retained or used, but what their tests showed. Here at the college there was no cheating, for there was nothing to cheat *at*: no all night cramming sessions, no circulated advance copies of final exams, no punitive reductions of earned grades, and no pattern of cram-forget. A massive, systemic evil had been exorcised.

Instead, at the end of each college term, reports were made by three individuals: the instructor, the student, and the student's faculty counselor. A non-letter, non-numeric evaluation was composed from these three opinions and filed in the student's record. And that was it.

Or so it had been claimed in the college catalogue.

Paul had believed it throughout his residence at the college: four years. Freed from that grade incubus, he had explored other aspects of education, such as folk singing, table tennis, and the frustrations and joys of association with the distaff sex. He had not, however, neglected the formal classes; in fact he had learned a great deal at them that served him well in subsequent years. But the classes had been merely *part* of his education, not the whole of it. He had never regretted this approach and had always appreciated the college's readiness to allow him to find himself in his own fashion. A student could not really grow in the strait jacket of "normal" education, but here it was different. He learned what it pleased him to learn, in and out of classes, and had continued the habit since. Learning was still his major joy, now more than ever—because he had learned at this college not facts, but *how to learn.* All the other tribulations faded in importance, but this ability grew.

Years later, in the course of his novice training for the Holy Order of Vision, Father Benjamin had set before him a thin folder. "This is Temptation," Father Benjamin had said.

Brother Paul looked at him. "I don't understand. I had expected to meditate this hour." Meditation was serious business: another form of learning.

"Indeed you shall, Paul," the Father said with a certain obscure smile. "You shall meditate whether to open that folder or to let it be."

Was the Father joking? This was hardly the standard definition of meditation! Yet it seemed he was not. "How shall I know what is right? I don't know the nature of this folder."

"It is your college transcript." And Father Benjamin departed.

Meditation? This was turmoil! Brother Paul knew this transcript was, for him, classified material; he was not supposed to see it. In order to remove all competitive pressure, the college concealed the records from the individual students. Of course, Paul knew generally how he had done, for his own opinions were part of the record.

Now, however, he wondered. If he knew what was in his transcript, why should it be secret from him? What difference did it make?

He pondered, and the doubt grew. No one kept his age a secret from him, or his weight, or any other aspect of his own being or performance. Generally Brother Paul felt that any person had a right to information about himself; it was after all *his* life. What purpose was there in a secret, ever?

But surely the college had reason to restrict this document. The pointless frills had been eliminated there in favor of the genuine education. If some aspect had to be concealed, it was necessary. Wasn't he honor bound to obey the rule and leave the folder alone?

Then why had Father Benjamin presented him with this material? Was this a test of his basic integrity, whose result would determine his progress in the Order? Was Father Benjamin playing the Devil's Advocate, subjecting him to temptation? Would he, like Jesus Christ, prevail and remain above reproach—or would he, like Eve in the Garden of Eden, succumb to the lure of the fruit of the forbidden Tree of Knowledge?

That introduced another aspect. Brother Paul himself had never condemned Eve for tasting that fruit, though it had cost her and Adam their residence in an earthly paradise. Knowledge was the very essence of man, the thing that distinguished him from the animals. A person who eschewed learning of any type sacrificed his heritage. Eden had been no paradise; it had been a prison. Ignorance was *not* bliss. Surely God had intended the ancestral couple to eat of the fruit; it would have been wrong *not* to do it. The point of the legend was that the price of knowledge was high—but it had to be paid. The alternative would have been to remain an animal.

This was not, perhaps, an orthodox interpretation. But the Holy Order of Vision, like the college, encouraged widely ranging thought. If man's insatiable curiosity were the Original Sin, how could he expiate it, except by finally satisfying it?

Was it significant that Satan had tempted Christ with power, wealth, and pride, but *not* with knowledge? "If thou be the Son of God, command that these stones be made bread." Jesus had responded: "Man shall not live by bread alone, but by every word that proceedeth out of the mouth of God." And to the offer of worldly power if he would worship the Devil: "Get thee behind me, Satan . . ." Why *not* knowledge?

He looked at the folder again. The thing seemed to glow with evil light despite his reasoning. Could it be that knowledge was power and, therefore, had been included in the temptations Christ withstood? What had Father Benjamin done to him, putting this manifestation of the Devil within his grasp?

No, he had no Biblical reference here. The verdict on knowledge was inconclusive. Each specific case had to be judged on its merits.

By what right did the college decree that everyone *except* the person most concerned should know the details of his education? There was an inherent unfairness in that which should be manifest to any objective person. By what irony were the educators themselves blind to this wrong?

Yet he knew from his experience that educators were human too, with human assets and failings. They did not see right and wrong with perfect clarity. And why should they? Their purpose was to enable the students to grow; if they succeeded in this, they had met the requirement of their office. Could God himself demand more of them? Probably it had been the college administrators, not the instructors, who had classified the documents.

But again: *why*? So the students could not complain? Why should any student complain about the simple record of his progress that he himself had helped write? Something was missing. . . .

He remembered his encounters with Exec and with the Vice Squad. Secrecy had been the hallmark of illicit dealings there. Secrecy was so often invoked to protect the guilty.

Was it the simple record? Or was there some sinister secret buried in this folder, known to all except him? Brother Paul recalled the frustrating joke about the man who was given a message written in a foreign language. Each person to whom he took it, who was able to read that language, refused either to tell him its meaning or to associate with him further. Thus the man remained forever in doubt. Was this college transcript like that? Surely he should find out!

He reached for it—but his hand hesitated. Did the end justify the means? The end was enlightenment, but the means was the violation of someone's trust. The college was a mere institution, true—but trust was trust. It did not matter what dark secrets lurked within this folder; the unveiling of them would be a personal sin, an affront against morality, rightness, and justice.

"Ah, but the flesh is weak," Paul murmured, opening the folder.

Soon he wished he had not. *Yea, Pandora!* he thought. Pandora was the girl who had opened the box (was she merely another incarnation of Eve?) and thereby loosed all things upon the world, retaining only one: hope. Paul had now let hope itself escape. For the cherished ideals of his college days, that had survived all the buffeting of campus politics, flawed faculty members, and a questionable suspension, were now revealed as delusions.

First, *this transcript had grades.* Straight letter grades, *A, B, C,* of precisely the type the college never used. Oh, there were paragraph evaluations too—but each was followed by its translation into the letter, the kind that computers could manipulate for numeric grade point averages, just as at any other school. But at other schools the grades were posted openly; each student knew exactly where he stood. Here they had been posted secretly so that not only was the student not advised of his rating, but he did not even know that he was being graded. Thus he was at a competitive disadvantage in the remainder of his life. As though he were playing poker and every other player could see his hand, but *he* could not. Brother Paul understood poker all too well, and the analogy tortured him. Here was his message in a foreign language, and of all the parties who could have revealed its content to him, only one had done so: the Holy Order of Vision. Thus he had broken the terrible *geas* more or less by luck. Yet its prior damage could not be undone. "Alma Mater, how *could* you!" he cried with a sensation like heartbreak.

At the beginning of the transcript was a note saying that the college preferred not to use grades, but owing to outside requirements had had to do so. Another note cautioned the reader against allowing the subject to see this record. No wonder!

Paul had traveled more or less innocently through the curriculum for four years without thought of grade or competitive standing; that had been the beauty of it. He had learned eclectically, *for the sake of learning*—and now via this hyprocrisy it had come to nought.

No, no—that was an unfair verdict. The gradeless environment had forced on him a peculiar discipline. It was so easy to sink into stagnation, deprived of the goad of tests and grades and the printed-letter esteem they brought. A number of students had done just that and in due course washed out of the program. But others considered it a challenge—to learn, profit, and grow *without* a formally structured stimulus. And a few, like Paul, who were well able to compete for grades if that were required, had discovered instead the sheer joy of knowledge. Knowledge of *things* was one route leading into knowledge of *self*. A grade in itself was nothing; it was, at the root, the *attitude* that counted.

The process had hardly been complete when Paul left college. He had had serious problems when he departed that protected environment, as his experience with the drug mnem had shown! But the foundation had been laid, and in time he had built upon it, and now he was learning more and growing more every year than he ever had in college. This was no denigration of that educational system; it was the fulfillment of it. Learning to learn—*that* was real, though the system turned out to be false.

From good must come good, and from evil, evil, he thought, remembering Buddha. Instead, he had encountered a set of statements, one saying the other was true, the other saying the first was false. A paradox. Good, somehow, had come from evil.

"If only you had believed in it yourself, O College Administration!" he murmured, more in regret than ire. "You wrought so much better than you knew, had you but had more faith!"

Yet they had made the letter grades under protest and

hidden them under this shield of secrecy. So it was a partial lack of faith on their part, rather than a complete one. The flesh of colleges, too, was weak.

Paul looked at the individual grades for the courses —and received another shock. They were not the correct ones!

He delved more deeply, reading the evaluations. Slowly it came clear: these *were* his grades—but not as he had understood them. For they hardly reflected his own one-third opinion or what he had known of his counselors' opinions. (He had had three faculty counselors before Will Hamlin.) They were the opinions of the course instructors—just as at other schools. Thus the courses having greatest impact on Paul's thinking and development were marked by *B*'s and *C*'s—and the course dearest to the heart of a particular instructor was marked *A*. That last had been completely worthwhile—but so had the others, receiving lesser marks. The variation had lain not so much within Paul, but within the instructors. Thus the evaluation system, too, was false.

On top of that, Paul had been given no credit for some of the courses he had taken; they were not even listed. Drama and music, where he had learned stage presence, voice projection, and artistry of sound—all supremely important to his later development—gone. By error or design—quite possibly the latter, as they were considered "minor" courses, heedless of their impact on the student—those parts of his college growth had been excised. Neatly, like a circumcision. Had he known, he would have protested. But the veil of secrecy had prevented him from knowing.

Was there *ever* justification for secrecy? Or was the seeming need to hide *anything,* whether physical or informational, an admission by the hider that the thing being hidden was shameful? Surely it was the *act* of hiding that was shameful! That would bear further meditation.

Yet the inadequacy of this sorry record could not take away the *fact* of his learning. Paul had profited, and profited greatly, from his experience at this institution.

Wasn't that the real point of education? The college by distorting the transcript had not really denigrated or deprived him; it had merely diminished its own estimate of its impact upon him. If he failed in life, that had not been warned by the transcript; if he succeeded, the transcript showed no prediction. As with so many conventional transcripts, distorted by conventional factors, this one was largely irrelevant. The college had cheated itself by publishing a document of mediocrity instead of the document of accuracy it should have. The good the college had done him would never be known though the transcript.

Paul completed the transcript and closed it, bemused. It was not after all a work of the Devil, merely of fallible people. Perhaps its greatest failing was its subtlest: in all the welter of statistics, test scores—yes, there *were* some there!—and comments, the authorities had somehow succeeded in missing the essential *him*. A stranger, reading this transcript, would have no idea of Paul's actual nature or capability. In this print he was nondescript, possessing no personality and not much potential.

He had known at the time that a number of instructors (including, to Paul's regret, Will Hamlin) had not seen in him, Paul, any particular promise. Perhaps even today they would not consider his present course as representative of "success." He had suspected at the time that this was because they had not made any real effort to know him—and that had they made this effort, they would have lacked the intelligence to complete the job. The Vice Squad matter had shown their level of comprehension of human values. Paul was intelligent in nonconventional ways and indifferent in conventional ways. He was not easy to measure by a set standard. This transcript confirmed this: it represented *them*, not *him*.

"Transference," he said.

"What?" Carolyn asked.

Suddenly he was back in the present, such as it was. He had thrown a complex concept at the child. "Transference. That is when a person attributes his feelings or actions to someone else. If he dislikes someone, he may say 'that person hates me.' If he feels tired, he says 'They made these steps too steep.' It is a way of dealing with certain things that he doesn't want to recognize in himself. He simply shifts the burden to someone else."

"Like Voodoo?" she asked brightly.

"Uh, no. You're thinking of sticking pins in dolls, and the person the doll stands for hurts?"

"Yes. Maybe the doll hurts too. *Mine* would."

Naturally she had sympathy for the doll! How hard it was to avoid falling into the same trap he had rehearsed here, that of failing to know the learner, and so misjudging his (her!) progress. "That's not really the same. Then again—" Then again—wasn't that whole transcript basically a voodoo doll? The college administration—and institutions of similar nature all over the world—thought that by calling this document "Paul" and sticking the pins of their secret opinions into it, they could define what he *was*. Well, perhaps it had satisfied them at the time. Next year new students had come, and he had been forgotten, buried in the office files. The irony was that his case was no doubt typical not only of the students at his college, but of the students in *all* colleges and universities. The great majority of them surely remained unknown. No status for any of them—or for their institutions. And people wondered why the educational system was failing! Straight Voodoo would be better than this. "It's close enough, sweetie," he told her.

Father Benjamin had never inquired into Paul's decision about the transcript. He knew the experience sufficed. It was not what Brother Paul had done, but how he felt about it that counted. He had to answer to no one, ultimately, except himself—and God.

But now he was returning to the college after twenty years with his daughter. For despite the erstwhile opinion of the administration, who had seen fit to suspend him and deceive him, he had succeeded in life. Now the college wanted him back, as a kind of authority in his field, to participate as a consultant for a weekend conference.

It was no laughing matter—but wasn't the last laugh his?

The little airplane dropped, bringing his attention to lower levels too. Now Brother Paul's ears hurt. Suddenly he appreciated precisely what his daughter had gone through.

"Blow your nose, Daddy!" she recommended solicitously. *She* understood!

He blew, but only the right ear cleared. The left remained blocked. It felt as though his eardrum would burst. He invisioned it bulging inward with the intolerable pressure of the atmosphere. Still the craft descended, as it were into Hell. Where could he find relief?

Finally, as the plane touched the small landing strip, he blew with such desperation it seemed his brain was squeezing out through his inner ear—and with an internal hiss of frustration, the pressure equalized. Lucky he hadn't caught a cold!

"I like Pandora," Carolyn remarked. "I would have opened that box too."

VI
Will: 14

Sex classically becomes involved for the child at a very early age, in Western civilization, with the realization that parents are hypocritical and unfair; that there is one law for the big and another for the little. That the only thing worth being is big, *and strong*; and that later, when one is big and strong, one will have one's innings and one's revenge not only by doing all the forbidden things, but by forbidding them in turn to one's own children, who will be littler than oneself and therefore proper to dominate and harass. Underneath this not-so-innocent dream of 'growing up' runs along the hopeless admission that one is still pretty little, and the anxious realization that one's sexual life is a dangerous matter indeed. Like playing with food or feces, or refusing to do what one is told, or speaking in a loud and demanding way (as do adults), sex can cause one to be unfairly rejected or severely punished by those whose love one very much needs. This is the real sexual enlightenment of the child, and of just as serious a nature as that concerning the birds & bees, or even human genitalia and what they do.

—G. Legman: *Rationale of the Dirty Joke,* First Series, New York: Grove Press, 1968.

*   *   *

They walked across the strip and entered the small terminal building. It was empty. Already the airplane was putt-putting back into the clouds.

"Who was supposed to meet us?" Carolyn asked.

"A man named David White," Paul answered. Had there been a foul up?

Then a tall young man, bearded and informally dressed, hurried up. "Father Paul?" he inquired, extending his hand.

"David White?" Paul inquired in return, taking the hand, recognizing Lee in another role. He was relieved to have this confirmation that this was an Animation; any alternative explanation would have been most disquieting in its implications. "This is my daughter, Carolyn."

"Sorry I'm late. I saw the plane coming down—"

They hustled to David's small car and piled in their handbags. Carolyn clambered into the back seat with enthusiasm, clutching her little handbag and big octopus doll. The car zoomed out of the airport.

On the way to the campus they chatted about inconsequentials, getting to know each other. David was a senior student, on leave to serve in the Admissions office. He was not satisfied and planned to complete his degree, then seek employment elsewhere. His program at the college, appropriately, was just twenty years later than Paul's. Here, in certain respects, *was* Paul—twenty years ago. Half his life ago! He was glad David was likeable for this purely private, selfish reason.

The college, he learned, had grown from less than a hundred students to almost two thousand, though the majority did not reside on campus. And that campus had expanded; what had been forest to the north was now a collection of dormitories. It was to one of these unfamiliar buildings they came. Paul knew the college had changed, yet he felt disappointment to *see* it changed. Change was a vital aspect of life and of the universe, yet an emotional countercurrent wished it were not so.

They were issued meal tickets for the cafeteria—and

this was in the Community Center where Paul had eaten
for four years. This building had hardly changed; it
remained a converted barn. The cellar he had helped dig
out was now a dining room; he and Carolyn ate there,
and he met the other program participants there. It was
strange, being in this place that he remembered as the
depths of the earth; it resembled a fantasy room, the
kind that was not really there.

No faces were familiar; the turnover had been complete except for Will Hamlin, who was not at supper.
But these were educated, compatible people, centering
around his own age—which had, as it were overnight,
doubled. He had jumped from twenty to forty, from
student status to instructor status, though inside he felt
the same. He was as much of a rebel as he had been. At
least he liked to think so. The outward manifestations
of it had merely changed.

Carolyn was eating with excellent appetite. She had
two glasses of chocolate milk and was in partial heaven.
That made him realize, with a rush of feeling: he *had*
changed, for now he had his daughter. From the
moment of her birth, his life had been metamorphosed;
her existence was the single most vital aspect of *his*
existence. He had diapered her as a baby, he had
watched her put her foot in her mouth the first time (so
many people never outgrew that!), he had helped her
walk and talk and read; since she came into existence he
had never slept without consciousness of her
whereabouts, the assurance that she was safe. Not
graduation, not marriage, not the God of Tarot Himself
had transformed him as significantly. When she was
born, he was reborn. He could not conceive of the scales
on which she could be balanced, in terms of the meaning
of his life, and found wanting; as well to balance her
against the cosmic lemniscate, the ∞ ribbon symbol of
infinity. This was why he had brought her here; she was
part of him. Eight years old, nine in three months (oh,
my—another birthday coming up!), precious beyond
conception.

This was not a thing others understood or ever needed
to. They thought he was the original Paul aged by two

decades, though they had not known the original. Yet did anyone know *anyone*? A philosophic question, unanswerable.

He talked with these others, planning out aspects of the program. Paul knew Tarot; one of the others knew I Ching: common ground of a sort. "I threw the yarrow sticks for tomorrow's program," the other said. "The answer was: 'The Center is empty.'"

Paul laughed. "That could be literal!"

The man nodded soberly. Much student interest had been expressed in this program, The Future of Revelation, but it was uncertain how much would manifest when the hour came. In Paul's day some excellent programs had foundered because the students simply couldn't be bothered to attend.

They finished the meal and went upstairs to the Haybarn Theater. They passed the site of Will's old office, but the office was gone. Doubtless Will rated more than a niche, today, if less than a silo. Paul sniffed —and there was the odor of distilled Old Grandma liqueur still permeating the hall. *After twenty years?* Impossible. . . .

The Haybarn was as he remembered it. Carolyn was thrilled, running about the stage, trying to act like an Actress. Here Paul had painted scenery, here he had wrestled with stage fright. Public speaking had not come readily to him; hesitancy and a soft voice had been formidable obstacles. Finally during one session the drama coach had gotten through: "Say it again, exactly as before, but just two point three times as loud." Paul had done so—and it had worked. Never again had he been faint on stage. He still spoke softly in life—but he knew the technique of projection and used it consciously when it was required. Armed with that mechanism, he had found that stage fright itself faded. Now he could speak extemporaneously before an audience of any size and come across well. In fact, at times he had a better stage presence than he had a personal presence; private conversations could be awkward.

"We won't use the theater," David White said.

"We'll go out on the lawn; more pleasant there."
Translation: not enough audience to fill the barn.

At dusk they sat on the gentle hillside behind the
Haybarn. Carolyn ran off to explore other portions of
the campus. Paul assured himself she would be all right;
no one would molest her here, and she knew where to
find him. Part of raising a child properly was giving her
rein; she had to discover her own horizons in her own
fashion.

Each person introduced himself, but the names sieved
out of Paul's mind as rapidly as they were uttered, for
names and dates were not his forte. Not since he got off
mnem! They chatted amiably as more people filled in.
When there were about thirty, the main speaker arrived,
lay on the bit of level ground at the foot of the slope,
dispensed with his notes, and delivered a rambling
discourse about his experiences in the political
maelstrom of pre-exodus Earth. The entire period of the
exodus had fit within ten years, those years fitting
within the score of years between Paul's departure and
return to the college, but already it seemed like medieval
history. People called it the "Fool" period, and indeed
it had been mad; the whole of Earth's culture had been
shaken in a fashion that was difficult to believe. But the
exodus had not sprung from nothing; Earth had been
near the explosion point before matter transmission had
provided the apparent relief valve. The speaker made
this plain, using salty vernacular to spice his strong
opinions. It was an interesting discourse, but not at all
what was listed on the program.

Paul had pondered what he would find, here at the
college of his future. It had been regressing when he left;
his own suspension had been only a symptom of the
deeper malady. In the interests of growth and ac-
ceptability, it had been clamping down on personal
freedom, sacrificing the very qualities that had made the
college what it was. Now it had achieved that desired
growth; did that mean it had become obnoxiously conventional? It was too early to tell, but the preliminary
signs indicated that it had not. If this speaker were

typical of the new breed of professor, the present college was even more liberal than the original one had been.

As darkness closed in, still more people manifested, dotting the hillside. So did mosquitoes. A young couple sat down before Paul, seeming more concerned with their whispered dialogue than the words of the speaker. The girl kept breaking wind and giggling. There was a murmur of other conversations scattered around the slope. Three dogs cruised about, playing tag around the seated figures, doing the things canines did. Some people left. Evidently this was not considered to be a program to attend from start to finish, but a temporary stop, a kind of low-grade continuous entertainment to be absorbed in shifts. There were some questions to the speaker, reflecting quite individualistic viewpoints.

Paul marveled, internally, as he worried about the dampening grass staining his good habit. He should have worn blue jeans. No doubt about it: the swinging pendulum of conservatism had long-since reversed course. This was the way programs had been in his own day.

At last the program broke up. Paul moved on to the next location where he was scheduled to read a paper. The subject was the God of Tarot, of course. His was the second of two; the first took well over an hour. It was quite interesting—but this meant it was well past his normal retirement hour before his turn came. By this time Paul was not at all sure his material suited the audience. He had chosen it to be not too "far out," so as not to offend tastes more conservative than his. Now that the extraordinary fact had manifested that in many ways the current campus was less conventional than was Paul himself, he was suffering a diminution of ease. He had not changed that much and certainly had not become more conservative overall; the college had changed and in an unexpected manner. There was certainly nothing wrong with this, but it left him off balance, braced in the wrong direction. He would seem more dowdy than he was.

Then Will Hamlin entered. He was older, grayer, but

immediately recognizable. On two levels: the role-player was Therion. Paul jumped up to shake his hand. That was really all there was time for; it *was* the middle of the program.

Paul read his paper, explaining some of the astonishing ways in which the God of Tarot had manifested, and at last the program ended. There was no particular comment; the others were surely as tired as he was. He located Carolyn, and they found their way to the dormitory room. It was of course much farther past the little girl's bedtime than Paul's own, but she never went to sleep an instant before she had to and was enjoying this.

Too bad there had not been more opportunity to talk with Will, even in the surrogate mode of Animation. Twenty years—the whole world had changed about them both, yet circumstance had granted a mere handshake. It was not that Will had been much in Paul's thoughts during the long interim, and surely Paul had never figured fundamentally in Will's thoughts (fundamentals being prime concepts to Will); this just happened to be the juxtaposition of frameworks that time had caused to diverge widely. Twenty years ago, the chances of Paul's eventual success in life and Will's continued tenure at the college might have seemed equally improbable—yet both had come to pass, and this present meeting was the realization of this. The more appropriate unity of conscience hardly showed overtly—

"Daddy, are we going to read?"

They normally read together at night, and though it was very late, Paul thought it best to maintain the ritual. He tried to give his daughter a supplementary education by this means, as well as enhancing that closeness that was so vital to them both. She was a sensitive, hyperactive child; she needed a constant supportive presence, not the grim imperatives of forbidding parental figures, but loving help, and this was part of it. He had read her the entire *Oz* series of books, a complete story—adaptation of the Bible, and was starting in on an unexpurgated translation of the *Arabian Nights* with the

works of Lewis Carroll and *Don Quixote* to come.
There were those who did not consider this to be proper
fare for a girl her age, but Carolyn was a very bright
girl. He explained things carefully, and they both enjoyed the readings. They were good books, all of them,
and more similar to each other than many people chose
to believe.

"Of course, sweetie." In his suitcase was the book he
had packed for this purpose: an old fantasy about a
griffin that came to life, having been a stone statue, and
took a little girl flying. For these readings he did not
eschew conventional novels; anything that seemed
worthwhile and interesting was fair game and had been
so since she was two years old, ready to graduate from
Mother Goose. Paul had thought this griffin story
would complement the experience of the airplane flight,
relieving possible anxiety. Actually it did not; Carolyn
had enjoyed the flight, and the book did not reach the
flying part this night. But the story was interesting.

After that, Carolyn lay on her bunk and read the
book she had brought for herself while Paul read the
one he had brought for *him*self. They were very much a
reading family; he felt that a book was one of the most
versatile educational and entertainment instruments
available to man.

Reading, however, tended to put Paul to sleep. It
relaxed his mind which otherwise was prone to continuous charges here and there that prevented sleep. He
had hardly started his reading before Carolyn trotted
across in her nightie, took the book from his hand,
kissed him good night, and turned out the light as he
nodded off. He heard her little feet pattering across the
floor in the dark, quickly to avoid possible monsters on
the floor, as he faded out. Was he taking care of her, or
she taking care of him? It hardly mattered.

Paul woke at dawn. It was too early for breakfast,
and he didn't want to disturb Carolyn, so he dressed
and walked out around the surrounding campus. This
was, as it turned out, a co-ed cooking dorm with kitchen
and laundry facilities. Such dorms had not existed at the
college in Paul's day, and there had been no indication

that the institution was moving in that direction. Surely the Vice Squad would have moved Heaven, Earth, and participating students (yea, right off the campus!) in its frantic efforts to balk any such development. What had happened? Paul had known the members of the Squad reasonably well; one had been described as "as shallow as an empty bathtub" and another as a "medieval moralist." They must have been grossly out-maneuvered!

No, he had to be fair: he might not have known them well enough. Perhaps they had come to accept what they had rejected in his day. It was always dangerous to judge any person's character or attitude as fixed; new aspects often appeared.

There was a chill to the morning even in this summer, and Paul was inadequately dressed. He had to keep moving to generate heat. That was fine; he liked running anyway. The environs were lovely. There was a small lake behind the dorm where four ducks dwelt; the moment they spied him they waddled over with loud quacks, hoping for food. Alas, he had none. A canoe and a kayak were at the edge for the use of students. Elsewhere was a volleyball court. Packed-dirt paths led in various directions. Beyond these items, the forest closed in closely. There were birds in it and no doubt deer and porcupines: Nature returning. It was all very pleasant, this enclave of higher education on the brink of the wilderness. Would that the whole world were the same!

He returned to Carolyn. She took after her mother in this respect; she slept as late as she could and stayed up as late as she could. Paul was an early bird, she a late bird. But they didn't want to miss breakfast. "Up," he murmured in her cute little ear. "Chocolate milk." She stirred. "Ducks."

"Oh, ducks!" she cried joyfully. Waking up might be a fate hardly better than death, but here were four new friends to make it all worthwhile! Before they left the campus, Paul knew, she would be on close terms with every duck, dog, cat, and child on the premises. This was the nature of little girls, bless them!

Together they walked the path to the main campus. The route took wooden steps up a steep hill, meandered by a solar-designed building still under construction, through the barbell-shaped Arts building, past the modern new library, and through a pleasantly dense pine forest. Only the pines had existed in Paul's day.

"In the pines, in the pines," they sang together, "Where the sun never shines, And I shiver where the cold winds blow." And there was a chill little breeze, and they shivered. He pointed out the huge bull spruces to her with their myriad spokes radiating out, easy to climb, but the dirt and sap got on the hands and never came off. "So *don't* climb," he finished warningly. "I don't want the people to think I have a dirty daughter."

"I won't, Daddy," she promised, eyeing the spruces appraisingly. Those spokes were just like ladders. . . .

On through a fair field full of flowers, reminding him of the alliterative opening to the epic poem *The Vision of Piers Plowman*, wherein there was a fair field full of folk, representing mankind, going about their petty pursuits, heedless of the promise of the Tower of Truth above or the threat of the Dungeon of Wrong below. Carolyn of course wanted to pick the flowers, all of them; but he begged her to let them be beautiful in life instead of killing them by picking them.

Finally down to the main campus in time for breakfast. O joy! Carolyn found several kinds of cereals, sweet pastries, and of course chocolate milk. Paul found dishes of nuts, sunflower seeds and yogurt; he settled for the skimmed white milk and two fried eggs as well. All paid for by their typed meal tickets! Carolyn loved those tickets; they were like magic. Just show one, and the best of food was yours.

When Paul had been a student here, there had been no particular consciousness of health in diet. The meals had been good, but conventional; the dietitian had been getting old, but insisted on doing things her own way. No yogurt or seeds. She would let the griddle get too hot, so that her fried eggs burned on the bottom while remaining runny on top. Because of this, Paul had switched from "sunny side up" to "over"—but had discovered that she had by then perfected the art of burning fried eggs on both sides while the whites in the middle resembled fresh mucous during the hayfever season. But today—the eggs were good. He was almost disappointed.

Paul glanced curiously at the students in the dining room. The males were almost universally bearded, the females braless; most of both sexes were in blue jeans. In Paul's day there had been fewer beards and more bras; otherwise the aspect of the student body had hardly changed.

Before the meal was over, Carolyn had made friends with the ladies of the kitchen. "Daddy, can I stay here this morning?" she asked brightly. Paul checked; children and animals were not necessarily welcome in kitchens. It was all right with the ladies. So he made sure his daughter knew where to find him and let her be. Actually, David White had arranged for a student, Susan, to keep an eye on Carolyn while Paul was tied up in the program. Susan had a head full of ringlets and seemed like a nice girl; he was sure it was all right.

On to the morning program. *The center is empty*, he remembered. There were to be three discussion groups, each cohosted by two people. Sure enough: only six people showed up. The six co-hosts. No students. That aspect of college life had not changed at all; theoretically students came to get an education, but in practice any program that began first thing in the morning was doomed.

A quick consultation; then the three groups merged. They discussed which topics to discuss. A few other people wandered in, as though accidentally diverted from their routine pursuits, temporarily caught in this eddying current, until at last there were some fifteen people.

Paul shook his head inwardly. This, too, was exactly the way it had been in his day. The students wanted the degree—the piece of paper that authenticated their education—without actually having to participate in the drudgery of classes. This happened to be the first really nice day in some time, and everyone was out with his girlfriend appreciating nature. Which was no bad thing. Paul well knew that growth could not be forced. Had his own transcript reflected his real educational experience, it would have listed the whole of his classroom participation as perhaps one third of his grade. And that would have been a higher classroom ratio than the average, for he had an intellectual bent.

Actually, it was a very good discussion, and he enjoyed it. He contributed minimally—not because he was shy or bored or uninformed, but because he was *not*. He did not need to prove anything by dominating the program. The uninterested and immature students were absent; only serious ones were present. Paul could see that many participants knew much more about their areas of expertise than he did; he could learn from them, and he liked listening to them. He liked interacting with those who were intellectually aware. So though this session might be a technical loss for the college—in fact a disaster because it really educated so few students—it was a profitable experience for him personally.

Carolyn wandered in a couple of times, just checking on him. Reassured, she buzzed off around the campus again. Just like a student. She liked it here, as he had known she would. She did not care about the deep significance of the college or about the fact that his presence in this very room at an earlier hour than he had stayed last night had gotten him suspended. To Carolyn, the entire college was a giant playground with interesting people doing interesting things all around. It was barely possible that she would one day attend as a student here; then the other meanings would begin to form.

The attendance of the program swelled, then petered out into assorted sub-dialogues. Finally, by common consent, the remainder was canceled. The college had made the program available to its students, but could not make them attend—and it was right that it do this. There were principles more important than formal education, as Paul well knew. Institutions that lost sight of that fact might post high ratings on paper that only

partially masked their fundamental failure. This college
had been, and remained, devoted to the quest for a
better reality.

In the afternoon, Paul took Carolyn down to the
moraine on the southern border of the college. He had
learned of this typical formation in a geology class here,
and it had stuck with him ever since. "You see," he told
her as they walked the path ascending the narrow ridge
through pines with the sides falling off steeply on either
side, "once huge masses of ice covered much of this
continent. That ice was two kilometers thick. It was
called a 'glacier.' At the edge it pushed up a pile of
stones, sand, and debris. When it melted, it left this pile
of rubble to show where it had been. The river ran right
below it, formed from its melt, and the river is still here.
So here we stand, on the glacial moraine." He knew she
was more intrigued by the trees, slope and path, and the
blackberries growing along it, than by the theory. But
he was often surprised by her retention, and he hoped
that some of the geologic background would stick with
her. How much the teacher he had become, profiting
from his own experience as student! (They should have
put the moraine in that transcript. . . .)

On the way back, Paul picked up an article printed
about the college. "There are two rules," it claimed;
"no pets and everybody works." Ho, ho! Minor
hypocrisy had not abated either! Just so long as they did
not try to expel any more students by selective en-
forcement.

After supper, Carolyn went up to the dormitory while
Paul remained on the main campus to talk with people.
The girl knew her way around now, so he didn't worry
about her going alone. After all, there were ducks to
feed. She had carefully saved her dinner scraps for
them. He gave her the key. "And don't lock me out!"

Returning late, he found the door locked with a note
on it. "FATHER PAUL—Carolyn could not locate you
and was upset, so she is with me." A female name was
signed and an address in another dorm.

Um. He didn't want his little girl upset. She tended to

overreact and hated to be alone. He set out for the listed dorm.

"Oh, sure," a boy in the lounge said. "They were here a moment ago. Here, I'll take you to her room." He led the way down the hall.

The room was empty. "I think they went to the other dorm," a girl said. "The little girl was crying—"

Crying. . . . "Thank you," Paul said. No question about the co-ed status of these dormitories; the boys and girls mixed freely throughout, and not merely the married ones. Paul only regretted that it had not been so in his time, as his suspension testified. The college had now admitted, in effect, that he had been right all along. Yet perhaps it had been his effort that encouraged them to change course; they must have been at least partially aware that they were fighting the most intellectually and socially aware students, not the misfits or crass ones. If the college admitted only those students who would obey restrictive and/or illegal rules, what would have been its future?

Ah, but would Paul send his innocent daughter to such a college with its carefree attitude toward the scholastic aspect and its completely open dormitories? Indeed he would, if her will and his finances permitted. He had fought for this very sort of freedom—freedom to learn to learn, to master real life—and still believed in it. The Vice Squad had won the battle and lost the war, and he was most gratified to see this.

He returned to his own dorm—and there was Carolyn. "Daddy!" she cried tearfully. "I thought you'd been killed in a car accident!"

Because she hadn't been able to find him. Her hyperactive imagination had brought her low. "I was in the Community Center, where you left me."

"I tried to call there, but they said you were gone."

How nice! Had anyone ever *looked*? Yet the same sort of thing had happened in his day. Paul himself had unwittingly caused much inconvenience to a visiting family because a phone call had come for a girl and he had not been able to go to the girl's dormitory (yea, and be suspended again?) even to call her from the lounge. He had explained this to the caller. Too late, he had learned that the girl, expecting the call, had been waiting—in the Community Center. He had not looked there, having no reason to believe that she would be there; one could not comb the entire campus every time the phone rang in the hope of such a random discovery.

The young lady who had taken charge of Carolyn accompanied them into the room. Amaranth in co-ed guise, of course; she had portrayed Susan too. All young women were the same, under the stage makeup, here in Animation. Paul was glad he had made the beds and kept the room neat, even to placing Carolyn's octopus doll on her bed. He had hardly expected female company at midnight! A friendly dog also wandered in, an Irish Setter, reminding him of another long-ago episode and recent hypocrisy. Carolyn was immediately cheered. Paul thanked the the student for her kindness; she said good-bye to Carolyn and departed. All was well again.

Next morning Carolyn found a girl her own age to play with. It was the granddaughter of the cleaning lady. The two set off for the kitchen to scrounge for food for the assorted animals of the campus, especially the voracious ducks. Carolyn also wangled a ride in the canoe on the little lake, another marvelous experience for her. *To be eight years old again, carefree . . .* yet there was more even to childhood than this, as the prior evening had shown.

Paul's programs were over. Now he was following up on other matters of interest: the college's new solar-power facilities, the resident water-dowser, the specialized Savonius-rotor windmill under construction, and the experimental crops grown on sludge. All these things had been exploited massively during the Exodus years, of course, but now that pressure was off, there was time to work out refinements and ascertain what was best for the long haul. They were raising crayfish as a crop and using wood for supplementary heating. All these things paralleled what the Holy Order of Vision was doing, and all were vital to the modern world. This

was another new direction for the college, and he
strongly approved. The years of wasteful, mechanized
pollution were over, and it was good to see the college
being so realistic. Institutions could learn and grow in
much the same manner as individuals!

Then he set out to run down Will Hamlin. The man
was as coincidentally elusive as all things were, here, but
finally Paul caught him in his office in the library
building. The door was marked "Dean"—was that his
position now?

"I have seen the college of my future, as it were,"
Paul said. "It has been twenty years, but my life has
been elsewhere, so to me it is very like yesterday. I note
many changes—and many similarities." He wondered
whether the evaluation system was still faked and
whether Will had any part in that, but decided against
bringing that up. He was, after all, not supposed to
know. "But you have been here throughout. I wondered
how the college development has seemed to *you*." This
was only an Animation, and he probably could not get
any genuine information, but it still seemed worth the
try.

Will was the only apparent survivor of that score of
years, although a couple of other instructors were in the
vicinity and Will's secretary was the wife of the other
student member of the Vice Squad in Paul's day. That
student had been an intelligent, sensible sort who had
known better than to get into the kind of rough-and-
tumble Paul had enjoyed. Paul had disagreed with him
on a number of matters, but always respected the individuality and perception of the man. To disagree
openly was no crime; it was hypocritical agreement that
was wrong. At any rate, there were some evidences of
continuity in the college. But the fundamental carry-
through, by the benificent irony of circumstance, was
Will.

Will, Paul thought privately. There were cards in the
Tarot deck identifying the concepts of Love, Victory,
and Justice. The card for Fortitude or Discipline had
been redefined by the Thoth deck as Lust; maybe two
cards were required there. Yet were Fortitude and

Discipline identical concepts? Perhaps they should be separated again, and a new card set up to cover Purpose—perhaps better titled Will.

Love is the Law, Love under Will. It was not necessary that anyone comprehend the pun; the concept was valid in itself. It had taken extreme fortitude to last it out here, surely. It had taken Will.

Paul's question, at any rate, was right in Will's bailiwick. Suddenly Paul was the student again, and Will the teacher, and the subject was the College: retrospect and prospect.

"It is hard to know where to start," Will said. "When you were here, the college was less than twenty years old—"

"Yes," Paul agreed. "When I came, it was fourteen; when I left, eighteen. Some of the students were the same age as the college." And the college had certainly been going through its adolescence then! Paul himself was four years older than the college; that was close enough for strong identification.

"I would say that at the outset the emphasis was on the college as community, and as involved in the larger community—about the first eight years," Will said. "Then a decade of concern with the nature of the learning process, and experiments with classroom methods derived from this concern—"

That was Paul's period. He remembered: philosophy class outdoors on the lawn, students falling asleep in the sun; geology, walking beside the river, learning to see it with phenomenal new awareness, its effect on the landscape, moraine and its own sedimented convolutions; art all over the campus, spending two hours looking at a landscape before making his first mark on the canvas, and the teacher had understood. Paul still had that painting today—not expert art, but another record of his learning experience. Drama, the plays and playlets performed on stage or in any available space on tour, once even in a private living room. Great exercise in versatility of expression! Dressing room facilities had not always been adequate; Paul's eyes had nearly popped the first time he had seen the very pretty leading lady blithely undress and change into her costume in the crowded backroom, while he and the others wrestled with make-up and cold cream and such. She had aspired to a career as an actress, but had later broken her leg in a skiing accident. That had, it seemed, destroyed her main qualification for the career. All classes had been discussion, not lecture, with all viewpoints appreciated. Yes, that had been worthwhile! Will called it "concern with the learning process;" Paul called it "learning to learn." How poignantly it returned, now!

"Then an eight year period when much effort went into curriculum experimentation," Will was saying. "There were strong influences from a number of social scientists and psychologists."

Those were the years immediately after Paul's departure. They sounded disorganized—as Paul's own life had been. Ages nineteen to twenty-six for the college: early maturity, but not necessarily the period of best judgment. A good age to heed the advice of specialists, certainly. Had that advice abolished the Vice Squad and started the trend toward dormitory deregulation? Had it returned the government of the Community *to the Community*, aborting the faculty oligarchy?

"Six years during which the college was trying to 'grow while staying small'," Will continued. "This was done by dividing its growing population into two relatively separate campus groups and by means of the organization of student-faculty 'living-learning' units."

Ages twenty-seven through thirty-two, Paul thought. Time to get married and settle down. But how could a college marry? Instead it reproduced by fission, like a creature of Sphere Nath, forming a satellite campus, propagating its species in its own fashion. Paul himself had gotten married in that period of his life after returning from his experience on Planet Tarot a changed man. But what man could visit Hell itself in his quest for God and not suffer change?

"And the past six years," Will concluded. "Involving growing program autonomy for the five programs developed, under an overall view of education as a rhythmic alteration of action and reflection, resident and nonresident experience, the analytical and the creative.'' Educationese came naturally to an educator!

Paul, too, had developed new programs. His daughter Carolyn was one of them. Now he was forty-one, almost forty-two, still four years older than the college. To the extent his life could be taken as a guide, the auspices for the college were promising. Its progress would continue, changing to accommodate the larger circumstance of a changing world. The microcosm always reflected the macrocosm; free will was to that extent a delusion.

Will produced a paper from his files. ''The philosophical ideals of the college have been reflected in its catalogues,'' he said. ''This first catalogue encouraged the education of young men and women for real living through the actual facing of real life problems as an essential part of their educational program. It urged the participation of students in the formulation of policies and management of the college. . . .''

''I believed in that,'' Paul said. ''But I was suspended for practicing it.''

''*You* were suspended? I had forgotten.''

Evidently the event had not loomed as large in Will's life as it had in Paul's! And why *should* it have? This did not subtract from its significance. Will had been true to the college catalogue he quoted when the rest of the faculty had seemingly lost sight of its precepts. Will had done it because that was the way he was. Perhaps he assumed that others who expressed similar ideals also practiced them.

''I had more trouble with practice than theory,'' Paul said. ''In theory we learned about practical life by finding work during the nonresident work term. In practice, it saved the college somewhat on the winter heating bill.''

Will looked at him. ''Didn't you find the work program beneficial?''

''It was an education—but I think not the way intended.'' It had proved almost impossible to get a job for just two midwinter months. Not if a person told the truth. Some students lied; they said they were looking for permanent employment. Then they'd quit when the work term ended. Those who told the truth could spend more time looking for a job than they did actually working. The obvious lesson was: to succeed in life, you had to lie.

Paul had not lied—and had almost lost credit for one of his work terms. An honest search and honest failure were not acceptable. One had to play the game by its rules! But no point in belaboring Will about this; life *was* rough and fraught with inherent unfairnesses, and he *had* learned this. The thoughtlessness of the college could be interpreted as an aspect of its accommodation to reality.

"Many things work out that way," Will agreed, not aware of Paul's thoughts. "The history of the college has other examples."

"Oh?"

"One such was the Action Group. It was composed of selected faculty and students who set up residence just off campus. Instead of academic sessions, texts, and papers, they sought to find, through action and facing problems, the real need for depth of study for each person's own competence and satisfaction."

"That hardly seems different from life itself," Paul observed.

"So it turned out. Some students proved less ready for the cooperation and interaction the project demanded than they had judged themselves to be. Two faculty members had problems. There was some romanticism about the group which led, among other things, to its welcoming wanderers who had no connection with the college. One was a young man with emotional and behavorial problems requiring professional help; another was an old woman who was soon observed to be both senile and physically ill. So it seemed the project was a failure after one year—yet later analysis showed that a significantly large number of Action Group participants had stayed on at the college to become some of its most serious, most hard-working students. Several important later projects originated in the Action Group, and these projects are still operating today. From these came the 'cooking dorms' in which students are responsible for planning and preparing their own meals."

There it was—the origin of the co-ed housing Paul had marveled at. The offshoot of a failed experiment.

"From them, too," Will continued, "came a number of special interest residences—houses for vegetarians, for the student-manned fire department, for feminists, political radicals, for persons interested in certain schools of philosophy or psychology, an organic-gardening group—"

"We saw one of the gardens!" Paul said. "All this seems good. I had been afraid I would find the college hopelessly conservative; that's the way it seemed to be going when I left. I am relieved to see I was wrong."

"Oh, the students wouldn't let us go conservative," Will said with a tired smile. "The politics of the world affected us too. When the college president asked male students to either get haircuts or leave campus during an accreditation survey, there was a protest. 'To thine own self be true!' Students moved into policy-making positions. They demanded appeal boards for administrative decisions."

"If we had had that in my day, three of us would never have been suspended!" Paul said. The memory still rankled. The student body had been overwhelmingly against the faculty position. Paul still had the tape recording of the complete protest meeting. But perhaps the matter had done some good, causing the administration to moderate its positions in subsequent years before things reached the crisis stage. Paul remembered a private conversation he had had with the college president after that. The man had inquired with genuine curiosity why Paul worked so hard to make so much trouble for the college. Paul had replied that he did not like trouble, but that his conscience compelled him to stand up for what he felt was right. That was all; had the president been a narrowly vindictive man, it would have been a comparatively simple matter to interfere with Paul's graduation.

In a very real sense, Paul thought now, the college president had resembled the Devil encountered on

Planet Tarot. The Devil was, after all, a fallen angel, an aspect of divinity; He had His honor too. In fact, in Hell the Devil was viewed as God, while the dominating force of Heaven had seemed wrongheaded. It was all a matter of perspective. Probably it was Paul's ability to appreciate the viewpoint of his opposition that had enabled him to survive his phenomenal quest—and his experience at this college had in a very real manner prepared him for the later trauma. Perhaps, after all, the situation leading to the suspension had been beneficial. . . .

"An administrative decision to put a small part of the college budget into paving an area for use as a volleyball court," Will was saying, "in response to a student request, actually resulted in a student picket line that stopped the bulldozer. The funds were needed elsewhere they claimed, and it was a violation of the natural environment." Will shook his head in mild wonder. "What appeared to be operating for both students and faculty was the memory of the very small, very personal college it had been in your day."

"That smallness was no bad thing," Paul agreed. "Everybody knew everybody, and that encouraged a special community unity. Though it was hardly all sweetness and light then." No; it had been like one big family, and contrary to the folk ideal, some of the most savage antagonisms existed in families. Yet it was better to be involved, positively and negatively, than to be isolated from life.

"There were some unfortunate manifestations. There was a series of attempted rapes of students, frequent visits to the campus by persons peddling narcotics, and uninvited guests moving into college buildings. Several campus patrolmen were hired. Some students welcomed them; others were irate, calling them the paid lackeys of the Provost or Company spies, and so on."

"There was some of that in my day," Paul agreed. He was ashamed of almost none of his actions of the time, but he did regret the remark "beyond the call of duty" he had made to the night watchman. For later he had learned that the watchman had considerable sympathy for the position of the students. The man had taken the job from pressing financial necessity, having been married abruptly when his girl became pregnant. He had not liked turning in students, but it had been a condition of his employment, and his honour required him to do his best. At the end of the year he resigned; he couldn't take it any more. Paul had blamed him and ridiculed him—when in fact the watchman had been very much a kindred soul. Now Paul turned his eyes momentarily inward: *Lord, may I never do that again!*

"This was more extreme," Will said. "A student burned down the 'guard house' by the campus gate, justifying his action with the claim that freedom of speech must, at some point, lead to action if careful argument and repeated requests brought no relief."

More extreme? Paul wondered. That student had destroyed property. Paul would never know for certain whether he had helped to destroy a life. A seemingly minor remark could have more impact than arson.

Will went on to describe the retirement of the college president, and the problems attendant on the selection of a new one; the revival of Community Meetings and their problems; the continued flux of new ideas; and the savagely defended individuality of Community members. The filibuster remained an instrument of legislation, in micro and macrocosm, and the college developed the motto "The Exception is the Rule." There were chronic financial difficulties. The disruption of world society brought about by the Exodus had had its effect here too. Yet the college had survived as an entity and perhaps would continue on to greater achievements. The details had changed, but it remained in essence the college Paul had known. Possibly it was stabilizing as it approached its middle age.

Paul thanked Will openly for his time and privately for just being Will. Then he went to round up Carolyn for supper. It was a good feeling, being caught up on the college; an aspect of his being that had been missing for twenty years was now complete. He was, in this subtle fashion, whole again.

Carolyn was playing with several other children in a

fancy student-made playground. There was a kind of cellar with a ladder going down and a connecting passage formed from about twenty suspended tire casings: sheer joy for a child. Carolyn resisted coming with him until he reminded her about the chocolate milk. He hoped she was not getting to like it here too much.

After supper they admired the graffiti above the stairs leading out the rear of the building—as it were, the structure's anus. "Can't fight shitty hall," one proclaimed appropriately. But others were more clever, such as the question and answer: "Name your favorite Rock Group. 1. Bauxite. 2. Shale. (etc.)" Paul had to explain some of the concepts to her; this was always a certain exercise in enlightenment, but it was his policy to answer any question she put honestly and in terms she could understand. Certain four letter words were real challenges though. He hoped that this policy would prevent her from experiencing certain brutal realities before she comprehended the concepts. He was not sure this would be successful, but it was worth trying. He did not want her to grow up in ignorance and pointless shame.

They followed the graveled path through the forest toward the north campus. Carolyn spied an offshoot path. "Daddy, let's follow it!" she cried. She had, it seemed, inherited his desire to explore all avenues, physical and mental. Blessed child! "Just a little way . . ." he said.

The path slid down the slope, petered out, then re-formed. "Just like the path you walked to school on," she said. She never tired of listening to the anecdotes of his youth. Paul had walked two and a half miles to school through the forest when he was Carolyn's present age. He had not told her this in any effort to demean her own status or supposedly easy life, but because she simply liked to compare his youth to hers. Now she had found a path like his; that added luster to her quest.

Did other children identify similarly with their parents? Surely they tried to—but in most cases legitimate comparisons were stifled, perhaps by parental indifference, until all that was left were the Freudian sublimations. If a girl-child could not relate to her father as either a mundane parent or a fantasy playmate, eventually she might relate sexually. That could have hellish consequenses for her subsequent life. How much better to let her *be* a daughter!

The path crossed a rickety little wooden bridge over a gully and meandered on. Carolyn charged along it, thrilled. How similarly he had ferreted out forest paths when he was eight—and indeed, he was enjoying this now! Still, dusk was approaching, and they had to get up early next morning to catch the plane home. This was no time to get lost! "I think we'd better turn back now," he said reluctantly.

"Just a little farther!" she pleaded, and he could not deny her. The twilight provided that special added luster to the scene, the visual purple of the eyes being invoked. Everything was so exciting, so wonderful, though unchanged. How like the quest for knowledge this was; every acquisition introduced a new riddle to be pursued until one could be led far from one's point of entry. Or, more somberly, how like the road to Hell, paved with good intentions He had traveled that road more than once, yet temptation remained. . . .

They continued more than a little farther, yielding to the present temptation. The path led merrily across decrepit slat bridges, around a fallen tree, and to a river. "Oh, pebbles!" Carolyn cried, squatting down precariously near the water. She had started a rock collection and was constantly on the lookout for new shapes and colors. "Oh, how pretty!"

Paul was fundamentally pleased by her interest in rocks. Prettiness was in the eye of the beholder, and she had a pretty eye. But this was not the time! "Either we must go back—or forward," he said, eyeing the darkening forest. Though he had spent four years at this college, he had never penetrated to this particular region. That evoked another parallel: surely there had also been available fields of knowledge at the college that he had similarly overlooked.

They decided to go forward, hoping to emerge before darkness trapped them, as the path was leading in the right direction. Paul had to put Carolyn's rocks in his pocket, for she had no pocket in her dress. They crossed a larger bridge that was in such a tenuous state of decomposition that some of the planks shifted out of place behind them; Paul had to hold Carolyn's little hand to steady her. "That's what Daddies are for," she said. They would certainly not go back now!

But now the path diverged. He took one branch, she the other. But when they separated too much, he became nervous. Suppose he lost her in the forest? The thought of her alone, frightened, crying—he experienced a resurgence of guilt for allowing her to lose track of him last night.

Then she crossed to join him. "There might be bears," she confided. Yes, indeed—and not merely physical one! *Here there be beares* . . . no, that was *tygers*. Same thing.

The path climbed up a steep piney slope out of the valley of the river, then curved left—which was not the way they wanted to go. But they continued, committed to it. It crested on an upper level, moved into a field-turning-forest, and divided again. "Look!" Paul cried.

It was a monstrous Indian style tent, fifteen feet tall, partially complete. Surely some ambitious student project; tools were present. A nice, serendipitous discovery.

Then, of course, he had to explain the meaning of the word "serendipity" to his bright daughter. So as they followed the path north through the fields, he told her of the three princes of Serendip who always found what they weren't looking for. How much better words became when their little individual mythologies were told! The next time he used that word, in whatever connection, she would say: "Oh, Daddy. The big tent!"

At last the path sneaked between high encroaching bushes—shoulder high on him, over Carolyn's head, so forward progress really was dependent on his adult perspective—and debouched into a more established trail they had used before. They were unlost!

"That was fun, Daddy!" she exclaimed.

Yes—it had been rare fun. He put his arm around her shoulders, and they walked on. Their college experience was essentially, fittingly over.

Yet that night his dreams were troubled. There was a letter for Carolyn, one she would like to have, lost on the way. A phone call for him, never relayed. The Vice Squad returned in force; unable to catch Paul, it turned its fury on Will, firing him from his position. All nonsense, of course, but disturbing.

They were up well before dawn. Paul worried about possible interferences to their return home: David White might oversleep, or his car might break down, or the plane would be late and they would miss their connection, or Paul or Carolyn might come down with a cold that would make flying perilous, or thy might lose their return tickets, or bad weather would—

David arrived on schedule to drive them to the local airport. One worry abated! "Bye, Ducks!" Carolyn said. "Bye, Dogs. Bye-bye, College." She began to cloud up. "Daddy, I wish we could stay here. . . ."

Paul didn't answer. He was glad she had liked it, but now they had to go home. He loved his daughter, but he loved her mother too, and that separation was becoming burdensome.

The car did not break down. They did not come down with colds. The board listed their flight as being on schedule. The weather was fine. Paul presented their tickets to the clerk at the Air Non Entity office. None of his foolish fears had materialized.

The man checked the listing. "Sorry—you can't board," he announced.

Paul's brow wrinkled. "These are confirmed reservations," he pointed out. "They're valid."

"Not for this flight."

Paul began to get heated. "We paid for those tickets three weeks ago! They are *confirmed*. We arrived on your flight from Boston, reserved at the same time. We are going to be *on* this flight, or there will be legal action."

"Don't threaten *me*," the man retorted. "I have to go by the list. You're not on it. I have no authority to bump a legitimate passenger for you."

And that was it. The man refused to honor their tickets or even really to look at them. In that way he protected himself from actually seeing the marks of their validity. But he did telephone Allegory Airlines to verify that they had two seats available on a flight to New York. However, their flight was from a larger airport, forty miles distant.

"I'll drive you there!" David volunteered.

Paul, conscious of the connection he had to make in New York, and worried about his wife's reaction if he should miss it, had to accept. He didn't like imposing on David, who had work to do at the college, and he was galled about letting Air Non Entity get away with what appeared to be illegal overbooking. "I thought Ralph Nader settled this matter decades ago!" Paul muttered. Oh, yes—there would be a reckoning!

"Aren't we going home?" Carolyn asked worriedly. "Why can't we get on the Air No Engine plane?"

"We're going home on a different airplane," Paul explained shortly. "Allegory Airlines. We're driving there now."

"Alligator Airlines!" she said, pleased.

It was a pleasant enough drive. The road had been improved since Paul's day. David spoke of graduating and finding another job. "Jobs can be hard to find, these days," Paul said, remembering his own experience before he joined the Holy Order of Vision. "Don't rule out a continuation of the college position." In ways David was like Paul of twenty years ago, but in this respect unlike: Paul had definitely not been on the college's list of prospective employees! Yet David was as much of an individual, as much of a rebel, were it only known. Certain remarks made by others, privately, suggested that the college still seethed with as much half-hidden dissent as it had twenty years ago; in fact, there were those who now looked back on the tenure of the College president Paul had known as the golden age.

Paul suspected that David's doubts about remaining with the college were well founded. Yet the outside world, too, was not an ideal situation.

They arrived safely at the Allegory terminal. There was no trouble at all; the ticket agent made out new tickets at no additional charge. Paul and Carolyn bade David farewell—his timely help had saved them from being stranded by the one problem Paul had *not* anticipated!—and boarded the plane. It was a much more pleasant craft than the Air Non Entity midget and provided a breakfast served by stewardesses.

"I owe Susan six cents," Carolyn announced.

"What?"

"I borrowed six cents from her."

Now she told him! "We'll mail it back to her after we get home." Could that be the lost letter he had dreamed about?

They landed in New York at the wrong time and in the wrong section of the terminal. Paul did not know his way around. He asked directions, and the girl at the counter pointed him down a busy hall. He followed it, Carolyn trotting along beside him.

A battery of signs pointed the way to the airline he wanted. He followed the direction indicated—and the next group of signs omitted that particular airline. He paused, perplexed.

"Daddy, where are we going?" Carolyn asked.

"I wish I knew!" He looked at his watch. Time was running out.

They backtracked, Carolyn dragging as she tired. The original sign still pointed the way. Where *was* their airline?

"Daddy, you acted like you didn't remember me," Carolyn said.

"Not *like*. *As.* As though I didn't remember you," he corrected her. Then: "What are you talking about?" He was distracted by the problem of the missing airline.

"When we were getting on. To start the trip. You said there was a confusion of iden—iden—"

"Identities." How could an entire airline vanish?

"Yes. Does that mean I'm not your little girl?"

"Whatever—" he started. Then he saw that she was close to tears. "Of *course* you're my little girl! You must have misheard me." She came up with the most awkward concepts at the least convenient times! "Right now we have an airline to find."

Between the signs was a large central collection area with stairs leading down and passages spinning off this way and that like a huge maze. "Maybe down there," he said uncertainly. Time, time!

They went down, but there were only more passages and more signs—wrong ones. "I can't make head or tail of this," he complained. He'd rather be lost in a forest anytime!

He went to a baggage checking window to ask directions while Carolyn weighed herself on the baggage scales. He had to wait impatiently for another passenger to check through his suitcase. At last Paul was able to explain his problem, and the girl told him where to find the correct waiting room.

"All right, Carolyn," he said comfortingly. "Now we know where we're going."

His daughter didn't answer. He turned, annoyed —and she was gone.

She must have grown tired of the scales, with her brief attention span, and moved away. Now she was separated from him, somewhere in these rushing throngs, lost. With a stabbing pang of worry, he searched for her. "Carolyn!"

He could not find her. The people hurring on, each intent on his own special interest. Most were adults; some were children. Paul saw a childlike form moving away from him, down the hall toward the exit. He ran after her. "Carolyn!"

The girl turned. It was a stranger-child, staring curiously at him. Embarrassed, Paul rushed on past her, as though he had called to someone beyond. But now he was at the great exit door. Beyond was the busy city street, its cars, buses, and vans zooming by, perilously close. Had she gone out there?

He pushed on out, his eyes casting desperately about. She was not here. "Carolyn!" he cried despairingly.

Maybe she had gone into a lady's room. Yes—she had never been able to pass a water fountain or a bathroom without indulging herself of its facilities. She had been that way ever since she first learned what they were for at about the age of two. She must have dodged aside and entered the room while he rushed heedlessly ahead. Then she might have been unable to open the heavy door from inside.

He backtracked, locating a bathroom. He was concerned that someone inside might—sometimes perverts lurked for little girls—no! But he couldn't go into the Lady's Room to check by himself.

A young woman approached. "Miss," he said abruptly. "Would you—" He faltered under her stare. She turned abruptly and departed.

"Carolyn!" he cried loudly. "Are you in there?"

There was no answer. He had no certainty she was in this particular facility; there must be dozens of them in this huge complex. How could he check them all?

An official-looking man approached purposefully. Paul knew the woman had complained; now he would be arrested for indecent behavior. He moved away.

Footfalls followed him. Paul hurried; if he got arrested now, he would never find his daughter! Already horrible specters were forming in his mind; if anything happened to her—

She had been worried about *him* that night at the college. Now he knew exactly what she had gone through.

He was at the exit again. Was that her out by the street looking for him? "Carolyn?" he cried, pushing out.

The little girl stepped off the curb. A horn blared; tires screeched.

"CAROLYN!" Paul screamed, lurching forward.

There was a crash.

VII
Honor: 15

Much of the ancient interpretation of Mosaic laws—indeed, the necessity for laws in the first place—was based on the need for larger and stronger tribes. The rule that women were to be considered unclean and untouchable during the five days of menstruation and for seven days afterwards (Leviticus 15) was undoubtedly based on the fact that these twelve days were (and are) generally considered to be unfavorable for conception; man should not, therefore, waste his sperm lest he be punished by God for not adding to the strength of his tribe. It also appears that the laws prohibiting bestiality and homosexuality, and the judgment that such sexual acts among men were considered to be much more reprehensible than if women were the participants, were based on the need not to waste precious sperm and thereby perhaps impede tribal growth. Since there is no loss of sperm in lesbianism, no such rigid prohibition against it developed as they did concerning homosexuality. . . .

Contrary to common belief, Jesus Christ himself taught very little on the subject of sex. The vast majority of sexual proscriptions associated with and attributed to Christianity are actually

*outgrowths of the thought and writings of later
Christian theologicians, and most of this moral
theology was not actually propounded until long
after Christ's death. Paul was probably the first
Christian to speak out specifically on sexual
morality. He emphasized the need for marriage as
a means to avoid fornication, although he apparently considered sexual abstinence a more ad-
mirable goal in life (I Corinthians 6 and 7). The
writings of St. Augustine during the 4th century
A.D. have probably had as much impact upon
prevailing 20th-century sexual attitudes as any
other single force, in that he severely condemned
premarital and extramarital sexual outlets, including beastiality, homosexuality, and especially
masturbation. The Roman Catholic Church in
time came to idealize celibacy, with the highest
level of male achievement being total rejection of
all life's pleasures, while women could expect to
reach their greatest glory only through permanent
virginity.*
    —James L. McCary: *Human Sexuality*, New
York: Van Nostrand, 1967.

Therion sat on top of a huge Bible. Even lying flat,
the book was about a meter thick and four meters long.

"So you are back," the acolyte of the Horned God
remarked. "Vacation's over, eh?"

What had happened to Carolyn? Brother Paul was
unmarried and had no daughter; he was sure of that
now. So she could not have been lost. Yet he was also
sure of Carolyn's reality. In that time, ten years in his
future. . . .

Well, he would have to worry about his future when
he got closer to it. "What is your concern?" he asked
the man. Therion of course was teasing him since
Therion had had a part in the recent sequence.

"You looked at other religions and other
philosophies, including your idea of an educational institution, and found them wanting," Therion said. "By

elimination, you are choosing the Christian God. But do you have the courage to view your Jesus and his cult as skeptically as you view the others?''

A grim but valid challenge. "I must be fair," Brother Paul agreed.

"Even though your Son of God was an arrant sexist?''

"What?" Brother Paul demanded, irritated.

"He dealt with men. He went to his cousin John the Baptist for the start of his ministry and gathered about him twelve men for disciples. Why no women? Didn't he think they were children of God too? Or were they just the servant class, not to be taken seriously?''

"Of course not!" Brother Paul snapped. But then he paused. Why *hadn't* there been some female disciples? "You have to understand: in those times the whole culture relegated women to a restricted status, especially in religious matters.''

"In *Christian* realms," Therion said. "Not among the Pagans. The Horned God welcomed women. The temples abounded with priestesses, and they were completely uninhibited.''

All too true. To Therion, the ultimate fullfillment of a woman was as a Temple prostitute or madam, a seducer of men. No use arguing *that* case. "Jesus was a Jew. He was not free to flout the established conventions of his people. He would have been mobbed much earlier than he was if he had female disciples, and his message would never have reached its audience.'' Those who preached a message whose time had not yet come always suffered; Paul had felt that backlash himself when he defended the free association of boys and girls at college. How well he understood! "Circumstances forced him to—''

"To preach salvation for men, not for women," the other finished snidely.

"Jesus *did* honor women!" Brother Paul said. "Some of them were missionaries for him—''

Therion sneered his best sneer. "Such as?''

"Such as the woman of the well!" Brother Paul said.

"She told of Jesus among the Samaritans and brought her relatives and friends to see him, and there were many converts—"

"The woman at the well," Therion repeated, as though that were a suggestively curious example. "You really think that proves anything?"

"Yes! It's right there in the Bible!"

Therion jumped down from the Bible. "Then take a look inside your own Good Book—between the lines." He heaved the cover up like the lid of a coffin. The pages flipped over by themselves, past the Old Testament, slowing in the New Testament. Matthew . . . Mark . . . Luke . . . John. Chapters 1 . . . 2 . . . 3 . . . 4.

" 'Now Jesus left Judea, and came again to Galilee,' " Therion read aloud with exaggerated emphasis. Around the Bible the landscape of that time and place formed. At first the scene was distant as if seen from an airplane—*No, not that!*—then it steadied. It was as though the cameras were being dollied along by a truck driving along a country road, the huge Bible being that truck. There was a field and a well.

"He had to go through Samaria," Therion continued as the camera oriented on that well. The giant open Bible faded out, becoming the built-up stone. " 'He approached a city called Sychar, near to a field Jacob had given to his son Joseph, and Jacob's well was there.' "

"Yes," Brother Paul said. He was confident that when it came to quoting excerpts from the Christian Bible, he could match any challenge made by this man. "That's the passage. The Samaritans were mixed people from many eastern lands, settled in Israel by the Assyrians after the Israelites were carried away. They brought in their own forms of worship, but when they suffered plagues they converted to Judaism, intermarried with Jews, and claimed descent from Abraham and Moses. This annoyed the regular Jews, and relations between the two cultures became bad. So it was quite significant when Jesus met a Samaritan woman and converted her though she was of ill repute, forgiving her her sins—"

"Or so the expurgated text would have us believe,"

Therion said. "Those Samaritans were eager to gain acceptance by Jews any way they could. Watch what really happened."

From the field a man came, dressed in a flowing off-white tunic bound by a dusty blue sash. The amount of material was necessary to ward off the burning sun. He was bearded and wore a flap of material over his head though his face shone with sweat. He was familiar in a strange double sense. "Lee!" Brother Paul cried, then covered his mouth.

"Do not be concerned," Therion said. "He is locked into his role; he can not escape it, no matter how it annoys him, until we release him from the script. You and I can not be perceived by any but ourselves; we are as ghosts."

That was only part of Brother Paul's concern. If the role could be forced on an individual by others in the Animation, while the person thought it was his own will—then Animation was potentially a horror unmatched in the annals of man!

Then another facet struck him. "Lee—as Jesus?" he asked, amazed.

"Why the hell not? It's only a part in a skit, and we need an actor. He knew it when he signed on."

Knew that he might be subject to horrendous indignities, even the loss of his life. Yes. Brother Paul had known the same. Nevertheless, Animation was opening disquieting doors to him. For now, it seemed best to let Therion present his case.

Jesus was grimy and tired; this showed in his slow gait and general demeanor. He came up to the well and sat down on the low wall beside it. This was a pleasant enough place, really an oasis, walled in to protect it from blowing debris and polluted runoff from storms, but with green vines overgrowing the walls. The city it served was visible in the distance; steps led up from the depression the well was in, and a well-worn path meandered toward the city. Brother Paul wondered why the well had not been situated nearer the city or vice versa; but he knew there would be many complicating factors, such as the lay of the land, the most fertile fields, the intersections of roads, and just plain ornery tradition. No doubt the women got good exercise, carrying their heavy jugs of water across that distance every day.

Jesus rested beside the well with evident relief. Soon, however, his tongue ran over dry lips; he was thirsty. He stood, crossed to the stone edge of the well, and leaned over to peer into it. The water was too far down to reach directly. There was a rope, but no bucket. Unless he wanted to jump in—which would be foolish, since he would be unable to climb out again (thirst vs. survival)—there was no way for him to fetch up water. Resigned, he returned to the other wall and sat again.

The sun bore down from almost directly overhead. Jesus sat alone, eyes downcast, his tongue playing again over cracking lips. "His disciples have gone into the city to buy food," Therion explained.

Now a woman came to the well, carrying her water jar: a large earthern crock with twin curving handles, shaped with archaic artistry. She was young and resembled her jug in the esthetics of her outline. She wore a faded blue skirt and a brown shawl tied in front like a halter for her full bosom, and her kerchief descended from her head to fall over one shoulder in front to her waist. Her dainty feet were protected by half-sandals, hardly more than straps about heel and sole, leaving her toes free. Woman of ill repute she might be, but an extremely fetching one. Of course, it was much easier for a homely woman to be of good repute; temptation did not constantly come courting.

"Amaranth," Brother Paul murmured. Every Animation scene was different, but the basic cast of characters was constant. But Amaranth would not be able to indulge her normal siren role here!

The woman trotted bouncily down the steps, glanced fleetingly at Jesus, and promptly ignored him. She stopped at the well, picked up the loose rope, strung it through an eyelet of her jar, and lowered the jar carefully its distance to the water. The sound of gurgling became loud as the air bubbled out.

Jesus emerged from his reverie. "Please give me a drink of water," he said.

Surprised, the woman looked directly at him. "Aren't you a Jew? From Galilee?" A person's accent and garb made him readily identifiable, geographically and culturally.

Jesus nodded. "Jews also thirst, even those from Galilee."

"You, a Jew, ask a Samaritan woman for a drink? Your people and ours have no dealings." Yet, vaguely flattered, she drew up the full jug and passed it to him. The hospitality of water was fundamental to this arid region.

Jesus drank deeply. At last he returned the jug, wiping moisture off his beard with his sleeve. "If you only knew the gift of God and who it is who asked you for a drink, you would have asked him for living water."

"What a come-on!" Therion remarked appreciatively. "Just like that he's hooked her curiosity. He'd make a good carnival barker."

Brother Paul repressed his reaction, knowing that Therion was baiting him.

The woman of the well smiled tolerantly as she lowered her jug to refill it. "You have no jug and no deep well; where would you get 'living water'? Do you think you're greater than Jacob who gave us this well?"

Jesus, refreshed by his rest and drink, smiled back. "Everyone who drinks of the water of this well will thirst again; but whoever drinks of the water *I* give him will never thirst again."

She set down her brimming jug and untied the rope. "All right, I'll bite, Jew: give me some of this living water."

Jesus lowered his hand to his own midsection, outlining through the cloth what rose up there. "What about your husband?"

Her eyes widened momentarily as she comprehended the nature of his offer. "I have no husband."

"Well spoken," Jesus agreed, taking her by the elbows and drawing her in to him. "You've had many husbands in your time, each only for a night. Now you may have one for a day."

She glanced about, making sure that no one was approaching the well from the city. "I see you are a prophet." She raised her lips for a kiss.

"Woman, believe me, the time is coming—"

"That's not all that's—"

Brother Paul could stand it no longer. "Stop it!" he cried. "This—this is appalling!"

"But you haven't seen the best part," Therion protested with mock innocence. "Wait till you see the Divine Erection. He really socks the Holy Ghost to her till she overflows with—"

"Jesus never fornicated with women! He—"

Therion frowned. "So you can't face the expurgated pages of your Bible? Where is your open mind?"

Flustered, Brother Paul had to take a moment to organize his thoughts. "There is a distinction between open-mindedness and sacrilegious pornography. I just don't believe Jesus would *do* such a thing! The 'Living Water' he referred to was the Holy Spirit. For you to distort that into a lascivious connection—"

"You don't concede the possibility that Jesus might have had a normal interest in the opposite sex?" Therion inquired evenly. "That he might be tempted on occasion to dally with a good-looking, lower-class woman who showed him some kindness? Not a Jewish woman, of course; that would be crass. But the Samaritans were not in the same class. Being a prophet is hard work; he had to take a break sometime."

"No!" Brother Paul cried, closing his mind to the superficial reasonableness of Therion's argument. He knew what this man's route led to! "There's no evidence in all the Bible that Jesus ever had sexual relations with a woman!"

Therion smiled nastily. "A very interesting qualification. Verrry interesting! You are implying he had sexual relations with a *man*?"

"No! I—" But Brother Paul knew he had plunged into another trap foolishly. It was not as though he had no hint of the proclivities of this worshiper of the Devil. Therion closed the jaws inexorably. "As you have

established, Jesus never touched women sexually. Had
the Samaritan woman at the well proffered her charms,
he would have cast her aside and never bothered to
make converts from the Samaritans. Therefore, he must
have vented his natural passions on those with whom he
felt greater kinship. And indeed your Bible establishes
that—"

"Impossible!" Brother Paul cried.

The huge pages flipped over again to the eleventh
chapter of John, and the picture formed. "Now there
was a man who was sick, the Brother of Mary, who had
anointed Jesus' feet with oil and wiped them with her
hair, and been forgiven of her sins.' " Therion looked
up. "You know, that's a most interesting use of
feminine hair; I shall have to try it sometime. Jesus certainly liked to forgive pretty women their sins, especially
when they kissed his stinking feet. In those days women
really knew their place. I dare say some of them were
very grateful to be allowed to tongue his toes, and had
he desired them to extend their oral attentions up his
legs somewhat—"

He paused, but this time Brother Paul refused to be
baited. It was folly to engage this man in casual debate.

"Well," Therion continued, "This brother of Mary's
name was Lazor or Lazarus. Jesus loved Lazarus, and if
we take that literally—"

The scene showed Jesus putting his hand on a man,
drawing him in for a kiss in much the same fashion as
the woman at the well.

"No!" Brother Paul cried. "This was normal friendship! You have no grounds to presume—"

Therion faced him seriously. "You balk at all
reasonable conjectures. That's part of the problem with
your whole weird religion. Now I submit to your objective mind this hypothesis: if Jesus did not indulge
himself with the fair sex or with men, he must have beat
his meat in private—"

"No!"

"What, then, *did* he do? Fuck his sheep?"

And Brother Paul was unable to answer. This devil

was overwhelming him with horror. How could he choose between fornication, homosexuality, masturbation, and bestiality?

Then, like a bright light, it struck him: "The Bible only covers a small portion of Jesus' life! Only his birth, his bar mitz-vah at age twelve, and his spiritual mission commencing at the age of thirty. Eighteen years of his youth and early maturity are missing. He could have led a perfectly normal life in every respect, which the framers of the New Testament were too prudish to mention—or simply didn't know about!"

"Which is what I suggested at the outset," Therion agreed. "That woman at the well was about as sexy as Samaritans come. Note how thereafter he told the Parable of the Good Samaritan. Obviously he was thinking of the good lay he had—"

"No!" Brother Paul was back in the first trap, sloughing through the muck of a degenerate's imagination. "No casual sex. He must have married—"

Therion raised an eyebrow. He had superb facial control. "Is there any mention of that in the Bible?"

Was there no way out? "No, no mention. But as I said, editing or oversight—"

"Do you really believe they could have missed something like that? A whole *wife* mislaid?" Therion smiled with satisfaction at his passing pun. "Not one Apostle, not one associate of Christ saying one word about the little woman? No widow at the crucifixion, no children orphaned?"

It was hopeless. "No, they could not have missed that," Brother Paul admitted heavily. "Jesus was not married." How tempting to conjecture a loving wife who died childless of some fever before Jesus commenced his mission—but futile.

"So we are back to the question. "What did Jesus do with his penis when he wasn't urinating?"

"I don't know."

"Don't you think you owe it to your mission to find out?"

Diabolical imperative! "Yes," Brother Paul said grimly. The honor of Jesus Christ had been challenged,

and Brother Paul had to vindicate it—if he could.
Failure would mean the elimination of the entire complex of religions deriving from Christ and leave the field
open to the Horned God.

"There's the record," Therion said, indicating the
Bible.

"Father, forgive me," Brother Paul murmured
prayerfully. "I must do it." He stepped toward the huge
Book, and the pages flipped over so rapidly that they
became a blur. He put one foot into that blur and then
the other, sank into it as into a bank of fog, and found
himself in Galilee, standing in a mountain pasture. He
looked about.

It was a typical semi-tropic slope with a few sturdy
trees and tall grass going to seed. In due course, he was
sure, a shepherd would guide his sheep here, and in a
few days they would crop the grass low. Then they
would go on to a greener pasture, allowing this one to
recycle itself. There were no fences of course; the land
was open to any who cared to use it and who had the
power to preempt it. Shepherds could be rough characters, he knew; little David had become master of the
sling, protecting his flock from wolves, and had used
that weapon to slay Goliath.

A man emerged from the brush down the incline,
walking in relaxed but purposeful manner. This was
Jesus; Brother Paul knew him at a glance, for he
recognized Lee's bearing. Naturally Jesus was coming
this way; Brother Paul's Animation had been crafted to
put him in the man's path.

Jesus spied him and paused. Brother Paul raised a
hand in greeting. This was a scene from a play, of
course, and not genuine history, yet he felt a thrill of ex-
pectancy. Even in a mere skit, the notion of meeting
Jesus Christ personally. . . .

"Hello," Brother Paul said as Jesus approached. He
did not speak in Jesus' native language, Aramaic, as
neither he nor Lee knew it. In a *real* jaunt into the past,
there would be a virtually insurmountable linguistic
barrier.

"Hello," Jesus responded. He was about Brother

Paul's age with shoulder length hair lightened by the fierce Levantine sun. His beard was short and rather sparse. He held his long staff ready, a weapon in abeyance.

Now it was awkward. Brother Paul did not feel free to ask Jesus directly about the state of his sex life, but he could not simply let the man go. "I—crave companionship. May I walk with you?"

Jesus looked surprised. "You wish to walk with a pariah of Nazareth? Don't you know that I am Jesus, called son of Joseph the carpenter?"

"I am . . . Paul," Brother Paul said, not wishing to identify himself as a follower of a religion not yet founded. "I . . . was raised by foster parents."

Jesus warmed immediately. "Foster parents! They are good people?"

"Very good," Brother Paul agreed. "But not quite—" He spread his hands. "There is always that shadow, however unjustified."

"Yes!" Jesus agreed. "Joseph is a good carpenter and a good man. Always good to me, despite—" He paused, took a breath, squared his shoulders, and resumed. "I am not really his child. My mother was gravid before she married him. He knew this, yet did not divorce her or demand the refund of the bridal price. He accepted me so as to protect her reputation and never discriminated against me in favor of his true children by her."

"Yet you suffer the stigma," Brother Paul said sympathetically.

"All my life! When I tend herd well, the villagers do not say 'There is an excellent shepherd who guides his sheep to the best pastures and makes them fat—' " Jesus paused, his eyes roving over the pasture around them speculatively. "They say instead 'The bastard was lucky.' When I excel at Scripture they do not hail me for my scholarship, but sneer privately at my presumption. I am the intruder, though I never sought to be so. I shall not be heir to Joseph's shop."

"The ignorant are cruel," Brother Paul said. He had

not realized how sensitive this issue would be. Bastardy. . . .

"Sometimes I get so angry—" Jesus clapped one fist into the other palm, making a sharp report. "Once a companion sneered at me half-covertly, and I threw him to the ground." He shook his head. "I should not have done that. But I have such a temper at times! It is written 'More in number than the hairs of my head are those who hate me without cause.' Yet when I respond to that derision, I become as they are."

"Yes," Brother Paul agreed. "Um—would you mind telling me the source of that quotation? I fear I am not as apt a scholar as you." Actually he knew it, but wanted to compliment Jesus again. Was he being a hypocrite, playing up to a man in order to learn his secrets?

"It is from the 69th Psalm," Jesus said. "It continues: 'Oh, God, you know my foolishness, and my sins are not hidden from you.' "

"Most apt," Brother Paul said. But privately he was disturbed. This was a perfectly serious, decent, human man—a far cry from any Son of God. There was no aura of divinity about him, no special atmosphere. How could this earnest country man found one of the major religions of all time?

"I was going to a special place," Jesus said somewhat diffidently. "An old temple, pagan I fear, yet conducive to meditation. If you care to come along—"

"I'd like to," Brother Paul said.

They proceeded to the place. This was an oddly uniform depression set in the side of a mountain, its rim overgrown by huge old cedar trees that Brother Paul was sure had been wiped out by his own time. It was well-concealed. This area was sparsely populated; only by accident was this meditation place likely to be discovered. In fact, without the trees it would hardly be worth discovering.

"You must have encountered this retreat while herding sheep," Brother Paul said.

"A shepherd has much time to explore," Jesus agreed. "And to think."

Brother Paul saw water at the base of the depression. "Is that a spring? It looks cool."

"No spring," Jesus said. "It fills when there is rain, then dries again. At the moment it is fresh, but soon it will be stagnant, not good for watering animals. Otherwise many more flocks would come here, for water is precious."

"Yes, indeed," Brother Paul agreed. "I'd like to take a swim."

"Swim?" Jesus was perplexed.

"My people live near fresh water," Brother Paul explained. "We enjoy swimming. Don't you?"

Jesus shrugged, embarrassed. "I cannot swim."

A mountain man, unused to deep water. Well, half the people of Brother Paul's own day could not swim; the ratio was probably worse here. "I would be happy to show you how."

Jesus considered. "As I mentioned, there are ruins here, perhaps of a pagan temple. The water covers them now, but if your faith forbids your approach—"

"I appeciate the warning," Brother Paul said. "But my faith is unlikely to be contaminated by a pagan ruin. Maybe Ezekiel's four-faced visitors had a base here. That would strengthen my faith because it would be a confirmation of the Scriptural description."

Jesus laughed. "Whoever exalts himself will be humbled, and whoever humbles himself will be exalted. I am not certain in which category you fit."

"There is no shame in swimming," Brother Paul said. "It is a good skill to have in case one should ever be shipwrecked. No sense in drowning when just a little preparation will save you." Of course the real Jesus had walked on the surface of the water—though that could have been an illusion. On hot days one could see water-like mirages in hollows of roads, and nearby objects were even reflected in that water. Had Jesus walked in such a place. . . .

Jesus nodded. "It is written: 'Truly, no man can ransom himself, or give to God the price of his life.' What will it profit a man, if he gains the whole world, yet forfeits his life?"

No question: this role was Jesus, later to be known as the Christ! Yet where was the magic that would compel men to drop their businesses to follow him, to give their own lives to promote his cause?

"Are you a teacher of Scripture?" Brother Paul asked cautiously. He did not use the word Bible because the formulation of the Bible had been accretive over many centuries, and at the time of Jesus its precise format or content had not been settled. In fact, the Bible was not originally a book at all, but a collection of canonical writings, a religious library.

Jesus smiled with mild self-disparagement. "I am not yet of the age to be a rabbi."

Not yet thirty, the age of intellectual maturity. "Still, you are *nearly* that age. You must have discussed your scriptural knowledge with others informally." Leading questions—yet it was important to ascertain how much of the Christian historians' view of Jesus was realistic and how much was hyperbole. Had Jesus *really* been a great teacher, springing into being at age thirty?

"Oh, yes, friend Paul, many times. But my countrymen are farmers, shepherds, and fishermen; they care little for the magic of the scriptures and regard me as—as a local boy, reciting verses tediously."

"But the ancient testament is not tedious!"

Jesus spread his hands. "Not to you, not to me. But how does it relate to farmers whose concern is rain and soil and seeds? There is the problem!"

"Seeds," Brother Paul mused. "What is the smallest seed?"

"The mustard," Jesus replied promptly.

"Couldn't you translate the message of the Scriptures into just such common terms? Take the little mustard seed and how it must be sowed in fertile soil, just as a human soul must—"

"And the tiniest of all seeds grows into the largest of all herbs, a tree for birds to nest in," Jesus finished. "Yes, *that* they might comprehend!"

"The power of the parable," Brother Paul agreed. "A little folksy story made up of familiar things to illustrate a Scriptural point. That way you could reach the common people who otherwise be by-passed.''

"I must think about that," Jesus said. "I do know Scripture, and I know the common life. If the two could be unified, religion and reality—"

"Many people might listen," Brother Paul finished. "And understand. And profit. Because for the first time a teacher spoke their own language, instead of seeming to try to conceal the word of God from them."

"Yet the high priests of the Temples would not permit—"

"Why stay cooped up in the temples? In my country those who refuse to relate their learning to the real world are called 'Ivory Tower Intellectuals.' It is as though they are locked in towers fashioned of burnished bone of their own making, perhaps very handsome residences—but they are out of touch with the practical aspects of life. Your message should be taken out to the field and forest and lake, where the living people are."

Jesus nodded. "To bring the message to the people. . . ."

Brother Paul stripped down and made his way to the pond. At the water's edge he paused and turned, waiting for Jesus.

The two naked men stared at each other. "You are a Gentile!" Jesus exclaimed.

"And you—" Brother Paul started, but could not continue. For Jesus' generative organ was strangely mutilated. Immediately Brother Paul tried to cover up his reaction. "Yes, I am a Gentile, not a Jew. I have never been circumcised. But I honor many of the tenets you honor, among them the validity of the Scriptures."

"But you are outside the Faith!"

Brother Paul smiled. "Is it not possible for a man to be outside the Faith, even to be a pagan, yet be worthwhile? Do not some, like the Samaritans, begin as pagans but seek enlightenment?"

Jesus considered, then nodded. "Yes, surely. There are people who walk in darkness, then see a great light. They are good people, needing only guidance. Perhaps even the Samaritans." He grimaced. "If only there *were* suitable guidance! The scholars have become hypocrites selling favors in the temple, mouthing Scriptures they neither comprehend nor practice."

"That is unfortunate," Brother Paul said. Jesus had an accurate notion of the problem, but seemed to have no present intention of doing anything about it himself. Where was that Divine spark? "Someone should go there and advise them of their error."

"Someone should go there and cast out the merchants and thieves and overturn the tables of the money-changers!" Jesus said vehemently. "The temple is supposed to be a place of prayer, not business!" But in a moment he cooled, glancing down at himself. "As for me—I was born in a stable, and some say this is reflected in my manner."

"And I was educated in a barn," Brother Paul put in.

Jesus smiled and continued. "That was in Bethlehem, in Judea, for my family had to go there for the census, for the taxing. Then they were afraid for my life because evil Herod had been told a new King was being born, and he feared he would be replaced and so was having babies killed. It was just a rumor started by some foreign astrologers who had observed an unusual conjunction of Jupiter, Saturn, and Mars—nothing ordinary people would notice, but as one who has watched the stars many clear nights I can assure you that those three never come together at the same time, so it would have been amazing if true—but it certainly set Herod off! The Romans took the matter lightly, and only a few babies were actually killed, but my family was quite alarmed at the time and had to travel to Egypt quickly because of it. They could not make proper arrangements for my circumcision, yet it had to be on the eighth day. The knife cut too deep, and there was an infection, and on the road they could not have it attended to. So—" He lifted his stricken penis momentarily, showing the gross scar on it and the imperfectly developed testicles. He was not castrate, but it seemed likely he was sterile, and more than likely impotent.

"This is a terrible thing," Brother Paul said sympathetically. "In my country there are medications—"

But obviously it was almost thirty years too late. Jesus had grown to manhood deprived, victim of unusual circumstances.

"I have long since become used to it," Jesus said. "At least I have never been tempted to sin." He frowned. "Though when I see the delight others have in such temptations, at times I am tempted to wish for a similar temptation."

Thus at one stroke (of an unsterile knife) all of Therion's conjectures had been nullified. Jesus had never felt the need of direct sexual expression and was quite certainly pure. *But why, God, did it have to be done this way?*

Jesus came down to the water and stepped in it. His feet plunged through to the ground beneath; there was after all no foolishness about walking on water.

Well, on to business, such as it was. "Swimming is mainly a matter of confidence," Brother Paul said. He squatted, immersing himself. The water was chill. "The human body in most cases is lighter than water, so it floats. Trust in that, and all else follows."

"One must have faith," Jesus said.

"That's it exactly! With faith, all things become possible. Now I'll demonstrate what we call the dead man's float." Was he making a pun there? The dead member Jesus had would never float.

Brother Paul stretched out his hands, ducked his head, and pushed off face down. He propelled himself by flutter kicking his feet. After a moment he raised his head and treaded water. "See how easy it is? If a dead man can do it, how much better for a living one!"

But Jesus had the caution of a man who had never before trusted himself to deep water. "I fear if I do that, I will soon *be* dead! How do you breathe?"

"Well, that's the next step. Let me show you the dog paddle."

"The dog piddle?" Jesus asked, frowning.

"Paddle." Brother Paul demonstrated.

Jesus watched and smiled with comprehension. "Yes, I have see a dog do that, too. But I am not a dog."

"Maybe we'd better start with a basic man-type survival technique," Brother Paul said. "With this you need never drown, no matter how long you stay in the water. Just take a breath, hold it, and float just under the surface, completely relaxed. Your feet will sink, but your head should be near the top. Then when you need air, stroke your arms down, so your head comes up, uncoil your body, take a breath—and sink down again. You may get cold, but you'll never get tired."

Soon, with Brother Paul's encouragement, Jesus took his first float-breaths, then made his first travel-strokes. He was unashamedly pleased. "God has borne me up! I have learned a skill I thought beyond me!"

"Yes," Brother Paul agreed. "But make sure you always have company when you practice it. Water *is* dangerous if it is unfamiliar. Now we'd better get out before we freeze."

Jesus glanced at him curiously. "I am not cold."

"I dare say you have spent many chill nights in the open tending your flocks." Where were those sheep now? Probably in the care of a younger brother, now that Jesus was approaching the age of citizenship. "I am not as hardy as you." An unfeigned compliment this time.

"You look strong," Jesus said. "But it is true, anyone who tends flocks must accustom himself to the heat of day and chill of night." He swam jerkily for the shore a few feet away, and Brother Paul, across the pond, stroked more efficiently to join him.

But as he swam, Brother Paul noticed something below. There was a disk of metal at the bottom of the pool, shiny and clear. That was odd; why was it not covered with sediment?

Jesus noted his reaction. "The bottom is like copper, always clear. I do not know why. That is the site of the pagan temple; all is gone now except that altar."

A copper bottom? Here in the first century? A pagan temple was possible, but copper on such scale was hardly to be believed! Brother Paul forgot the discomfort of the cold water. "I think I'll have a look at that!"

"Wait a few days," Jesus advised. "The water will go, and you can see it directly."

"I fear I lack the patience," Brother Paul said. He dived, stroking powerfully down to the bottom. The water was only about eight feet deep.

The metal seemed to shine more brilliantly as he approached. Copper? It looked like gold! His fingers quested through the clear water, moving down to touch that mysterious surface. What was such an anachronism doing here?

Contact! Something passed through him like an electric charge, but not painful. Pale light beamed up from the disk, forming a column in the water, bathing him. He felt strangely uplifted, though he did not move physically.

But his breath was running out. Brother Paul stroked for the surface, slanting up to leave the column. His head broke water, and he took a breath. "Jesus!" he exclaimed. "There is something here!"

"I see it, Paul! Did you light a lamp down there?"

Brother Paul snorted at the humor. "I only touched the metal, and it glowed! I don't understand it!"

"Let me look," Jesus said. Carefully, awkwardly, he paddled across the pool. In a moment he entered the glow that now extended beyond the surface of the water and disappeared above.

Suddenly Jesus himself glowed. Transfigured, he radiated his own light. He remained still, neither swimming nor breathing; then, slowly, he sank.

Brother Paul launched himself through the water. He caught the man below the surface, hooked one arm about his neck, and drew him up and along. Jesus was completely passive, unresisting. Soon they reached the shallow water of the rim.

Brother Paul put down his feet, stood up, and lifted Jesus in his arms. He staggered out of the water. Jesus was not breathing.

No time to consider the historical or personal implications! Brother Paul laid the unconscious man face down on the ground and applied artificial respiration. What a fool he had been to encourage a novice swimmer to venture into deep water the first time! Yet Jesus had seemed in control until that light—

*referring to the spark of divine spirit which he had
and all of us have in us. We know that he was bap-
tized by John the Baptist, and many years of his
life are unaccounted for, so it is possible that he
spent a considerable time in John's company. If
so, he would have learnt from him the doctrine of
the Essenes, who taught belief in that divine
spark.*

*There is another possibility. If he was indeed a
human being, like others he could have suffered
from delusions and honestly believed that he was
divine.*

—Dennis Wheatley: *The Devil and All His
Works*, London: Hutchinson, 1971.

Brother Paul emerged from the scene troubled.
Therion sat atop the Bible again, smirking. "Got your
answer?"

"I got *an* answer," Brother Paul said. "But I'm not
satisfied I can accept it."

"You were there; if you can't believe what happened—"

"I was in an Animation subscene, not the historical
reality. I suspect these scenes are the product of the
imaginations of all of us who are participants in this
quest. The effect of precession leads us into strange
bypaths."

"I was watching. I never heard of an ancient copper
plaque that radiates a column of Holy-Ghostly light.
You can't blame me for that one!"

"No, that was from my own mind," Brother Paul
agreed. "I encountered a—a person who informed me
about the powers of the so-called Kirlian Aura and of a
long expired civilization he termed the Ancients. He
suggested there might be potent Ancient sites or ruins on
Planet Earth. Thus perhaps it was natural for me to
conjecture this as the explanation of Jesus' power."

Therion nodded. "Imbued by a machine many hundreds or thousands of years old."

"Millions of years old."

"Millions! Beautiful! To primitives, that power

would seem God-like." Therion squinted at him. "I
think you mentioned the four-faced visitors of Ezekiel
in your Bible. That was a good notion. Those were
surely men in self-propelled space suits—"

"I don't believe the Ancients were human," Brother
Paul said. "In any event, they were no longer around
when man achieved prominence on Earth."

"Still, there could be other aliens, looking for those
powerful old sites, trying to tap their scientific riches
before the local yokels did. Ezekiel's visitors could have
been looking for the Ancient site that Jesus actually
found. But—do I have it clear?—only a creature with a
very strong aura like yours can key open such a site, so
those aliens failed. When you touched it, you activated
it, and then Jesus got the brunt of its force."

"So it appeared in the Animation. But of course we
were not really on Earth, so even if there *were* such a
site, I could not have—"

"Don't be so quick to explain it away! *That's* a
theory of Christianity I can accept! A local boy
shazamed into Superman by the sleeping robot—and
what a swath that boy cut with that power! But he
should have bathed in that alien beam longer until he
was invulnerable except for maybe his heel—though of
course it wasn't really Achilles' *heel* that was
vulnerable—so they couldn't crucify him."

Brother Paul shook his head. "The very fact you can
accept this notion—means that I must question it. If the
Holy Ghost becomes no more than alien technology,
God has no part in it."

"Ah, but God works in devious ways! Maybe He
operates through Ancient sites!"

"Maybe," Brother Paul agreed, again refusing to be
baited. "But I would prefer to think of Jesus as a mere
mortal man with an immortal message."

"Oh come *on*, Brother! The Son of God—a natural
man?"

"Enhanced by the Spirit of God. Without the Holy
Ghost, Jesus was quite mortal."

"Oho! So it is the Ghost that counts, not the man."

Brother Paul did not care to engage this alert,

devious, diabolic skeptic in theological argument. "Approximately."

"Then you have been looking in the wrong place. You were following Jesus when you should have followed that super aura."

Brother Paul looked at him, startled. "Yes! It was the Spirit that made Christ and Christianity what it was. What it *is*. If the Spirit is false, if it is nothing but alien technology, then Christianity is false, and—"

"And you must seek elsewhere for the God of Tarot," Therion finished. "Exactly my case."

"If that phenomenon was only an Ancient aura," Brother Paul continued, working it out, "it might have imbued an ordinary man for a time, perhaps during his life—but it would not have survived the loss of its host. It would have dissipated on his death or reverted to its machine. Yet the Holy Ghost would have survived the demise of the man and gone on to imbue his Disciples, as prophesied by Joel and described in the Acts of the Apostles. 'And it shall come to pass that I will pour out my spirit upon all flesh; and your sons and daughters shall prophesy, your old men shall dream dreams, and your young men shall see visions.' This *did* happen at the first harvest festival, the Pentecost, after Jesus was crucified. The Apostles went on to preach the Word and heal the sick and form the nucleus of Christianity—"

"Are you *sure* it happened?" Therion inquired sardonically. "Or did they merely pay their visits to that same Ancient site, bathe in the 'Holy Light,' and pick up more grace from the machine?"

"That's ridiculous! There wasn't any machine! That was just a product of my imagination—"

Therion merely smiled.

"All *right*, damn you!" Brother Paul snapped, conscious of the verbal irony. How could a disciple of the Devil be further damned? "I'll go back and follow that aura! Then will you be satisfied?"

"*You* are the one who needs to be satisfied," Therion pointed out. "You are the judge of the God of Tarot."

The man was infuriatingly correct. "I will follow that aura until the end." He stepped toward the Bible.

Therion hastily jumped off as the pages flipped over. Then Brother Paul found himself in the forming scene of—the Crucifixion.

"Oh, no!" he muttered. But of course he had to attend because this was where Jesus' aura would survive—or dissipate.

A crowd of people was walking along a road leading up a hill. In the center a man struggled under the weight of a huge wooden cross. Brother Paul moved forward, biting his lower lip. He hated this, but he had to get close to Jesus in order to verify the man's aura.

Ironic, that this mob of perhaps a hundred was all that the city of Jerusalem, with a population of 25,000, could spare either to ridicule or to mourn the greatest man of the age! The plain fact was that ninety nine per cent of the population was simply too busy with its routine pursuits to pay any attention to—

He banged into a bystander. "Sorry," Brother Paul said. "I was trying to see—" But the man took no notice of him.

Brother Paul made his way to the front, finally getting a look at the cross carrier's face. And stopped, surprised. It was not Jesus!

Then he laughed with sheer relief of confusion, though his underlying distress had not been abated. Jesus had not carried his own cross; he had been too weak after the beating they had given him so that another man had been impressed to carry it for him.

Brother Paul's laughter had attracted momentary attention. People shied away from him, and a Roman soldier scowled.

Now he saw Jesus walking a few paces behind, wearing the crown of thorns, eyes downcast. He was pale, and there was a trickle of blood on his forehead where a thorn had punctured the skin, but he walked unassisted.

"Oh, Jesus!" Brother Paul breathed. "Couldn't there have been some other way!" Yet then there would have been no Christianity. . . .

The group moved slowly on up the hill, limited by the pace of the man staggering under the burden of the cross. Brother Paul, wary of interfering with history even in Animation, walked with them, trying to get close enough to feel Jesus' aura without attracting further attention to himself. But the Roman soldier spied him and warned him away with a dark glance. Brother Paul fell back.

They come to the gate in the great city wall. Beyond this was the dread place called Golgotha. The meaning of the name, Brother Paul remembered, was "The Skull."

Now the crowd milled about as the soldiers prepared the ground for the crucifixion. It was necessary to dig a hole to stand the cross in and place a support to act as a fulcrum so that the cross could be erected. The immediate vicinity was crowded because two more victims had arrived with their crosses; the religious nut did not rate an entire ceremony to himself. Yet Jesus was the center of attention.

Women closed in, and the harried soldiers permitted this encroachment because the ladies were obviously harmless and were, after all, female. Brother Paul tried to move in with them, but again the soldier spied him and warned him back with a significant gesture. The Romans were businesslike and relatively dispassionate; they evidently did not like this business, but they had done it before, followed orders now, and did not intend to let the situation get out of hand. Brother Paul retreated again still unable to verify Jesus' aura by contact.

The ladies clustered about Jesus tearfully, some mourning most eloquently. In Brother Paul's day the term "wailing" had derogatory connotations, but here the wailing was genuine: a passionate voicing of utter bereavement that chilled the flesh and whose sincerity could not be doubted. Occidentals were unable to show emotion this candidly, and perhaps this was their loss.

Jesus stood up straight and spoke for the first time since Brother Paul had joined the party. "O daughters of Jerusalem, do not weep over me. Weep over yourselves and over your own children."

They became silent, surprised. Jesus continued

talking to them, but Brother Paul, straining to hear, was roughly interrupted by a hand on his shoulder. Startled, he turned about. There was a Roman legionary, impressive in his ornate helmet, armored skirt, and slung short sword.

"Governor Pilate will speak with you," the soldier said gruffly.

Oh, no! The last thing Brother Paul wanted was to become involved in history. Of course he could not affect actual history, but if his presence distorted the Animation, he would not be able to ascertain the truth he sought. Was the validity of the Holy Ghost something that was inherently unknowable?

No! Better to believe that there had been a man like him at the Crucifixion, who had spoken to Pontius Pilate. Brother Paul was merely occupying the body, the host, as it were in Transfer, as the alien visitor Antares would have put it. All he had to do was go along with it, acting natural. So long as he did not deliberately step out of character for this situation, it should be all right.

Pilate was resplendent in his official Roman tunic and embroidered cape, astride a magnificent stallion. Behind him the flag of Rome fluttered restlessly in the rising wind, its huge eagle seeming almost to fly. Oh, the trappings of power were impressive!

The Governor stared down at Brother Paul from his elevation. "You appear to be unusually interested in the proceedings, and you are not from Jerusalem. Are you one of this man's disciples?"

Brother Paul stood frozen. Was he, like Simon, to deny his faith? Yet he was not a disciple in the fashion Pilate meant; not one of the Twelve. "I am not a disciple," Brother Paul said carefully. "But I do believe in the divinity of Jesus Christ." Yet was that itself a lie? He was here to verify the aura Jesus hosted, to ascertain whether it was some artificial, machine-enhanced thing, or the living Holy Spirit of God. How could he claim to believe when his objectivity required that he hold his judgment in abeyance. "At least, I think he may be the—"

"The King of the Jews?" Pilate asked. Suddenly

Brother Paul recognized him: Therion! The Roman soldiers had been Therion too, but this was better casting.

"Perhaps," Brother Paul agreed tightly. The legionary beside him shifted his balance. (Could a single role-player play two roles simultaneously in Animation? Apparently so.)

"Are you literate?" Pilate asked.

Since the verbal portion of this Animation was in Brother Paul's own language, it seemed safe to assume the writing was also. "Yes."

"Yes, *sir*!" the legionary snapped. "Show respect to the Governor!"

Brother Paul reminded himself of his need to play along with the Animation. "Yes, sir," he repeated.

Pilate nodded benignly. "Excellent. I have a task for you. I am not altogether satisfied of this man Jesus' guilt; in fact I find little to condemn him other than intemperate words, most of which have been uttered by his accusers." He glanced aside, making an eloquest gesture of spitting. "The high priests of the Temple, who feel their authority threatened by one who preaches some modicum of decency and salvation, even for the poor. Pharisees!" And now he did spit. "I understand this man Jesus once rousted them right out of the Temple, kicking over their tables and scattering their money. Good riddance!" Then his gaze returned to Brother Paul. "But these Jews would have him die, and I do not wish to incite further unrest while passions are already roused during this local celebration, the Passaway. Passover, I mean. Relates to some sort of mythology concerning Egypt, I hear, though I'd like to hear the Egyptians' side of it! At any rate, the politics of the situation require me to accede to an act I do not necessarily approve, washing my hands of responsibility for the decision. But that others may at least know the claim for which this man is being crucified, rightly or wrongly, I propose to inscribe a plaque and set it on his cross. You will print the words on this plaque. Are you amenable to that?"

Brother Paul had not expected a statement of this

nature from either Pilate or Therion, yet it rang true. Besides which, the legionary was nudging him with a dagger-like knuckle. "I—am amenable," he murmured. Then, as the legionary reacted, he added "Sir."

Pilate looked away, dismissing him. Brother Paul got to work on the plaque. He seemed to remember it, historically, as having been made of stone, but what they provided was a rough wooden board. Well, that would have to do. "What shall I inscribe?" he asked the legionary.

The man shrugged. He seemed amiable enough when out from under the eye of the Governor. "What is he accused of?"

"Of being the King of the Jews," Brother Paul said, half facetiously.

"Then write that." Case closed.

Brother Paul took the heavy chalk and printed out the seven words as boldly and clearly as he could: THIS IS THE KING OF THE JEWS.

One of the Temple priests came by as he was completing it. "That isn't right!" the man protested. "He isn't *really* the King of the Jews. You should write that he *says* he is—"

"Go soak your head," Brother Paul muttered.

Angrily, the priest went a few paces to complain to the Governor. In a moment Pilate's half-ironic response sounded above the clatter and hubub of the proceedings: "What I have written, I have written."

Brother Paul smiled privately. By assuming authorship of the plaque, Pontius Pilate had squelched all further complaints.

The legionary also smiled, briefly. "Serves the hypocrite right," he said, glancing at the disgruntled priest. "I'd like to see the whole lot of them crucified." He studied the plaque. "Does it *really* say—?"

He was illiterate, of course. That was why Pilate had needed a literate volunteer. Otherwise Pilate would have had to write the words himself, and that would have been beneath his station as well as to a certain extent again involving him in the matter he had supposedly washed his hands of. "It really does," Brother Paul assured him.

"King Herod should see that!" the legionary remarked appreciatively. Obviously he resented the whole troublesome tribe of Jews and enjoyed a good insult to any of them. "Now go take it to the cross. Hurry, before they erect it."

Suddenly Brother Paul had a legitimate way to get close to Jesus. Yet now that the opportunity was upon him, he found himself hanging back. How could he participate so immediately in this abomination?

"Move!" the legionary snapped, fingering his sword hilt. "They're about to mount him."

Brother Paul moved. He brought the plaque to the cross where it lay on the ground. "The Governor says to put this—"

"Yeah?" another soldier said. "How'd you like to put it up your—"

"It's all right," the first legionary said from behind Brother Paul. "Governor Pilate did order it."

The soldier shrugged. "If you say so, Longinus. Here, you take over this spear; I'm going to need my hands."

Longinus took the spear. "Hammer it in above his head," he told Brother Paul. "They're stretching him out now."

And while Brother Paul held the plaque, they made Jesus lie down upon the cross, placing his feet on the partial platform near the base and stretching his arms out along the crosspiece. Jesus was nearly naked now; they had stripped all his clothing except a loincloth: part of the humiliation of this form of execution. It was not enough that a man die; he had to die with his pride effaced. Brother Paul's heart seemed to freeze for several beats, seeing him there. Was there no way to abate this horror? Yet of course there was not.

A soldier handed him a heavy, crude hammer—really a mallet—and a large iron nail. "Right above his head," he said.

Brother Paul laid the plaque on the upper projection

of the cross, set the nail, and pounded it in. It was a hard chore because the nail was handmade and somewhat crooked, but he made allowances and got it done.

"Okay," the legionary said approvingly. "Now do his hand."

Brother Paul stared at the Roman, appalled. "I couldn't—"

The legionary blinked. He seemed to have some trouble with his eyes. This was a mechanical thing, not related to the crucifixion; some infection that reddened the eyeballs and evidently gave him chronic pain. Brother Paul was sure this affliction did not improve the man's temper. "Come on, come on, we're wasting time. You've got the hammer, here's a nail—pound it through the wrist, well-centered so it won't tear loose. The Governor wants to get this job finished."

Brother Paul looked across at Pontius Pilate still astride his horse. The wind had picked up considerably, and clouds were coalescing. There might be a storm. Naturally the Governor wanted to wrap this up and get back to his palace! But for Brother Paul to have to do this thing himself—

Yet if he balked, he might be changing history, and lose sight of the aura. He had tried to exert his own will in prior Animations and suffered terrible precession; he could not afford to do that now. He had to let the vision take its own course, now that he was in it.

"Forgive me," he murmured brokenly. Then he took a new nail, set it on Jesus' pale wrist, steadied it with an effort of will, controlling the shaking of his hand—and with that contact felt the aura. It was the same one he had known in the other scene: incredibly strong, stronger than his own, electric and encompassing and wonderful. The Holy Ghost.

Jesus reacted. His eyes stared straight up into the swirling clouds and his body did not move, but he was obviously aware of Brother Paul's own aura. "Paul," he murmured. "The mountain pool. . . ."

Brother Paul dropped the hammer. "I can't do it!"

Still Jesus did not look at him. "Do it, Brother," he

said. "My flesh will not suffer when the hammer is wielded by the hand of a friend. Do not let the scoffers nail me to the cross."

And Brother Paul, unable to deny that plea, picked up the hammer and pounded in the nail. The flesh was no harder to penetrate than the board had been.

Then he turned his face to the side and vomited.

Rough hands hustled him off. By the time he regained his equilibrium, the soldiers had finished nailing Jesus and had erected the cross. Now they were packing in the dirt around the base, steadying the upright.

Jesus hung by the cruel nails, the demeaning plaque above his head. He had been crucified. "Father, forgive them," he said, grimacing with pain, "for they know not what they do."

Suddenly the storm struck. The noon sun, already obscured behind amazingly dense clouds, disappeared entirely, and the whole scene darkened. There was a shudder in the ground. The wind whipped so ferociously across the hill that it seemed the crosses would be blown down.

"A tornado," Brother Paul murmured. But that wasn't it; there was no funnel cloud. "An earthquake." But, though the earth rocked, that could not account for the darkness. Yet this was no ordinary storm. There was a strange, burning smell, as if Hell itself were extending its environs across this territory.

"A volcanic eruption!" he cried, finally placing it. Some deep venting of pressures, spewing ash voluminously, blotting out the sunlight until it cleared. A blast like that of Thera of 1400 B.C., occurring in the same region of the globe, affecting the entire Mediterranean basin, coincidentally with Jesus' execution—

Coincidentally?

Brother Paul looked up at Jesus, hanging on his torture stake. How could this obscuration of light, this groaning of the very earth, be coincidental? Yet if God so protested the sacrifice of His Son, why had He not acted before to prevent it? Even now, it would be far more dramatic to have the cross shaken down and apart, releasing its captive. Dramatic phenomena whose origin and purpose the spectators did not comprehend—such things were wasted effort. Most of the people of Jerusalem would never connect this with the crucifixion.

He knew the answer: because this sacrifice was necessary to His purpose. Jesus Christ had to die in this highly visible and final manner so that his Ressurrection would have meaning. God asked nothing of any person that He would not require of his own Son—and here was the proof in the form of the most horrible, demeaning, seemingly useless death this society was capable of inflicting. Here was the proof that *any* person, no matter how insignificant he thought himself, could achieve salvation. Provided only that he follow the example of Jesus and believe.

Yet Brother Paul dared *not* believe—for he was here to verify and judge objectively the presence or absence of the Holy Ghost. Without that Spirit there could be no survival of consciousness after the demise of the body. No life after death—for Jesus or any other person. Jesus' resurrection would seem like fakery and be meaningless if his death were not dramatic—but his death would be pointless without the Resurrection. So this was not the end of the story; it was the central nexus, the significant turning point, the key event in the founding of a major religion.

And what if the aura dissipated upon Jesus' death? If there were no Resurrection, no Holy Ghost? Where was his own faith then?

Brother Paul got shakily to his feet and walked toward the cross. No one interfered with him; the darkness and turbulence had scattered the crowd. Governor Pilate had hastily departed, leaving only a few guards at the crucifixion site. They had recovered enough from their initial surprise to revert to their natural pursuit: shooting dice. The stakes were Jesus' clothing, particularly his seamless robe: who would get what as booty.

The aura manifested as Brother Paul approached. He was now able to feel it at some distance. The closer he came, the more intense it became, until he stood immediately before the hanging man.

The hanging man: the card of the Tarot, one of the Major Arcana. Now he knew the ultimate referent for that presentation. Jesus—crucified. Upside down, on the card, because this whole thing was inverted: the innocent suffering in lieu of the guilty—willingly. Sacrifice.

Jesus opened his eyes, feeling Brother Paul's approach. "Where have you been, Gentile friend?" he inquired. "Four years I have looked for you since you disappeared after saving my life at the pool, and I have tried to perfect your suggestions—"

"No!" Brother Paul demurred hastily. "I have no responsibility!"

"Because of you, I learned to harness the power of the parable," Jesus insisted. "It has been my most effective teaching tool. Because of you I have ministered to Gentiles as well as to Jews. Always I have sought your aura—"

"No, no!" Brother Paul protested faintly. "You did it all yourself! I only passed by—"

"Except sometimes when my temper got the better of me. Once I cursed a fig tree because it had no fruit for me, and the tree shriveled and died. That was wrong."

"Siddhattha would not have cursed any fig tree," Brother Paul agreed. "Such a tree was the setting for his Awakening."

"Who—?"

"He was another great teacher, called the Buddha. Yet each person must seek his own enlightenment. You did what you were fated to do. I had no part—"

The eyes focused their lambent gaze upon him. "Do you also deny my friendship, Paul, now that the end comes?"

Brother Paul, stricken, reached up to touch Jesus' knee. "No, never that! I merely meant I deserve no credit for your accomplishments. You are the Son of God, the Savior; I am only—"

"A friend," Jesus finished for him. "And what greater accolade can there be?"

A soldier looked up. "Get away from that cross—he ain't dead yet!" he snapped at Brother Paul. But Longinus, leaning on his spear, murmured something, and the man relaxed.

"Farewell," Brother Paul said, his eyes stinging. He broke contact and stepped back—and something fell on the back of his hand. It was a drop of Jesus blood from the nailing Brother Paul had done.

"This was my destiny," Jesus said.

"Anything I can do—" Brother Paul said, looking at the blood. Yet what *could* he do?

He walked numbly away and sat on the ground, awaiting the inevitable. Time passed slowly. The air cleared, and the afternoon sun emerged. From time to time people approached the cross to speak with Jesus, and sometimes Jesus cried out in pain and despair as the weight of his body dragged at the nails, but he did not struggle. Brother Paul tried to close his ears to the horror of it and felt guilty for doing so. "Christ equals Guilt," he murmured. "If he can suffer, I must at least pay attention."

Then, clearly, Jesus said: "I thirst."

A soldier dipped a sponge in vinegar, put it on a pole, and lofted it up to Jesus lips. Jesus took some. Apparently this was not an additional torture, but a mechanism to moisten parched lips. The tang of vinegar might distract the attention of the dying man momentarily from his situation.

"It is fulfilled," Jesus said.

The body on the cross sagged—and the back of Brother Paul's hand itched. Distracted by his horror of the end, he rubbed that spot—and felt the blood, sticky on his fingers. The blood of Jesus.

Brother Paul stared at it, feeling as though the nail had penetrated his own flesh at that spot. His whole hand became hot as if held in fire. The sensation spread up his arm and into his shoulder, not unpleasant but strangely exhiliarating. It was like heartbreak in reverse.

Abruptly Brother Paul felt the presence of a second aura, inhabiting his body beside his own. "Hello, friend," Jesus said inside him.

"This—this is Transfer!" Brother Paul exclaimed, amazed.

"There are things I have yet to do in this realm," Jesus said, "before I return to my Father."

"But this isn't—I'm not supposed to—" Brother Paul was unable to organize his protest. "Historically, I wasn't—"

"I understood you were willing to help," Jesus replied with gentle reproach.

"I—had hoped to ascertain—you see, I'm not of your framework," Brother Paul tried to explain.

"I understand that—now," Jesus said. "I can perceive your thoughts, for I share your body. Without you, I might have been unable to complete my mission on Earth. I shall not intrude long; will you not indulge me so that the work of my Father and yours be accomplished?"

Brother Paul could hardly turn down this plea, no matter how it complicated his investigation. "I will help you."

The soldiers were breaking the legs of the two thieves on the crosses to either side of Jesus' own so that the felons would die sooner and not extend the torture into the next day, the Sabbath Saturday. The body of Jesus was spared because it was already dead: a phenomenon the spectators found remarkable.

The legionary Longinus, skeptical about so sudden an expiration, took his spear and stabbed it into the side of the corpse. Fluid poured out, running down the shaft of the lifted spear. Longinus danced back, while the others laughed, but still got splattered across the face with blood.

"Shame! Shame!" a Jew cried, rushing up to try to catch the blood in a cup. "The sacred blood must not be spilled on the ground!"

"Who the hell are you?" Longinus demanded, wiping his face and blinking.

"I am Joseph, a—an interested party. I have—I have a tomb in a cave over there, and—if you will let me bury the body there—"

Longinus considered. "Oh, all right. Here, I'll help

you take it down." He blinked again. "The day is certainly getting bright! I never saw things so clearly before."

"Let us depart this vile place," Jesus said. Brother Paul was glad to oblige.

Under Jesus' guidance, Brother Paul went to the temporary residence of Mary Magdalene. "I am a friend of Jesus," he told the grief-stricken woman. "I came late and have no place to stay."

She hesitated, peering closely at him. She had been at the Crucifixion; he recognized her now. But her eyes had been only for Jesus; Brother Paul had been lost in the crowd. Then, without a word, she gestured him in, making space for him in the crowded room. Mary's friend, also called Mary, and other Disciples were there, but Jesus did not make himself known. "I suffer at their suffering, but it is not yet time," he said to Brother Paul.

They rested all day Saturday, the Sabbath, as was required by the Jewish religion. "You know," Brother Paul said in passing to Jesus, "in my day we rest on Sunday, the first day of the week. I believe that custom stems from an adjustment in the calendar somewhere along the line."

"What the day is called does not matter," Jesus said. "So long as one day in seven is set aside to honor my Father."

They slept, for it had been a tiring occasion. Brother Paul had nightmares of humiliation and agony, and woke to realize that these sufferings were from the mind of Jesus, not his own. Strangely, it was the thirst that was worst, not the nails or ridicule.

As evening came, Jesus roused Brother Paul. "Come, we must go to the tomb."

Quietly, they departed, leaving the room and then the city, walking toward the Place of Skulls where Jesus body had been sealed in a tomb. Night was closing in; the guards at the gate looked curiously at Brother Paul as he went out because few people cared to leave the city at night.

Suddenly the ground shook. It was another quake!

Brother Paul was flung to the ground, alarmed—but soon the earth quieted. He was only bruised and somewhat dirty. They resumed their walk.

The quake had done other damage. The great stone sealing the entrance to the tomb had been rolled aside. "Thank you, Father," Jesus said. Then, to Brother Paul: "we must remove the body and bury it separately so that it will never be found.

Brother Paul did not question this. Once he started asking questions, he would never stop! He entered the silent tomb.

The body lay there, tossed askew by the tremor, unpretty. Brother Paul nerved himself, put his hands on it, stripped off the clothing, and dragged it out of the tomb. He tried to close his nose against what he thought he smelled. He hauled it well into the foliage of the garden, then found a fragment of stone and scooped out as deep a grave as he could. The work was grueling in the dark, and every time he heard a noise not of his own making he paused, holding his breath, afraid the guards were returning. They had evidently been frightened away by the quake, but that would not keep them away forever.

Finally he got it deep enough. He set the body in, scooped the dirt over, and tamped it down. But the fresh grave would be too obvious by daylight. To conceal it, he had to uproot an adjacent bush, plant it directly over the grave, then scatter the surplus earth so that there was no giveaway mound. If anyone dug below the hollow where the bush had been, they would find nothing of course. Would this ruse be good enough to hide the body? Time would tell!

Again there was a noise. Someone *was* coming this time! It was not yet dawn; only a wan glow showed in the east. Brother Paul hurried from the grave and went to stand near the open tomb, trying to wipe the guilty dirt from his hands.

The person approached the tomb—and saw that it was open. There was a little scream. "Mary Magdalene!" Jesus exclaimed to Brother Paul. "She I would have married, if—" There was a mental image of a surgeon's scalpel, the blade that had destroyed Jesus' prospects for a normal life long before he had been aware of such things.

As the sun showed, Mary returned with two of the male Disciples. The men ran toward the tomb, exclaiming. They found the burial clothing Brother Paul had left, then hurried back to the city, excited. Only Mary remained, standing wistfully outside the tomb. She buried her face in her hands.

"To Hell with history!" Brother Paul said. "She must be consoled." He walked up to her. "Woman, why do you weep?" he asked.

She looked up, startled. She was a comely young woman, and he knew who played the role. She did not recognize him, grimed and disheveled as he was, despite his day at her house; he was now a stranger, but her grief excluded fear. Mary had been numbed by the immediacy of it, the day before, two days before; now she was trying to come to terms with it. "My lord, if you are the one who has taken him away, tell me where you have laid him, and I will—"

Now Jesus spoke through Brother Paul's mouth. "Mary!"

Mary's eyes widened. "My Teacher!" she cried, stepping toward him.

"Do not come near me," Jesus said, retreating. "For I have not yet ascended to my Father. Go to my brethren and tell them I am going to my Father and your Father, my God and your God."

Dumbly, she nodded, love and hope shining in her eyes. Then she turned and fled toward the city.

"But is it historical?" Brother Paul demanded when they were alone again.

"Have faith," Jesus said. "Even as a mustard seed."

In the course of the next few days, Jesus appeared similarly to a number of people, spreading the news of his Resurrection in the manner he thought fit, and Brother Paul had to trust him. Then they traveled to Jesus' homeland of Galilee, making more appearances. Finally Jesus returned to Jerusalem. "This is where we must part at last," he told Brother Paul. "It is time for me to give my spirit to the Disciples at the Pentecost so that they may continue my work on Earth."

But when that had been done, a small portion of that Holy Aura remained. "I do not understand," Jesus said. "I had thought I would at last be free."

Suddenly it came to Brother Paul: "Saint Paul!"

"Are you to be a saint, friend?"

"Not I! Paul of Tarsus, the Pharisee. You may know him as Saul."

"I do not know any Saul of Tarsus, and I doubt that I would want to give my last remaining Spirit to any Pharisee."

"Trust me," Brother Paul said. "We must journey to Damascus."

"Friend, I fear for your sanity," Jesus said. "But I see in your mind that this thing must be. I will meet this Pharisee of Tarsus."

IX

Change: 17

Man is born to die. Perhaps alone of all the animals on Earth, he is conscious of his own inevitable demise. This may indeed be taken as the curse of the fruit of the Tree of Knowledge of Good and Evil. The moment man's intellect lifted him above the level of the ignorant, complacent beast so that he could improve his lot by planning ahead, he was able to perceive the fate Nature had prepared for him.

Psychologists say that when a person is faced with untimely death, he typically goes through five stages. The first is DENIAL: he simply refuses to believe that this horrible thing is true. The second is ANGER: why should he be treated this way when others are spared? It simply isn't fair, and he is furious. The third is BARGAINING WITH GOD: he prays to God for relief from this sentence and promises to improve himself if his life is only reprieved. Sometimes it *is* reprieved, and sometimes he honors his bargain. But when this appeal fails, he comes to the fourth: DEPRESSION. What is the point of carrying on when the sentence is absolute and there is no escape? But at last he comes to the fifth: AC-CEPTANCE. At peace with his situation, he

wraps up his worldly affairs and comports himself
for the termination.

It seems reasonable to assume that man's whole
life is governed by similar stages of awareness,
even when his death is not expected to be untimely. As a child, he denies death; it is beyond his
comprehension. But as he matures, the deaths of
relatives, friends, and strangers force awareness
upon him, and he responds angrily by indulging in
death-defying exploits of diverse kinds,
"proving" he is immune. With further maturity
he becomes more subtle; he becomes religious, accepting the thesis that physical death is not the
end, but merely another change in his situation, a
transformation to an "afterlife." Perhaps all
religion derives from this urge to negate death;
one cannot bargain with God unless God exists.
Yet the fear of death is not entirely abated by
religion; the services of assorted churches may be
perceived as mere ritual, and his confidence
erodes. The inexorable approach of death in the
form of advancing age depresses man; he longs for
his youth again. But in the end he resigns himself
to his situation, makes out his will, arranges for
the disposition of his remains, and departs with a
certain grace. He has accepted the inevitable.

They stood on the road to Damascus, staring in the
direction Paul of Tarsus had gone. The man, already
lame and scarred by disease, had been blinded by his experience and was sadly out of sorts, but Brother Paul
knew he would recover. Brother Paul found himself
shaken by his contact with the man whose name and
principles he had adopted. The name remained—but
Brother Paul could no longer consider himself a
follower of those principles.

"Still I am with you," Jesus remarked. "Why have I
not dissipated? I long to rejoin my Father in Heaven."

"I don't know," Brother Paul admitted. "I'm not
sure why I haven't returned to my own framework.
These Animations seem to continue long after their pur-

pose has been accomplished. Their *immediate* purpose.
I thought return would be automatic once you—
finished.''

"But I *haven't* finished," Jesus said. "My life and
death are only the beginning, showing the way. Now the
rest of the world must follow to achieve Salvation."

"I—doubt that will happen immediately."

"But the Scriptures say—"

"Sometimes things take more time than anticipated.
We really don't know how God measures time."

"Then I must remain to watch. I cannot let the people
drift alone."

Brother Paul shook his head. "Jesus, I fear you
would not like all of what you might see."

But Jesus had decided. "Come, friend Paul; you and
I will watch it all. Return your body to its place, and we
shall go together in Spirit."

Brother Paul tried to protest, but the will of Jesus
prevailed. "All right—we'll watch it together. But I
don't think we'll be able to participate directly because
you are physically dead and I have not yet been born."

"Come," Jesus said.

Brother Paul's body shivered and dissolved. It had
returned to its frame—but he and Jesus remained,
standing side by side.

"Come," Jesus repeated, taking Brother Paul's
ethereal hand. "We follow the lame Pharisee."

They flew through the air like the spirits they were, invisible to all others except each other. When that
became tedious, they simply jumped through space and
time, fading out in one location and fading in at
another.

They followed Paul of Tarsus. Though physically un-
pretentious and a rather poor public speaker, the
Apostle Paul turned out to have a fine if narrowly chan-
neled mind. His logic was powerful and his written
material eloquent. He also had a remarkable determination, a perverse courage that absolutely prevented
him from deviating from his set course. In some cities he
was ridiculed or even mobbed; he carried on. Many of

the other Christian leaders distrusted him and plotted against him, but he made converts everywhere.

"But this is not my message!" Jesus protested. "I was not attempting to found a new Church, but to show the way—"

"I said you might not like it," Brother Paul reminded him. "Yet if it is necessary to start a new religion in order to show people the way to Salvation—"

Jesus sighed. "I suppose so," he said dubiously. "Since the world will soon end, it may not matter."

Brother Paul did not comment. It was obvious that the Christian Church was not the initiative or desire of either Jesus or the Disciples who had known him personally. Thus, it seemed, it was necessary that a man who had never known Jesus personally assume a leading role in the propagation of the new faith. As with a failing business: a professional organizer had been brought in from outside, and he was doing his job without catering unduly to the foibles of the existing order.

But the Apostle Paul, it became apparent, was shaping that faith into his own image—and that was an unfortunately narrow one. Jesus, sexually voided, had not made stipulations about sex. He had treated all people equally, gladly accepting women as well as men, regardless of their station or the prior state of their conscience. Rich men *and* prostitutes were welcome, provided each renounce his/her liabilities. The Apostle Paul was far more restrictive, almost anti-woman; he permitted them to join, but never to exercise responsibility.

Jesus shook his head sadly. "I had not supposed it would be like this," he murmured, as he watched the Apostle Paul quarreling with the other Apostles. Brother Paul had mixed emotions. How much better to see his namesake from the perspective of history, rather than as this sometimes small-minded person! "He has written some excellent Epistles," he said.

Then, looking ahead in history, they discovered that not all of the Epistles written by Paul the Apostle had been collected in the Bible and that not all the fourteen collected had been authored by Paul. Jesus watched the Epistle to the Hebrews being clothed with the Apostle's name so as to make it acceptable for publication, and suddenly he laughed. "Even as Paul credits me with attitudes I never held, so now he himself is being credited with letters he never wrote! Truly my Father is just!" But he soon sobered, for all of this only elaborated the distortions of Jesus' own message.

"Let's view some other aspect," Brother Paul suggested. He had liked to think that the fourteen cards of each Tarot suit reflected the fourteen Paulean Epistles in the Bible, but if some of these were invalid—

"Perhaps they are doing better in America," Jesus said.

Brother Paul was startled. This was a gross anachronism; America would not be discovered by Europeans for some centuries yet! Lee had fluffed his line. "Did you say Rome?" Brother Paul inquired, giving him the cue.

"I said America. The opposite side of the globe—but we can get there in a moment."

Sometimes it happened: a mental short circuit that became established. What did the actors in a play do in such a case to correct the situation without alerting the watching audience? There was no audience here, but it seemed a fair analogy. They could not trace true history if they inserted discontinuities.

Brother Paul tried again: "I'm not sure I know that city."

Jesus glanced at him. "More than a city, friend Paul. A *continent*. Come—I will show you."

"Ah—yes," Brother Paul agreed weakly. At least he had tried.

They flew up high, a kilometer, three kilometers, and on up. "It seems you do not know of the Jaredite and Nephite Nations," Jesus said.

"I am afraid I don't." Was there any hope of putting this scene back together, or was precession simply too strong?

"I shall explain while we fly." They were now ten

kilometers up, looking down at the drifting clouds;
Brother Paul thought poignantly of his un-daughter
Carolyn in the airplane, enjoying a similar view. "At
the time of the confusion of tongues after the Tower of
Babel, a man named Jared and his brother, who was a
prophet, importuned the Lord my Father that they and
their tribe be spared from the impending disruption.
The Lord granted their prayer and directed them to the
ocean, where they constructed eight great barges and set
sail. Their only inside light was from luminous stones.
After almost a year they landed on the shores of
America about two thousand four hundred years before
my birth."

"2400 B.C.," Brother Paul murmured, fascinated by
this strange story from the mouth of the Phantom
Jesus. He had never heard a parable like this! Now they
were so high he could see the curve of the Earth below.
They were flying east over the great land mass of Asia
near the edge of the Indian Ocean. What was this
Animation coming to?

"In America they multiplied and became a
flourishing nation," Jesus continued. "But they fractured into warring factions until after eighteen hundred
years they died out. But at just about this time, a second
expedition set out from Jerusalem six hundred years
before my birth. This was led by a Jewish prophet of the
tribe of Manasseh named Lehi together with his family
and some friends. They marched to the Arabian Sea and
built and provisioned a ship, then sailed east across the
South Pacific until they landed on the western coast of
America. This was their promised land—but like the
first colony, they split into two tribes, the Nephite and
the Lamanite. The Nephite advanced in the arts of
civilization and built prosperous cities while the
Lamanites degenerated. They forgot the God of their
fathers, became wild nomads, and became benighted in
spirit and dark of skin like the accursed children of
Cain."

"The children of Cain?" Brother Paul inquired. They
were now over the middle of the Pacific, still bearing
east.

"The evil ones. The black races," Jesus clarified.

Brother Paul was taken aback. "Do you mean the black races of Africa?"

"The same. They rejected the power of the Holy Priesthood and the Law of God. Thus they have been cursed with black skin to match their black hearts."

This was Jesus Christ talking? Far from it! It had to be Lee the Mormon. Brother Paul had not realized the Mormons viewed the Negro in such a light. "Surely there is some error. Since all people except Noah and his family perished in the Flood, no descendents of Cain would have survived—"

"It carried on through Noah's line, some of that foul blood," Lee insisted. "Ham, the son of Noah, fearing that there would be additional heirs to share the earth after the Flood, conspired with his two brothers Shem and Japhet to castrate their father. But they refused, for they were good sons. So he did it himself when Noah was drunk—"

"The Bible says Ham only saw his father's nakedness!" Brother Paul protested.

"The Bible has been expurgated," Lee said darkly. "But even so, it provides the punishment: the children of Ham became servants to the children of the good sons. races Thus the black races achieved their just deserts—"

"I am part black," Brother Paul said. "I had thought that was understood." But he realized now that Lee had played no part in the Dozens Animation where he had made an issue of his race, and the matter had not come up elsewhere. "Am I also cursed?"

Jesus paused in his flight, and from his eyes Lee looked out, shocked. "*You* have black blood?"

"About one-eighth, give or take a smidgen. Technically, I am a light-skinned Negro."

Jesus shook his head. "No, that can't be true. You are a good man!"

"I hope I am a good man, or can become one. But I am also a black man. I don't see the conflict—"

"No!" Jesus cried. "Corruption is not to be tolerated in the sacred places! Am I to throw the moneylenders out of the Temple only to be affronted by such insinuations? You must not joke this way, Paul!''

Brother Paul spread his hands. ''I prefer to be neither a joker nor a liar. I'm sorry if it bothers you, but I can not and will not deny my ancestry.''

Jesus/Lee turned on him a strange look of disbelief phasing into wrath. ''We shall discuss it at another time!'' Then he turned away, and Brother Paul sensed a kind of cold withdrawal in him, a rescinding of proffered friendship. Brother Paul had thought he was inured to this type of reaction, but he found it stll hurt. Lee was such an intelligent, upstanding, clean-cut person; how could he be a conscious racist? How could he reconcile this wth his portrayal of Jesus who preached Salvation for all men, no matter what their birth or their prior sins?

Then he recognized the pattern of reaction: this was similar to a person's response to the news that he must die. First disbelief, then anger. Lee's Mormon religion cursed the black races; the notion that someone close to him could have black ancestry, however small in proportion to the white ancestry—that was fundamentally intolerable.

It would take time for Lee's emotion to run its course, especially since it was not one that the role of Jesus Christ facilitated. But Brother Paul was very much afraid he had lost a friend.

Jesus angled down sharply, and Brother Paul corrected his flight to follow. Down they went toward the western coastline of the double continent of America. Faster and faster: ten thousand kilometers per hour, fifteen thousand, twenty thousand, and still accelerating. Jesus was really working off a head of steam! Twenty five thousand—''Hey, I think we're approaching orbital velocity!'' Brother Paul warned. But still Jesus accelerated, passing thirty thousand KPH—and now they were slanting in toward the land only a hundred kilometers ahead. Ninety kilometers ahead. Eighty—each second knocked off more than ten kilos. Still Jesus drove on.

They skimmed the ocean, leveled out, and ap-

proached the coastal mountains. Suddenly the peaks
loomed large—and there was no time to decelerate.
Though these forms had little mass, Brother Paul had
the crazy notion that their extreme velocity was
magnifying that mass because acceleration toward the
speed of light increases the mass of an object toward the
infinite. Jesus shot straight in to them, unslowing, and
Brother Paul had to follow. But what would happen
when—

Collision!

"And it came to pass in the thirty and fourth year . . .
there arose a great storm . . . behold, the whole face of
the land was changed, because of the tempest and the
whirlwinds and the thunderings and the lightnings, and
the exceeding great quaking of the whole earth. . . . And
many great and notable cities were sunk, and many were
burned, and many were shaken till the buildings thereof
had fallen to the earth, and the inhabitants thereof were
slain, and the places were left desolate. . . . And it came
to pass that there was a thick darkness upon all the face
of the land . . . it did last for the space of three days. . . ."

"What *is* this?" Brother Paul demanded in the
darkness, unable to see anything at all.

"This is the cataclysm that came upon the world at
my death," Jesus said beside him.

"That much I gathered," Brother Paul said. "Fire
and water and air and earth—the four basic elements
running wild in the form of volcanoes and floods and
storms and earthquakes. And now a fifth element,
darkness. But why did these nations of ancient America
have to suffer; they had no knowledge of you or responsibility for your death! And what were you quoting
from just now?"

"Chapter 8 of the Third Book of Nephi," Jesus answered. "Of *The Book of Mormon*."

Suddenly it fell into place. "*The Book of Mormon*!"
Brother Paul exclaimed. "Of course!" For Lee, as a
Mormon, would naturally believe in the version of
history and religion presented by his own Holy Book.
Brother Paul had reviewed Mormonism along with the
other religions in the course of his studies with the Holy

Order of Vision but had not actually read *The Book of Mormon*. Now, belatedly, he recalled the summary. Christianity had come to the New World, and the history of these converted tribes had been recorded on gold plates by the last surviving member of those tribes, a man called Moroni. The tribes had faded out about 400 A.D., and the plates had been buried in the side of a hill in the state of New York, America, until revealed to the founder of the modern Mormons, Joseph Smith, in 1823. Smith, and later Brigham Young, led the Mormons to Utah where most of them remained until the current extra-terrestrial colonization program provided new worlds to conquer.

Well, why *not* view the Mormon version of Christian history? The Mormons had been able to justify many of their claims through discoveries in archaeology, linguistics, and ethnology. *The Book of Mormon* did not conflict with the Bible; rather it augmented it.

Light returned upon the blasted land. Jesus stood up tall and spoke, and his voice reverberated through all the continent. "Behold, I am Jesus Christ the Son of God. I created the heavens and the earth, and all things that in them are. I was with the Father from the beginning. I am in the Father, and the Father in me, and in me hath the Father glorified his name."

"I came unto my own, and my own received me not. And the scriptures concerning my coming are fulfilled."

"And as many as have received me, to them have I given to become the sons of God; and even so will I to as many as shall believe in my name, for behold, by me redemption cometh, and in me is the law of Moses fulfilled."

"I am the light and the life of the world. I am the Alpha and Omega, the beginning and the end. . . ."

Brother Paul listened, fascinated. Lee had played the part of Jesus-the-man before; how he played the part of Jesus-the-Deity. He was far more effective this way, in his familiar text of *The Book of Mormon*. Yet Brother Paul thought he preferred the man.

"And ye shall offer for a sacrifice unto me a broken heart and a contrite spirit."

And what of racism? Brother Paul wondered. Suppose a black man had a broken heart and a contrite spirit?

Jesus went on to deliver the Sermon on the Mount, adapted directly from the Old World Gospel according to Saint Matthew. Then he commissioned twelve Disciples and founded his Church. It was an auspicious announcement.

At last Jesus and Brother Paul returned to the Old World. They looked at the broader history, seeing the new Church of Christianity infuse the Jewish Diaspora, the region where the Jews had been scattered by the deportations of assorted conquerors. But as the missionary message of the Apostle Paul took hold, there were an increasing number of non-Jewish Christians. The Jewish Christians did not view these with favor—but soon the Gentile Christians outnumbered the Jewish Christians, and eventually that latter faded and disappeared.

Jesus shook his head. "I hardly know what to think," he said. "I preached the dedication of self to the ends for which we live, rather than to the means by which we live. Ceremony misses the heart of religion. Thus I never set special restrictions, but—"

"We are far from Galilee," Brother Paul reminded him.

Indeed they were! Now the center of the stage was Rome, and Rome was in a centuries-long struggle against the empire of Persia to the east. The battle line swung back and forth, and for a time Rome governed sections of Asia Minor, importing their slaves, prisoners, soldiers, and merchants into the Imperial City. With these people came their religion: Mithraism, the faith of the Magi, later called "magicians." They worshiped earth, fire, water, winds, sun and moon; and men completely dominated this religion. Perhaps for this reason, Mithraism spread like wildfire through the Roman Empire after its two-thousand year quiescence and sometime persecution in Asia. Rome never conquered Persia, but the Persian religion bid fair to conquer Rome. Except for the competition of

Christianity! The two religions soon became rivals for the spiritual domination of the Empire.

Mithraism had a lot going for it with its essential monotheism and magic. But its exclusion of women weakened it. Christianity did not treat women well, but at least it allowed them to join. Thus the man of the family might worship Mithra, while his wife had to be content with the religion that would accept her, however grudgingly. Slowly and subtly, Christianity gained.

Jesus and Brother Paul came to stand in a Mithraic chapel in the city of Rome. It was a subterranean vault, lighted only by a torch. Its chief feature was a magnificent carving of a bull-slaying scene, brilliantly colored. There were several altars, one of which was evidently used for the sacrifice of birds. There were benches of stone with space allowed for kneeling during the service. The chapel was small, but well made.

"This is pagan, yet I would not condemn it," Jesus decided. "Worship should be an internal experience rather than a public display, and this private chapel is a step in the right direction. I wish I could talk to these people, and tell them of—"

There was noise. "I think they're coming," Brother Paul said.

But it was not a body of worshipers who came. A mob of Roman soldiers charged in. They overturned the altars and attacked the great bas-relief carving with hammers. In moments they had destroyed the chapel.

"But this—this is horrible!" Jesus cried, a tear on his cheek. "Religion is a principle, not a law. Those who have not found the way should be converted, not brutalized! Who has done this thing?"

They soon found out. The Christians had done it. They had made a deal with Gracchus, the Urban Prefect of Rome. Persecution of the Mithraists followed throughout the Empire, and the religion was essentially shut down in favor of Christianity.

"But this is not my way!" Jesus protested. "Religion is inseparable from morality. How can there be persecutions of others in my name?"

Yet it was so. Other religions shared the fate of

Mithra, and Christianity was supreme in Rome. As people of the northern European tribes were converted, they brought their pagan values with them and their pagan holidays. Christian titles were applied to these celebrations: Christmas, Easter—but their essence remained pagan and, therefore, were easily commercialized.

"By their fruits ye shall know them," Jesus said sadly. "They have made of my ministry—a business!" Yet he could only watch.

Now Jews were persecuted by Christians and so were heretics: other Christians who differed from the official Church line. Yet the Church itself squabbled and split, following the pattern of the Empire. Later, armies of pagan Christians were sent back to the Holy Land itself to fight civilized non-Christians: the Crusades.

"I cannot stand by and watch!" Jesus cried. "Where is there now the sympathetic understanding I preached, treating others as one would wish to be treated himself? My name has been attached to a monstrosity! I must correct—"

History rushed on heedlessly. The Church fashioned in the name of Jesus no sooner became established than it began to fragment in the nature of human (rather than divine) organizations. Disagreements arose about the specific nature of Christ. Schismatic churches fissioned from the main mass: the Arians, the Nestorians, the Monophysites. Finally the Church itself split into an Eastern and a Western branch. Jesus and Brother Paul chose to follow the West—and it fractured into Catholic and Protestant groups, and the latter into multiple splits. The Lutherans, the Calvinists, Episcopals, Presbyterians, Puritans, Baptists, Congregationalists, Quakers, Methodists—on and on until there seemed to be no counting the individual sects. The nineteenth and twentieth centuries saw no abatement of the proliferation until it reached the situation on contemporary Planet Tarot.

"No, no!" Jesus protested. "I am not certain *any* of these fragments really relate to my ministry. Go back; I want to talk to someone before—"

They went back. "Here," Jesus said, more or less randomly. History paused in place.

France and England, two Christian nations, were making war upon each other. The lot of the majority of people in both nations was worsening. "If I can stop it here, set them right—" Jesus said with somewhat wild-eyed hope. "I can not stand idly by; I must do something."

"You can't do anything physically," Brother Paul pointed out. He understood some of Jesus' agony but doubted that it was wise to attempt to change history even in Animation. Precession might make things worse than before. "Maybe you could generate a vision—"

Jesus stopped where he was. They happened to be in a small village of France. "I will speak to the first person I see!"

Soon a country girl came into sight, going about her chores. She was dressed in dirty peasant clothing and could not have been more than thirteen years old. "Lots of luck," Brother Paul murmured sadly.

Jesus appeared to the girl. He manifested as an intangible but visible presence. At first she was amazed, then frightened, but in due course she responded. She began to take action in the world. She got an army and went to fight the British.

Her name was Joan of Arc.

Jesus and Brother Paul watched her fate with intensifying dismay. "She tried to spread the Word of God that I had given her—and they burned her for heresy!" Jesus cried.

"That is the nature of politics and of the Inquisition," Brother Paul said grimly.

Further along, in time and geography, they spied a Christian city adding a new level to a protective wall that had sunk into the porous subsoil. "We shall never make it stable until we offer a sacrifice," the superstitious people said, and the Christian authorities agreed. So they made a vault within the wall, placed a table and chair in it, and loaded the table with toys and candy. Then they brought an innocent little girl to this play area.

"Uh-oh," Brother Paul murmured. He recognized the child: Carolyn, lost as he departed his college Animation. "I don't like this—"

"We cannot interfere," Jesus reminded him.

The child was thrilled with the things. They occupied her whole attention. And while she played merrily, making exclamations of discovery and joy, a dozen masons efficiently and silently covered the vault and finished the wall. The priests blessed the proceedings and went their way—and the wall was stable.

Jesus looked at Brother Paul. "In my name, this too?" he inquired, almost beyond shock.

"Let's go get that girl out of there," Brother Paul said tersely. "We can do it, now, without changing history." But Carolyn had already departed the role by the time they got there; the chamber was empty.

"The center is empty . . ." Brother Paul murmured, beginning a chain of private reflection.

Abruptly Jesus turned to him. "I have been praying to my Father for enlightenment on this problem. I see that my sacrifice did not bring salvation to the world, and this is why I was not released to Heaven when I died. The sins of the world continue unabated, defiling my name and that of my Father. Yet there is also good in the world, as there was in the city of Sodom. I cannot deny you are a good man and an honest one; I must therefore believe you when you inform me you are a child of Cain. How can there be one good son of an accursed race? I have begged God for a resolution to this paradox—and He has answered my prayer."

Brother Paul remained silent, uncertain what was coming. Was this the bargaining-with-God stage of an adjustment that seemed more difficult for this man than death itself? Or was it acceptance?

"It is true you are damned," Jesus continued. "But only one-eighth of you is guilty. Seven-eighths of you is innocent, and that is the portion I have come to know as friend. It is as though a demon inhabits you. Since you were born with that demon, it can not be excised—yet I cannot allow the good in you to be relegated to Hell for the sake of your evil portion. Yet I know it is not possible to separate the good from the evil; both are part of you. I could cast out an ordinary demon or heal an ordinary ailment or forgive an ordinary sin. But I cannot grant a place in Heaven to a Son of Cain. It is beyond the power of the Son to reverse a dictum of the Father."

Jesus' eyes seemed to glow. "But I can save you," he continued. "All that is necessary is for me to assume the burden of your sin. I must go to Hell—so that you may go to Heaven. For the sake of the friendship we have and the good that is in you, O lone man of Sodom, I do this willingly. It is my bargain with God."

Brother Paul understood the context—that of a single good man in a corrupt environment—but he wished Jesus had not used "Sodom" as an analogy. The word "sodomy" derived from that, and that prior scene with Therion. . . .

"The decision is final," Jesus continued. "The only question remaining is the manner of my entry to the Infernal region. I choose to make it in a way that will help expiate the regenerated sins of the rest of the world. If I am successful this time, the world will soon end, and my confinement in Hell will not be long. But in any event, *you* shall be saved—and for that I am prepared to trade the world. Farewell, Friend." And Jesus/Lee put forth his hand.

Brother Paul, amazed, could only accept that hand and shake it solemnly. Here he had been reacting to a coincidental term and missing the serious import. Jesus was going to Hell—for him! Brother Paul could not at the moment even speculate on the larger meaning of this man's sacrifice.

Jesus turned away. Before him opened out a vista of contemporary America in an area where high technology remained. In the distance was a hydrogen fusion atomic power plant, and there were people manning a computer in the foreground. Jesus walked toward that scene.

Brother Paul realized what Jesus intended. He was

going to renew his ministry on Earth, this time utilizing the physical host available to him: the body of Lee. This was the Second Coming.

"Don't *do* it, Jesus!" Brother Paul cried. "They aren't ready for the Kingdom of God! They will crucify you again!"

Jesus paused on the verge of the scene, turning to face Brother Paul momentarily. Bright tears made his eyes lambent. "I know it," he said.

Then he turned again and walked on—into the present. His body solidified about him as he moved into the hall of the computer and around a corner, out of sight.

Brother Paul closed his eyes, remaining where he was. It seemed only a moment before the terrible clamor began, and the hammering of nails.

X

Vision: 18

And behold, a Philadelphia lawyer stood up to test him, asking, 'Teacher, what shall I do to inherit eternal life?' Jesus said to him, 'What is the law? How do you interpret it?' The lawyer said, 'You must love God with all your heart and with all your soul and with all your strength and with all your mind, and your neighbor as yourself.' Jesus said, 'Correct! Do this and you will live.' But the lawyer wanted to justify himself, so he asked, 'And who is my neighbor?'

Jesus replied, 'Once there was a man who made a business trip from New York to Washington. He stopped at a restaurant to eat, and when he returned to his car a hijacker rose up from the back seat, put a gun to his head, and forced him to drive to a deserted alley where he shot him in the stomach, took his wallet with all his money and identification, and drove away in his car, leaving him dying on the pavement.'

'A priest came through that alley by chance, and saw the man, and stepped over him and went on, averting his gaze from the blood, muttering something about being late for his service. Then a young woman passed, a secretary; she heard him moan and was horrified, and skirted him and got away as fast as possible. Then there came a garbageman, stinking of his trade, a son of the race of Cain, black as a tarred feather. When the wounded man saw him, he said to himself, "This nigger will surely finish me off!"'

'But the black man had been mugged himself in the past, and had compassion on the businessman, and stopped and cleaned up his wound and picked him up and put him in his garbage truck and drove him to a doctor and said, "I don't know who this guy is, but he needs help bad. If he can't pay you, I'll make it good next payday; here's five bucks to start off." '

Jesus turned to the lawyer. 'Now which of these three people, do you think, was the best neighbor to the suffering man?' The lawyer said, 'The nigger.' And Jesus said to him, 'Go and do likewise.'

Brother Paul stood amid the temporary chaos of shifting Animations. Jesus was gone, surely to Hell —but what of Lee? Had he stepped out of Animation—or was he stuck in a self-made inferno?

It did not seem wise to take a chance. It was possible to set up a given Animation more or less by choice, but once inside it, control or departure became problematical. As with boarding an airplane—as he had done!—it might be the right or wrong vehicle, but there was no getting off until it landed. Wherever that might be, safely or in flames. Lee might never escape Hell without help.

Brother Paul concentrated on a virtually intangible object: Lee's likely concept of Hell. It was probably a fairly artistic, literary notion, definitely Christian but not necessarily Mormon, for that would be too obvious. What Hell would a Mormon envision Jesus Christ attending? That was where Brother Paul needed to go.

The scene firmed around him. It was a field, half-plowed, about a fifth of a hectare in extent. Beyond it, to what he assumed was the east, the sun was rising in the sky. In the distance stood a tower, seeming to lie directly under the sun—perhaps the same tower he had seen in his first Tarot visions. "The Tower of Truth," he murmured.

He looked to the west and saw a deep valley with dangerous ditches and an ugly building in the lowest reaches. His field lay between tower and dungeon, the only arable land in sight. But he had no horse or ox to draw his plow; he would have to go to a neighbor to borrow his team, and that meant leaving his field unattended.

Now a motley crowd of people moved along the slope toward his field. Exactly his problem: they were apt to trample it flat, ruining yesterday's plowing, if he didn't stay here to ward them off.

Then he had a notion. Maybe some of them would help him plow!

But as they came closer, he lost confidence. The people seemed to be drifting aimlessly. Some were fat, others sickly, and others morose; none of them looked like reliable workers.

From the other direction came a more promising prospect: a pilgrim in pagan clothing with a sturdy staff. As the Animation would have it, the pilgrim arrived at Brother Paul's field just as the throng surged in from the other side.

"Whence come ye?" someone cried.

"From Sinai," the pilgrim replied. "And from our Lord's sepulchre. I have been a time in Bethlehem and Babylon and Armenia and Alexandria and many other places."

"Do you know anything of a Saint named Truth?" someone asked eagerly. "Can you tell us where he lives?"

The pilgrim shook his head. "God help me, I have never heard anyone ask after *him* before! I don't know—"

"*I'm* looking for Truth," Brother Paul said. "I saw his tower a moment ago. I can point out the way."

They looked at him dubiously. "You, a simple plowman? Who are you?"

"I am Paul Plowman," he said—and was shocked to hear himself say it. Now he recognized this scene: it was from the *Vision of Piers Plowman*, a fifteenth century epic poem by William Langland. And *he* was stuck in the title role!

"Yes, Paul," the people said. "We'll pay you to take us there."

But that wasn't really where he wanted to go. Not right now. First he had to locate Lee; then he could search out the Tower, now hidden behind clouds. Lee was more likely down in the Dungeon of Wrong, this Animation's version of Hell.

But now that he was in this vision, Brother Paul found himself constrained to follow the script. But maybe he could stall them while he figured out some way to rescue Lee.

"No, I won't take any money, not a farthing," he told them. "I will tell you the way—it's over there to the east—but I must stay here to plow my field."

They looked toward the east. The clouds were thickening into a storm. "We need a leader. You'll have to come with us."

"I have a whole half acre to harrow by the highway!" Brother Paul protested in the alliterative mode of the epic. "But if you help me to prepare and sow my field, then I'll show you the road." That should turn these idlers off!

"That would be a long delay," a young lady protested. She was in a fancy dress and wore the kind of hat called a wimple. Amaranth, naturally. And the pilgrim was Therion. "What would we woman work at while waiting?"

Now there was a challenge! Obviously this lady had seldom soiled her hands with common labor. "Some must sew the sack to stop the seed from spilling," he told her. "You lovely ladies with your long fingers—"

"Christ, it's a good idea," agreed a knight—another version of Therion. "I'll help too! But no one ever taught me how to drive a team."

Then they were all volunteering. It seemed the plowman's job would soon be done! Which was not exactly what he wanted. Well, he was stuck with it now.

But it turned out that many people were not good workers. Brother Paul had to keep after them, bawling them out, before the job was done.

He remembered that this epic meandered through a great deal of symbolic dialogue, while people dubbed Conscience, Reason, Wisdom, and Holy Church debated moral issues with others titled Liar, Falsehood, Flattery, and Mede the Maid. It might be a great work of medieval literature, but it wasn't taking him where he wanted to go. He had to break away from this story and seek another that would serve his purpose better.

Probably a direct effort wouldn't work; the Animations tended to precess when opposed as he knew to his chagrin. But maybe a slanting push, a shift into something similar, that might cast him into a more suitable role. . . .

What offered? Piers Plowman had tried to get men to earn their salvation by reforming themselves. Was there another epic with similar thrust and symbolism?

Suddenly it came to him. "*Pilgrim's Progress*!" he exclaimed. Bunyan's allegory even shared the alliterative *P*! In it, the character Christian sought the celestial city, buttressed by such bit players as Help, Worldly Wiseman, Legality and Evangelist. Would anyone know the difference if he phased into that vision? The genuine, fictional, Piers Plowman could take over here. Why not give it a quiet try! Not a hard shove, just a nudge. . . .

It worked! Brother Paul found himself in the Valley of Humiliation of *Pilgrim's Progress*. He was alone, but carried a good sword. He should be able to make his way to—

His thoughts were interrupted by the appearance of a monster. Oh, no! Now he had to face the hazards of *this* vision, and they were no more pleasant than those of the others. This was the thing called Apollyon, and he knew he could not escape it. He would have to fight it if he could not bluff it back. So he stood his ground.

The monster was hideous; it had scales like those of a fish, wings like a dragon's, bear's feet, a lion's mouth, and a bellyful of fire. Its face, however, seemed familiar: could this be Therion again?

Apollyon gazed on him disdainfully, blowing out evil smoke. "Whence come you? and whither are you bound?"

"I am from the City of Destruction," Brother Paul replied, "which is the place of all evil, and am going to the City of Zion.'' He was locked into the action and dialogue of the classic; only his thoughts were free. What a circuitous route he was following to locate Lee's Hell!

Apollyon spread out his legs to straddle the full breadth of the way. ''Prepare thyself to die; for I swear by my infernal den, that thou shalt go no further; here will I spill thy soul.''

With that the monster threw a flaming dart at Brother Paul's breast. But Brother Paul had a shield, round and coppery like a great coin (had it been there a moment ago?) and intercepted the missile.

He drew his sword—but Apollyon was already hurling more darts at him. Brother Paul tried to block them off, but they come like hail, magically multiplied. One flew directly at his face; he threw up his sword to fend it off, not daring to raise the shield and expose his legs, and it wounded his hand. Brother Paul gave a cry of pain and shook it loose; the wound was superficial, but it stung like fire. But then another dart speared his left foot, making him dance about in agony. What was *on* those barbs—essence of red ant, hornet, and scorpion? His shield dropped low—and a third dart caught him in the head, just above the hairline on the right.

Brother Paul fell back. He was being destroyed! He had somehow thought he was invulnerable to attack by mythical monsters since he was only passing through. False notion! The Animations could and did kill; he had known that from the outset. Apollyon might be a creature of the imagination of John Bunyan, but this was the realm of imagination, and the monster was being played by another real person. If *Pilgrim's Progress* decreed the death of this character, Brother Paul was in trouble. Unless he could shift stories again, get into a surviving role—

He tried to concentrate on that, but could not. The dreadful darts were still coming at him, and his head, hand, and foot still hurt. A trickle of blood was dribbling into his right eye. Apollyon was striding forward to match Brother Paul's retreat; any attention diverted to other literature could be immediately fatal here!

No help for it: he would have to fight right here and now. He obviously could not win by playing the monster's game; he would have to convert it to his own style. That style, of course, was judo; let him get his bare hands on Apollyon, and—

But that hadn't worked too well against the dragon Temptation back in the Seven Cups. Judo was geared primarily to handling *men*, not monsters. So maybe it was best to save that for a last resort and use his sword meanwhile.

Brother Paul stood and fought, swinging his sword back and forth, forth and back in flashing arcs. It was a good weapon, beautifully balanced, and its edge was magically sharp, and this was a heroic fantasy Animation. Apollyon retreated, fearing this new imperative. Brother Paul advanced, trying to cut the monster in half.

But the sword was also heavy. His arm was tiring. If he didn't cut down the enemy soon, he would wear himself out, and then be vulnerable. So he doubled his effort, trying to finish it now.

Apollyon stepped in close. Brother Paul dropped his shield and swung a two-handed blow at the monster's head to cleave him in two lengthwise. And hesitated in mid-stroke: it was Apollyon he aimed at—but would it be Therion he killed?

In that moment Apollyon dodged to the side, turned about, caught Brother Paul's arms in his own, emitted a stunning scream KIIAAIII!—and executed a perfect *ippon seoi nage* shoulder throw. Brother Paul, fool that he was, had walked right into it! These throws had been designed to handle warriors in armor and to disarm armed attackers. He had been beaten at his own game.

The fall was bruising. Brother Paul's sword flew out of his hand, and the wind was knocked out of him. Half conscious, he felt the monster dropping down expertly to put him in a holddown. It was *Kami shiho gatame*, the upper four quarter hold, one of the most effective in the judo arsenal. The monster was bearing down, putting the weight of his torso on Brother Paul's head, pinning it, forcing him to turn his face to the side in order to prevent suffocation. The fish scales of Apollyon's body stank in Brother Paul's nostrils and rasped against his cheek. He tried to struggle to throw the monster off, but the hold was cruelly tight. Apollyon really knew his business! No man could break this hold!

This was no judo match, however. The monster was not about to let him up in thirty seconds in polite victory. "I am sure of thee now," Apollyon said, pressing down harder. The weight of his body increased magically, becoming more than the mere position could possibly account for. Brother Paul thought his skull was going to crack open. His eyeballs were being squeezed; they seemed about to pop out of his head. He was in a vice, and the invisible handle was being cranked tighter. . . .

Then he saw the sword. It had not flown far; it was within a meter, lying flat on the ground. Had he turned his head the other way, he would not have been able to see it. Pure luck! Desperately he flung out his left hand—and caught the handle.

"Rejoice not against me, O mine enemy," he gasped. "When I fall I shall arise." Then he made a left-handed stab at the monster's side. It was not a really effective stroke because Brother Paul had poor vision and poorer leverage, but the good sword gouged out a patch of scales and laid open the dark inner flesh.

Apollyon gave a cry of agony. His hold loosened, and Brother Paul heaved him off. Brother Paul rolled to his hands and knees, shaking his aching head, and saw brown ichor leaking from the monster's side. Brother Paul raised himself to his knees, gripped the sword again in both hands, and raised it high. "Nay," he cried. "In all these things we are more than conquerors through Him that loved us." And he brought the sword down in a conclusive smash.

But Apollyon, defeated, scuttled back, escaping the blow. "Spare me, great Hero!" he cried. "I will make it worth your mercy!"

Brother Paul hesitated. Was this in the script? Could he trust the monster—*or* the man who played it? Well, he still had the good sword and could use it the moment Apollyon made a false move. The monster seemed to be out of darts anyway. "What do you offer, O fiend?"

"Information!" Apollyon cried eagerly. "I know these realms as you do not. I can direct you to anything you seek. Riches, weapons, pretty nymphs—"

Hm. "I am looking for someone in Hell."

The monster spread his wings, momentarily startled. "I could have sent you there ere now, had you not thwarted me."

"I don't want to be *sent* to Hell—I want to rescue someone who may be there. Locate him for me, and you can go free."

Apollyon fluttered his wings again in a gesture very like a shrug. "I see you know little of Hell, O mortal! If it took you such a tussle to overcome me (and then only because I neglected to kick your blade aside), who am the least of fiends, you would survive only seconds in the infernal region. You would need to have a thorough comprehension of the history and psychology of Hell before you could even guess where your friend might be, for it is larger than all the world, and then you still durst not venture there yourself."

Brother Paul considered. The monster was making sense! "Very well—tell me that history and psychology."

A snort of fire issued from the leonine nostrils. "Mortal, that would require a lifetime!"

"Abridge it," Brother Paul suggested, lifting his sword.

Apollyon sighed smokily. "I will try. I believe John Milton said it best—"

"You are familiar with the works of Milton?" Brother Paul asked with surprise.

"Naturally. He and Bunyan were contemporaries, the two great figures of the Puritan Interlude of seventeenth century British literature. The one wrote the great allegory, the other the great epic. Some scholars (bastards!) choose to ignore Bunyan in favor of Milton, but—"

"Yes, all right, okay," Brother Paul said. "Tell me about Milton's Hell."

"Well, if I may quote from *Paradise Lost*—"

"Not the whole epic!" Brother Paul protested.

"I will edit the selection," Apollyon assured him, though he evidently had had no intention of doing that before. Then the monster set himself up, spread his bear feet like an actor on a stage, and declaimed:

> The infernal serpent; he it was whose guile . . .
> Had cast him out from heaven, with all
>   his host
> Of rebel angels, by whose aid aspiring
> To set himself in glory above his peers,
> He trusted to have equaled the most high,
> If he opposed; and with ambitious aim
> Against the throne and monarchy of God
> Raised imperious war in heaven and battle
>   proud
> With vain attempt. Him the almighty power
> Hurled headlong flaming from the ethereal
>   sky,
> With hideous ruin and combustion down
> To bottomless perdition, there to dwell
> In adamantine chains and penal fire,
> Who durst defy the omnipotent to arms.

"Fine," Brother Paul said. "I appreciate the grandeur of Milton—but what about Hell?"

"I'm getting to it," Apollyon said, annoyed. "Satan picks himself up in the nether chaos and says:

> . . . What though the field be lost?
> All is not lost; the unconquerable will
> And study of revenge, immortal hate,
> And courage never to submit or yield:
> And what is else not to be overcome?
> That glory never shall his wrath or might
> Extort from me. To bow and sue for grace
> . . . that were low indeed.
> So spake the apostate angel, though in pain
> Vaunting aloud, but racked with deep despair. . . .
> Forthwith upright he rears from off the pool. . . .

Then with expanded wings he steers his flight
... till on dry land he lights. ...
Is this the region, this the soil, the clime,
Said then the lost archangel, this the seat
That we must change for heaven, this mourn-
　　ful gloom
For that celestial light? Be it so ....
... Farewell, happy fields,
Where joy for ever dwells: hail, horrors, hail
Infernal world, and thou, profoundest hell
Receive thy new possessor: one who brings
A mind not to be changed by place or time.
The mind is its own place, and in itself
Can make a heaven of hell, a hell of heaven.
... Here at least we shall be free; ...
Here we may reign secure: ...
Better to reign in hell, than serve in heaven.

Brother Paul nodded his head, impressed. "Yes, I can appreciate Satan's determination. He didn't give up at all; he had a fighting heart. So he fashioned Hell into a place of his liking—"

"Precisely," Apollyon said. "Now how can you expect to descend into this Hell, to the infernal city of Pandemonium, and gain any power over the fallen Archangel? He defied God Himself; only if your power rivals that of God can you hope to extract any soul from Hell. Frankly, you don't measure up."

"Well, I'll just have to find a way," Brother Paul said.

Now Apollyon spread his dragon's wings and lofted himself into the air. He sped away, and in a moment he was lost in the distance.

What now? It would be foolish to venture directly into Hell; Apollyon had shown him that. Yet he could not in conscience give up his mission. Was there any alternative?

He snapped his fingers. "Dante!" he exclaimed. "*He* went to Hell—on a guided tour. He had a guide, the Roman poet Virgil. If I had a similar guide—"

But Dante had not sought the extract anyone from Hell—least of all a prisoner of the status of Jesus. Virgil would probably not have assisted him in such an attempt, and it would have voided his visitor's visa.

Brother Paul would be better off taking his chances alone. If he could sneak in—

No! That would be dishonest. The end did *not* justify the means. Jesus himself would not accept rescue by questionable means. If he could not do it legitimately, he could not do it at all. So—

So he would go to the top—to Satan Himself if need be—and ask permission. This was, after all, a special situation.

You're crazy! a voice inside him cried. Was it his conscience—or his diabolic self? *Satan will grab you and put YOU in Hell!*

Um, yes. So he would have to be extremely careful. But still he had to make the attempt. He concentrated. "Lord of Hell! Prince of Darkness! I crave audience. . . ."

And the Sphere of Fire manifested about him. There was light like a blazing river, coursing through its winding channel, throwing out bright sparks that glowed like rubies. If this were the River Styx—or, rather, the River Acheron—then Hell was a much prettier place than he had imagined.

Well, maybe his imagination had been fantasy! He had heeded the propaganda of the Angelic side and pictured Hell as ugly; no doubt the souls in Hell were told Heaven was ugly too. Black is white, white is black, doublespeak, mindthink, whatever. Which was beside the point. Now all he had to do was locate the Demonic headquarters—

As he watched, the radiant river changed course and formed into a spiral, a vortex, whose center shone like the sun so brilliantly that he was unable to look directly at it. The outer loops became patterned, each swirl resembling a fresh flower—yet these flowers were winged creatures. Satan's host of demons? Strange; even though he knew them for what they were, they still looked beautiful!

One detached itself and flew to him. It was a female spirit, lovely beyond anything he had supposed possible for Hell, seeming absolutely chaste. "Paul," she called, as she came to rest beside him. He stood, he realized, on the top of a mountain, facing the glowing white rose of figures as though before a whirlpool in the sky, and she had come from that celestial image.

She was familiar. Amaranth, of course, the chronic temptress. Naturally she would turn up in Hell! Yet her face shone with its own pure radiance, and she was beautiful in a special way, more like an angel than—

"Where *is* this?" he demanded abruptly. "Who *are* you?"

She smiled graciously. "This is the Emphyrean, the Tenth Heaven—and I am Mary."

"Tenth what?" he asked stupidly. "Mary who?"

"The Tenth Heaven of Paradiso," she replied with another gentle smile. "Mary, mother of Jesus."

Something had gone wrong. "I—thought I was in Hell."

She looked at him with tolerant wonder. "You gaze upon the Court of God—and confuse it with Hell?"

"Precession," he muttered. Then, trying to reorient: "I meant to seek out Satan to—to make a plea. I—have no business in Heaven. I—must have stumbled through the wrong door."

"Cannot the Lord of Heaven serve as well?" Mary inquired. She looked familiar in a hauntingly evocative way, not at all like the person who portrayed her. Maybe she had been patterned after a painting.

Brother Paul considered. "I, uh, had not intended to bother God, uh, at this time." He was here in Animation to judge whether the God of Tarot was genuine; why did he hesitate now that he had a chance for a direct interview? Was it because he was unprepared (and who was *ever* really prepared for that encounter?)—or because he feared that beyond that unearthly radiance in the center of the rose of light was an answer like that he had found within his glowing Grail? All he was sure of was that he did not want to interview God right now!

"Perhaps if you informed me of the nature of your quest . . . ," Mary suggested compassionately.

He clutched at that with grateful speed. "Uh, yes. It—he—I—that is, your son Jesus—he meant to—" He could not continue. This was ludicrous!

"Jesus is absent at present," Mary said. "He has a mission with the living, and we have not had recent news of him. I am concerned, as a mother must be."

"He's in Hell," Brother Paul blurted. "He—I was slated to go there, but because of our friendship he went in my stead, and now I want to get him *out*."

She contemplated him with angelic solemnity. "You wish to exchange places with him?"

"No! I don't want either one of us in Hell! I feel his gesture was mistaken because I am not destined for Hell. Not for the reason he thought anyway. So I want to persuade him of that and take him out—if I can find him."

She considered. "This would be most irregular. Hell cannot hold him without his consent. Yet, as his mother, I am grieved to have him suffer. I know he is willful; I remember when he ran away as a child of twelve and picked an argument with Temple priests—he never was too keen on some of the activities of the Temple, the moneychangers, you know. . . . " She trailed off, her eyes unfocused reminiscently.

"If I could just *talk* to him," Brother Paul said.

Mary made a sudden decision. "I think God would not object if you made a little survey of the spirit regions. There is such a constant influx of personnel, we tend to lose track. Are you apt at counting?"

"I don't care *how* many spirits there are in—" He stopped, seeing her silent reproach. He brought out his calculator. "Yes, I can count," he said.

"But you would have to be circumspect," she cautioned. "God does not like to have disturbances. If anyone became suspicious—"

"That's the point! I don't want to sneak in, I just want to go and speak to—"

"You will go openly," she said. "If you wait for a pass from Satan you may wait forever. Bureaucratic delay is one of the specialties of Hell. But as a surveyor, you can begin immediately. God understands."

In short, this was a method of cutting red tape. He would have to do it. "Uh—is there a map? I wouldn't want to get lost—"

"You will need no map," she assured him. "There are ten Heavens in Paradiso, each indicated by a planet or star, for the Angels, Saints, Righteous Rulers, Warrior Spirits, Theologians, Lovers, and such. You have merely to descend past them in order, making your notations. You will then be atop the mountain that is Purgatorio with its seven levels for the Lustful, Gluttonous, Avaricious, Slothful, Angry, Envious, and Proud. Then, inside the Earth, you must pass around Satan and enter the deepest ring of Hell: the icy realm of the traitors. After that you have merely to ascend to each of the other rings. There are nine in all, and in one of them you will find him." She looked at him with disturbing intensity. "Take care, Paul."

"I will," he agreed. What *was* there about her? Not that she was the mother of Christ; he had seen her weeping at the base of the Cross, there at the Place of Skulls, and there had been no magic. Something more personal—

He cut off the speculation. He had a job to do. He looked about—and Mary was gone. She had rejoined the Heavenly Throng.

Very well: he would take a census of Dante's Paradise. Except—how could he count these sparkling myriads, let alone record them? All the souls of all the people who had ever existed! But as he looked at his calculator, he saw numbers appearing, changing. It was totaling them itself, filing them in its little memory. All he had to do was look.

He started down the slope. He seemed to be made of spirit stuff himself so that he more or less floated with no danger of falling. The great circles of the Heavenly Host receded, looking like the stars of the Milky Way, and now he became aware of their music: "Gloria in Excelsis. . . . "

Rapidly he traversed the regions of the Fixed Stars,

Saturn, Jupiter, Mars, the Sun, Venus, Mercury, and
the Moon and arrived at the boundary of Purgatorio.
He really would have liked to interview some of the
souls in these Heavens, but feared that any delay would
imperil his other mission. He did not want Jesus to burn
in Hell any longer than necessary.

Purgatorio, however, was much more solid and
somber. The atmosphere was gray, the shadows deep;
gnarly trees reached high in nocturnal silhouette. He felt
the weight of physical mass settle about his own being.
No angelic choirs here!

This was the Seventh Level, the top of the grim mountain, the habitat of Lust. He had no need to tarry here
any longer than needed to record the spirits. He already
knew the mischief blind lust could lead to.

Then he saw a wagon or chariot, set by a tree. From
the sky a great eagle swooped, diving to attack, once,
twice—but it sheered off at the last moment, and
feathers floated over the vehicle. A crack opened in the
ground, and a dragon strove to climb out of its depths.
The monster's tail swung up and smashed the chariot,
stirring up the feathers and leaving the bottom knocked
out.

But lo! the chariot regenerated. Each broken part of
it sprouted animal flesh: grotesque monsters, winged,
horned, serpentine bodied, ferocious. And upon this
half-living platform appeared a woman, busty, brassy,
bold-eyed, looking about acquisitively. Her eye caught
Brother Paul's, and she gave him a wanton come-hither
signal, patting the chariot beside her. A prostitute,
surely, played by the one who played all such roles: for
this was the Circle of Lust.

Brother Paul was not tempted this time. But even as
she gestured to him, a huge man appeared by her side, a
veritable giant. He began to kiss the harlot, and she met
him eagerly—yet simultaneously kept an eye on Brother
Paul. The giant followed her gaze, saw Brother Paul,
and scowled, now resembling the monster Apollyon. He
seemed about to jump down from the chariot and attack
his supposed rival, but Brother Paul quickly retreated.
He was wasting time here anyway. Then the giant took a

whip to the monster portion of the chariot and drove it some distance away. As soon as the animals were under way, he turned his whip on his paramour, scourging her savagely. Brother Paul moved on. Once he was done with this mission, he would have to read the *Comedy* and discover who these people were and what their little act meant.

He crossed the river Lethe, wading through the shallowest section he could find, careful not to drink even one drop. The last thing he needed now was to forget his mission! He passed on down through the gloomy wilderness, making sure his calculator was recording all the souls there. This was certainly a contrast to Paradise! There were not too many overt tortures, apart from a group of naked people walking through a fire, but there was a great deal of misery. The Gluttonous of the Sixth Circle were being starved; the Avaricious were without creature comforts; the Slothful stood perpetually idle—and bored. The Proud, down in the first Circle, were bearing heavy stones up a hill.

If this were only Purgatorio, what was Inferno like? He was about to find out!

Brother Paul came to the place where Satan's huge legs projected from the ground. But it was only a statue; the living Devil was evidently off duty at the moment. Or on business elsewhere; the Evil One was *never* off duty! Between those legs and the ground was a narrow space; this was the entry to Inferno: Hell as Dante conceived it.

Brother Paul made his climb. At first it was down, but soon his weight shifted, and he had to turn about and proceed headfirst. He was passing through the center of the world right at Satan's colossal genital! Now he was climbing up—into Hell.

It grew cold. When he emerged into an open chamber, he was about chest high on the Devil-statue and in a frozen lake. Dante's Inferno, ironically, was locked in ice.

Shivering from more than the cold, Brother Paul moved out across the lake. The ice was so frigid it was not slippery; it might as well have been rock. He paused to look back—and for the first time he saw Satan in perspective. Hugely spreading bat's wings—and three faces, one white, one crimson, one black. The black face was looking right at Brother Paul. One eye winked, deliberately.

This was no statue. This was Satan Himself!

All Brother Paul could think of at this moment was: suppose Satan had had flatulence at the time Brother Paul was traversing the nadir? He would have been blown to Kingdom come!

Brother Paul turned about and ran. There was no pursuit. And why should there be? The only escape from Hell was back the way he had come—and Satan would be there, corking the bottle.

Toward the edge of the lake, he discovered bodies. They were frozen in the ice, face up, staring—yet not quite unconscious. These were the Traitors to their Benefactors.

Brother Paul hurried on, letting the calculator make its own tally. It hardly seemed that Satan had been fooled, but so long as Brother Paul remained free, he would act. Maybe this would turn out to be his own Hell: the tabulations for each section would be fouled up so that he would have to do them over, and over, and over, touring Hell perpetually.

The edge of the pit that contained the lake was ringed by giants—not as huge as three-faced (not two-faced?) Satan, but six times the height of a normal man. Each had a beard some two meters long, covering his hairy chest, so that it was hard to tell where the beard left off and chest began.

Brother Paul approached the nearest. "I'm doing a survey," he called, showing his calculator. He was not sure the giant could either see it or hear him. "If you will assist me to the Eighth Circle. . . ."

To his surprise, the giant bent and extended one hand. Brother Paul climbed aboard and was quickly lifted to the top of the cliff. "Thank you," he said—but the giant turned his back, ignoring him.

He moved on, passing people who had their arms, legs or even heads cut off—yet they remained conscious and in pain. Falsifiers of some sort. Would Lee be among these because he had acted the role of Jesus? What was the definition of falsification? Surely not this!

Where *would* Lee be? Apollyon had been right: there were so many categories of evil in Hell and so many souls in each that he might search of the rest of his natural (or even his immortal) life and not find his man. Maybe that was what Satan had in mind. Brother Paul had to get smart and narrow it down, drastically. Carnal Sin? No, not Lee! Miser? No, probably not. Wrath? Well, maybe. . . .

Brother Paul paused, struck by the obvious that had not been obvious until this moment. It was not Lee and not Jesus he should be orienting on, but the *combination*. What part of Hell would this pair be in? Surely not among the Heretics, though after what he had seen of the Church Jesus' name had spawned—

Suddenly he had it. "The Schismatics!" he exclaimed. "Those who separated from the Mother Church." That would fit both Lee and Jesus—for Lee was a Mormon, certainly a schismatic sect, and Jesus himself could no longer accept without reservation the church that had tortured and even killed in his name.

The Schismatics were right here in the Eighth Circle along with the Seducers, Sorcerors, Thieves, Hypocrites, Liars, Evil Counselors, and other Frauds. Brother Paul did not agree with Dante's classifications, but had to work within the framework that obtained here. After all, the Romans had crucified Jesus between two thieves. When in Rome, when in Hell. . . .

He closed in on the Schismatic region, searching for Jesus/Lee's face. It seemed to be morning here—time varied magically in Hell—and a number of souls were rising from their uncomfortable slumbers on the rocks and ground. They seemed to be queuing up to pass around a certain big rock. Breakfast, maybe?

Why should anyone need to sleep or eat in Hell? They were all spirits! Well, neither literature nor religion had ever felt the need to make sense!

Brother Paul walked parallel to the line, his calculator

tabulating merrily. The men were naked, so he could not tell from observation what schism they were associated with. He wondered where the women were; didn't any females belong to the sects Dante frowned on? Dante had been fairly open-minded for his times, but circa 1300 was not a liberal period in Europe, as they had seen.

He circled the rock in the other direction from that taken by the line of souls. He came upon activity at the far side—

God, no! he cried internally. But it was so: a demon was wielding a great sword, striking at the people coming through. Not randomly, but with malicious precision. On one subject he lopped off the ears and nose; on another he laid open the chest; the next he disemboweled with a terrible vertical slash from neck to crotch.

The souls suffered these injuries without resistance, evasion, or even complaint. Gasping with agony, they clutched themselves and staggered on, bleeding. One had his entrails looping out through the wound in his stomach, dangling almost to the ground—yet he continued moving.

Brother Paul stepped out to intercept him, for the man looked familiar. "Sir, let me help you!" Yet he was not sure what he could do in the face of this horror.

"There is no help," the man responded. "This punishment is eternal for me. Help he who follows me; he is new here, not yet injured."

"Who are you?" Brother Paul asked, recognizing the actor now: Therion.

"I am Mahomet, founder of the Moslem Schism."

"Mohammed! But you're not even a Christian! You have no business in a Christian Hell!"

The man made a wry smile, forgetting his agony for an instant. "You may know that, I may know it. But Allah seems to have another opinion." He paused to suck in some of his gut. "Of course, Dante is in Muslim Hell, as befits an Infidel. So perhaps—"

"Paul!"

Brother Paul whirled around at the sound of his name. "Jesus!"

Jesus was a horrible sight. The demon had slashed him in the pattern of a cross, exposing his pulsating lungs, heart, liver, spleen, and part of a kidney. Yet he lived and moved. "What are you doing here, Paul? I thought I had exonerated you."

Brother Paul's shock at the sight of these gruesome wounds translated into baseless anger. "Nobody can exonerate me but *me*! I don't consider myself a sinner in the way you suppose—and if I did, I'd damn well suffer the punishment myself! No one else can be my surrogate!"

Jesus was silent. "Perhaps I can mediate," Mahomet suggested. "I have no direct interest in your quarrel."

"Who are you?" Jesus inquired.

"I am Mahomet, Prophet of Allah."

"I don't believe I know of you."

Mahomet smiled—a somewhat grisly effort since he was still holding in his guts. "Naturally not, Prophet. I came six hundred years after your time."

" 'Prophet'? I don't understand—"

"I call you that because that is how I regard you. There have been many prophets in the history of men, and you were—*are*—a great one. But the final prophecy to date is mine."

"Uh, perhaps a change of subject—" Brother Paul interjected.

"No, this man interests me," Jesus said. "There is nothing like a good philosophical discussion to take a man's mind from his physical problems. Please tell me about yourself, Prophet Mahomet."

Brother Paul shut up. What these men needed most at the moment was relief from their physical agony—and maybe while they talked he would be able to think of a more persuasive argument to get Jesus *out* of here.

"Gladly, Prophet Jesus! I was born in the city of Mecca—you may know of it as Mekkeh or some other variant—570 years after your own birth. That's approximate because of changes and errors in the calendar. My father died before my birth, and my mother passed on six years later, so I was raised by relatives.''

''You had no father?'' Jesus inquired.

''In a manner of speaking,'' Mahomet agreed. ''Allah may be the ultimate sire of us all, but a man requires human paternity too—a man to protect him and show him right from wrong.''

''Yes!'' Jesus agreed. ''That he may not be mocked.''

''That he may pass from the space of time in the womb when his life is a blank, and be shown how to seek refuge in the God of men, from the mischief of the slinking prompter who whispers in the hearts of men.''

''The mischief of Satan,'' Jesus agreed. ''You speak well, Prophet.''

Mahomet started to shrug, winced as his guts shifted, and aborted the motion. ''I speak only to guide men to the straight path, the path Allah favors.''

''Did you—marry? How did you die?''

''I married as a young man of 25,'' Mahomet said. ''She was a rich widow fifteen years my senior, but a good woman, and she put her commercial affairs in my hands. I was grieved when she died when I was 49.''

''But how could a Prophet share his love of God with a mere woman?'' Jesus asked.

''How could he fail to do so? Was not your blessed mother a woman, beloved of God?''

Jesus was not wholly satisfied. ''What do you know of my mother?'' And Brother Paul, who had met the lady in Paradiso, wondered also.

''She left her people and went out east alone,'' Mahomet said. ''God sent his spirit to her in the guise of a handsome man. When she saw him she was alarmed, fearing mischief. 'May the Merciful protect me! If you fear God, leave me alone!' she cried. But he replied 'I am the messenger of your God, and have come to give you a holy son.' And she, still alarmed, asked 'How shall I bear a child when I am a virgin, untouched by man?' But he said—''

''Uh, I'm not sure—'' Brother Paul broke in, remembering the manner Therion had Animated questions of sex before.

"But he said, 'Such is the will of your God,' " Mahomet continued firmly. " 'Your son shall be a sign to mankind, a blessing from Me. This is My decree.' Thereupon she conceived you, and the rest followed. Mary was blessed above all women—and blessed was the man Joseph who married her and gave the child of God a home. I would have had no shame to dwell in the house of Joseph the Carpenter, rather than in the house of an uncle."

"Yes," Jesus agreed, and it was evident what an impact these kind words from this unexpected source were having on him. "How did you come to serve directly, Prophet?"

"I was troubled by the iniquities I perceived about me," Mahomet said. "God had revealed His Will to the Jews and the Christians through chosen apostles. But the Jews corrupted the Scriptures, and the Christians perpetrated atrocities in the name of Jesus—"

"Yes!" Jesus echoed fervently.

"One day when I was forty, in a vision the Angel Gabriel came to me. 'Recite!' he charged me, and when I did not understand he repeated it three times, and said 'Recite in the name of God, who created man from clots of blood.' Then I understood that I must recite God's words, and so I spoke them and wrote them down and called that book *The Recital* or the Koran. Actually it was put together from my writings after my time, by idiots who simply arranged the pieces in order from the longest to the shortest, but still it serves."

"The Bible's organization is little better," Jesus murmured. "Accounts of my life and sayings were written a century after my time and ascribed to my Disciples and called Gospel. The major portion of my life and ministry was omitted. But I know now that matters little, for the people who call themselves Christians do not pay attention even to the fragments that were recorded. They do not love their neighbors." He grimaced. "And so you became a worker of miracles, a Son of God? Were you crucified also?"

"I never had the power to work miracles, and I was not the Son of God—and indeed I condemn the Christians for worshiping *you* as the Son of God."

"But—"

"I did not say you were *not* the Son of God. You were and are—"

"We *all* are," Brother Paul put in.

"But God commanded the people to worship Him, and none but Him. When they started worshiping you and all the Saints, they were perverting His directive. Because they had gone astray, the Angel Gabriel came to me and directed me to bring them back to the true religion as preached by Abraham, to absolute submission to His Will."

"Yes," Jesus agreed a trifle doubtfully. "And yet—"

"Yet the Christians have confined me in their Hell," Mahomet finished with a grim smile. "Because the true heretics are not those who schismed from the main mass of Christianity in order to worship God more properly. The true heretics are in charge of the Christian Church —and the Jewish Church. And—"

"And the Moslem Church?" Jesus inquired gently.

"*And* the Moslem Church," Mahomet agreed. "Do they think I do not see their hate, their alcoholic drinking, their sins? And those heretics of all churches condemn to Hell all who seek to expose their iniquity. God is merciful; the rulers of these Churches are not."

"And so you were killed?"

"No, I died naturally when I was no longer needed on Earth."

Jesus made a decision. "Prophet, I like your attitude. Your beliefs are not mine in all ways, but I believe you are qualified to settle the differences between Brother Paul and me."

"I will be happy to try," Mahomet said. "So long as it does not require much physical exertion. Our wounds will not heal until the night—and then each morning we must walk past the demon again. At the moment I cannot do more than talk."

They turned to Brother Paul. Well, why not? If this were a possible route to the release of his friend from this place. . . . "It is this," Brother Paul said. "I am of mixed descent. I have some, uh, Nubian blood. He feels this damns me, so for the sake of friendship, he endures my punishment. But I feel there is no crime in heredity, except perhaps in Original Sin, which taints all men equally. *Is* black blood a sin?"

"There is no crime in heredity," Mahomet said. "Any person who practices right belief and action is welcome to the house of Allah, the Compassionate, the Merciful. I regret that many who profess to follow my own prophecy do not seem to believe this, but it is so." He turned to Jesus, gesturing toward Brother Paul. "Is this such a man? One who honors God in his heart as well as with his lips?"

"Yes," Jesus said. "But—"

"I *seek* God," Brother Paul said. "I do not claim to have found Him or to be worthy of—"

"But if he were in some way flawed," Mahomet continued, "I would neither send him to Hell nor go in his place. I would forgive him."

"Forgive him . . ." Jesus said, as though this were a phenomenal revelation. "As God forgave man. . . ."

"Therefore," Brother Paul said quickly, "having done that, there is no need for you to suffer the tortures of Hell. Let's get out of here."

Jesus almost agreed. But then he balked. "You are forgiven—but who is to forgive *me*?"

"You? You are blameless!"

"Jesus is blameless, except perhaps for a matter of a fig tree. But the one who plays the role—and plays it imperfectly—that is another matter."

Brother Paul felt a premonition of disaster. He fought it off. "Let's get out of here. Then we can discuss it at leisure."

"No," Lee said with growing conviction. "I see now that I deceived myself and you. It was for my own crimes I came here. I am a Mormon, and—"

"What has that to do with it?" Brother Paul demanded desperately. "You have honored your creed."

"That has not been proven," Lee insisted. "I—"

"Then let's put it on trial," Mahomet said. "We shall have the proof soon enough."

A female demon appeared. In lieu of clothes she wore bright paint: rainbow rings around her breasts and a clown's mouth at her nether bifurcation. Another prime role for Amaranth! "Jesus Christ may leave Hell," she said. "His host may not, for his heritage is tainted."

"Ah, but *is* it?" Mahomet demanded. "What do you hold against him or his religion?"

"I passed through Utah once," the demoness said. "I saw a handsome man. 'Who is that?' I inquired. 'That is Brigham Young, leader of the Mormons,' my companion informed me. 'He has twenty seven wives.' 'Why, he ought to be hung!' I cried. My companion smiled. 'Lady, he *is*!' he replied." The demoness pointed to Lee. "His Church is polygamous!"

"But that is no sin," Mahomet protested. "Every man should have four wives, or more, depending on circumstances."

"Score one for the defense," Brother Paul murmured, hiding a smile. No, the Mohammedans would not condemn polygamy!

"Well, try *this* on for size!" the demoness said angrily. She whirled, made an obscene gesture with her bare posterior—and from it a cloud of smoke issued. The cloud developed color and character, and became a picture of a wagon train of the nineteenth century, wending its way through western America. "It is short of supplies," the demoness said from behind the picture. "The local inhabitants, intimidated by the Mormons, refused to see to it. They believed the train carried a shipment of gold, and they wanted that wealth." In the moving picture, Indians attacked. It seemed they would overwhelm the wagon train, but the men, women and children fought back desperately, and finally drove the Indians off.

The scene shifted. Now the leaders of the wagon train were talking with the Mormons. "The Mormons were on good terms with the Indians," the demoness explained. "They promised to guide the train safely through the hostile territory if the travelers surrendered their weapons so as not to seem to threaten the Indians." The picture showed the turnover of weapons and the resumption of travel.

"No!" Lee cried in the throes of an agony that seemed worse than that of his wounds.

"Yes!" the lady demon insisted gleefully. "It was a trap. The guide led the train into an exposed place. Indians attacked it again, and the guide joined the Indians, and this time massacred the defenseless travelers. The attack was led by Mormons, whose leader was John Doyle Lee."

"My namesake!" Lee said brokenly. "Betrayer and murderer! That name was passed along to me with such pride—"

Brother Paul winced. No wonder Lee was hurting! "But the fact that your namesake Lee may have been guilty of such a crime does not make the whole Mormon Church guilty," he protested. "Did the Mormons defend Lee's action?"

"No," Lee admitted. "He was tried and condemned. But—"

"And you can not be blamed for something that happened long before your birth," Brother Paul continued. "Can he, Mahomet?"

"I would not accept this version of original sin," Mahomet agreed.

"I'm not finished!" the lady demon said, reappearing. "This man is a member of a plagiarized faith."

"Plagiarized faith!" Lee exclaimed. "That's a hellish lie!"

"Say you so? Watch this," she cried, doing her bit with the smoke again. This time the scene was of a man writing a manuscript. "This is Solomon Spaulding, a Congregationalist minister and would-be author, writing a novel in 1810," she announced. "He wrote several novels, but never had them published. His interest was in the origin of the American Indians—the Amerinds, and he liked to conjecture about their possible connections with the people across the Atlantic Ocean. He died in 1816."

"That has nothing to do with me or my religion!" Lee protested.

The scene shifted. Now it was a blanket stretched

across a cabin. "This is Joseph Smith, founder of the Mormon Church," the demoness said. "He hides himself so that his amanuensis can not perceive him plagiarizing from Spaulding's novel, and the King James Bible, and other sources to fashion *The Book of Mormon.*"

"No!" Lee cried. "*The Book of Mormon* is a divine revelation!"

"And when it became too cumbersome dictating these divine revelations to the scribe, Smith simply used sheets from Spaulding's original manuscript. 'First Nephi' is an example."

"No!" But the cry sounded like that of a man with his neck in the guillotine.

"Then *you* explain the origin of *The Book of Mormon*," she challenged.

"It was written by members of the Nephite Nation, the last of whom was Moroni, who concealed the records at the place later called Cumorah, New York State. There these engraved plates of gold remained from A. D. 400 until A. D. 1827, when the resurrected Moroni gave them to Joseph Smith for translation and publication. This translation is *The Book of Mormon.*"

"The prosecution rests," the demoness said. "Do you still believe that moronic legend?"

And Lee was silent.

"That *is* a problem," Mahomet said. "If your entire religion is based on a lie—"

"No!" Brother Paul cried. "Maybe the origins of the Mormons are suspect, or maybe it is all a great libel. It doesn't matter! What matters is what the religion is *today*. Many worthy religions have foundered when their adherents forgot their original principles—but here is a religion that became greater than its origin! The Mormons today constitute one of the most powerful forces for good on Earth. Their uprightness stands in stark contrast to the hypocrisy of so many of the more conventional religions. Therefore, there is no crime in this man who has faithfully honored the fine principles of his faith. Let us crucify no more people for being better than *we* are!"

Lee seemed stunned. The demoness, a look of sheer fury on her pretty face, faded away. Mahomet shook his head thoughtfully. "Yes, Brother, I believe you are correct. We must judge what *is*, not what *was*. On that basis—"

"To hell with what was!" Brother Paul cried. "This man is as much like Jesus Christ as a contemporary man can be. He belongs among the living."

"What *is*," Lee repeated. "I have been haunted by what *was*." Then his face glowed—literally. "We have no further business in Hell," Jesus said. "Hell itself has no business existing. Prophets like Mahomet and good men like Brother Paul—what the Hell are they doing in Hell! I never preached hellfire; I preached forgiveness—for men and for institutions." He stood straight, and his horrible wounds closed and healed in seconds. He gestured to Mahomet—and the Prophet's guts folded back into his body cavity, and the skin sealed smoothly around them. "Come, friends—we must abolish this atrocity." And he strode back toward the rock where the demon was still hacking helpless souls apart. All along the way he gestured at the wounded: "Rise, take up your bodies, and follow me!" And they were restored.

The demon glanced up as Jesus approached. "What, healed already?" it exclaimed. "I'll split you in two!" And it struck hard.

The sword bounced off Jesus's flesh and broke into two fragments. The demon stared, then backed away. Then, as Jesus continued advancing, the demon screamed in terror and fled.

The healed souls gathered around. "We are saved!" they cried joyfully. They closed ranks and marched behind like a swelling army. They sang hymns of victory. Before them all the legions of demons were seized with terror and scrambled out of the way. Hell was in revolt.

Down they marched into the frozen Ninth Circle— and the ice cracked and shattered as the souls buried within it came to life to join the throng. Even the giants ringing this circle merged with the marchers, and the sheer cliff crumbled to form a gently sloping ramp.

They came in sight of monstrous Satan Himself.
Jesus paused. "O Thou Prince of Destruction," he
cried indignantly, "the scorn of God's angels, loathed
by all righteous persons! Why didst thou venture
without either reason or justice to bring to this region a
person innocent and righteous? Suffer now the penalty
of—"

"No, wait!" Brother Paul cried, putting a restraining
hand on Jesus' rising arm. "Even Satan has only been
doing His job. You must forgive Him also!"

"Forgive *Satan?*" Jesus was amazed, and so were
Mahomet and all the multitude of regenerate souls.

"Besides," Brother Paul continued, remembering. "I
haven't finished my survey of souls." And he showed
his calculator still zipping through the numbers. "It
would be false pretenses to start a survey and then incite
a riot."

Jesus paused, glancing at Mahomet. Then, as one,
they burst out laughing. Suddenly all Hell was laughing,
even the demons. A mad tangle of bodies formed as
laughing souls collapsed upon each other. And,
overriding it deafeningly, came the laughter of Satan
Himself: "HO HO HO HO HO!"

Hell dissolved into chaos. Like smoke it lifted,
leaving them standing in a valley, laughing un-
controllably.

XI

Transfer: 19

There is a story about a man who wished to reward three of his faithful employees. To each he offered the choice between a lump of gold worth a small fortune—and a Bible. The first employee considered both, but he was not a religious man, and so he took the gold. The second employee wrestled with his conscience for some time, but finally, apologetically, explained that he had a family with sick children and many debts and had to take the gold. The third, though obviously tempted by the gold, finally settled on the Bible. When he opened it, bills of high denomination fell out from between the pages. In their aggregate, they amounted to much more than the value of the gold had been.

The obvious moral of this story is that by seeking faith instead of worldly riches, a person may acquire more riches than he would otherwise have done. The problem is that this justifies the Bible not for itself, but for the profit that may be in it. That is a perversion of the Bible's meaning. When people use the Bible as a means to promote the acquisition of wealth, the moneychangers have surely taken over the Temple, and Christianity has become merely another business.

In the distance the two outside watchers stood. "This time let's make sure we have the child," Brother Paul said as his laughter subsided.

But it was all right, for Amaranth and a smaller figure were walking toward them. This time all of them were emerging!

"The child!" Mrs. Ellend exclaimed as the parties joined. "You found her!"

"You all have emerged," Pastor Runford said darkly. "But are you all sane? You were laughing crazily when the mist lifted."

"We are all sane," Brother Paul said. "But it wasn't easy."

"Not easy at all!" Lee agreed shakily, running one hand cautiously over his chest.

"You must rest," Mrs. Ellend said. "Tomorrow we shall hear your report."

"I'm not sure we're ready to make a full report," Brother Paul said, glancing at Lee.

"You make me very curious what occurs within those Animations," Mrs. Ellend said. "We perceive only the fringe effects. When you went in this time, there seemed to be a landscape with a river and a tree, but then a storm obscured the tree. When it cleared we saw the Sphinx."

"And the Great Pyramid," Pastor Runford put in gruffly. "The Bible in Stone. Analysis of its measurements reveals the coming of Armageddon. Jehovah inspired Pharaoh to build it according to a secret key—"

"But the Pyramid is Matter," Mrs. Ellend protested. "The realm of the real is Spiritual, not Material. Matter is an error of statement. All disease is illusion; Jesus established this fundamental fact when he cast out devils and made people well."

"Jesus was a good man," Lee murmured, his eyes closed. "We would do well to pay better heed to his values today."

"At any rate, after a time the Sphinx faded, replaced by what seemed to be an Earthly airline terminal," Mrs. Ellend continued. "Then it became opaque until just now when there seemed to be giants moving in flames. Could that have been someone's concept of the Infernal Region?"

"There *is* no Infernal Region!" the Pastor exclaimed. "The concept is a mistranslation of the Hebrew word *Sheol*, meaning the grave."

"There is Hell," Mrs. Ellend said. "It exists in life. It is error, hatred, lust, sickness, and sin."

"Yes!" Lee agreed. "Nothing in the Afterlife can match the tortures we inflict upon ourselves in *this* life."

"Oh, I don't know about that," Therion began. "Satan has resources—"

"Please, can we go home?" the child asked plaintively. "I'm very tired."

"Of course, child," Mrs. Ellend said, softening. "Your father will be happy to see you—" She broke off.

"Condition unchanged?" Lee inquired guardedly.

Mrs. Ellend nodded gravely. "I shall try to talk to him; perhaps I can make him understand that his malady is illusory. But perhaps—" She turned to Amaranth. "Perhaps this child could stay with you tonight. You have shared much experience—"

"What's the matter with my father?" Carolyn demanded. She was a brown-haired girl of about twelve, somewhat dark complexioned in contrast to the rather fair girl of the Animation. Her dress was rumpled and soiled by her long stay in the wilderness, and her locks were tangled.

"The Swami is unconscious," Pastor Runford said. "He sought you during the last rift in Animation and suffered himself."

Brother Paul was chagrined. "The Swami—her natural father?"

"He was opposed to this experiment," Pastor Runford said. "As many of us were. I differ with him on many things, but on this he was reasonable. But since we were overruled by the majority, he felt a representative of our view should be within the Animation area. His daughter agreed to be a Watcher. When all emerged safely except her, he must have been distracted. He has already suffered grievously from the things of this planet."

"Bigfoot killed my mother," the girl said. Brother Paul still thought of her as Carolyn.

"This is horrible!" Brother Paul exclaimed. "I never suspected—"

"Perhaps we should have informed you of these things," Mrs. Ellend said soberly. "But under the Covenant—"

"Come home with me," Amaranth told Carolyn.

"No! I want to go with Brother Paul," she cried.

Surprised and flattered, Brother Paul put out his hand to her. "I am staying with the Reverend Siltz. I'm not sure he would approve."

"Go with him," Lee said. "We can make other arrangements as necessary."

Carolyn flashed Lee a grateful smile. "Thank you, sir."

"The group of you appear to have developed an unusual rapport," Mrs. Ellend observed. "My female curiosity wars with my scientific detachment. I wonder whether the entire colony would benefit from immersion in Animation?"

"Appalling!" Pastor Runford exclaimed.

"We have undergone phenomenal mutual experience," Therion said. "But I doubt the full colony would survive it, let alone profit by it."

Now they reached the village and separated. Brother Paul took Carolyn to Siltz's house. The Reverend was not there—but Jeanette was. The diminutive suitor of the Communist's son sat with her back against the door, weaving a basket from flexible strips of wood. "I am lurking for the Reverend," she announced. "I want to know what he thinks of trial marriage."

Reverend Siltz would explode! But this was not properly Brother Paul's business. "I think it would be all right to wait inside," he said. "I am his house guest, and if you could help—" He indicated the bedraggled Carolyn.

"What is the Swami's child doing with you?" Jeanette demanded.

"She is tired from a long ordeal in Animation, and

her father is ill,'' Brother Paul explained. That was an oversimplification, but it would have to do.

"Of course I'll help,'' Jeanette said, deciding in a flash. "Come on in, child; we'll get you cleaned in a jiffy.'' She took the girl by the arm, guiding her. The woman was barely taller than the child, but there was no confusing the two: Carolyn was thin and somewhat awkward, while Jeanette was full-bodied and decisive. In moments they were busy in the wash area, and Brother Paul sank into a wooden chair, relieved.

Soon they joined him. Carolyn was now clean, and her hair was neatly brushed. "You're awful nice,'' she told Jeanette. "Since my mother died, I never—''

"No need to dwell on that,'' Jeanette said.

"I *have* to,'' Carolyn said. "When I get tired I get scared, and I'm awful tired, and I have to tell *someone* or I can't sleep.''

Jeanette's brow furrowed. "What are you afraid of?''

"Bigfoot. He prowls around, and he killed my mother, and now he's prowling for me. I hear him coming, and I scream—''

"I would have thought that was a foolish fear,'' Brother Paul said. "But I met Bigfoot when we were searching for you. He went after Amaranth—''

"Who?'' Jeanette asked.

"The woman of I.A.O.,'' Brother Paul explained. "I don't know her real name, but she watches the amaranth field, so—''

"She does look a little like my mother,'' Carolyn said. "Bigfoot probably got confused.''

"I tried to stop Bigfoot,'' Brother Paul continued. "But it was stronger. If the Breaker hadn't come—''

"I know,'' Carolyn said. "I was coming out, but then I saw Bigfoot, and I had to run back into my fantasy city.''

"Bigfoot ran into the Animation too,'' Brother Paul said. "I'm glad he didn't catch you.'' Understatement of the day!

"I made a big river, and he couldn't get across,'' she

said, smiling. "When I was alone, I could control the effect some. Bigfoot stormed and ranted, but it couldn't get me. But oh, it scared me!" Her shoulders shook.

Brother Paul got up and put his arm around her shoulders, holding her close. "You father the Swami can surely protect you."

"Bigfoot only comes when he's away!" she cried. "That's how Bigfoot got my mother! It waited until my father was away, and—"

Jeanette frowned. "Bigfoot does prowl around a lot. I thought it was just a nuisance from when the storms bring the Animation fringe. But with your father out of circulation—" She glanced up. "Why is Bigfoot after you? Why did it kill your mother?"

"I don't *know*!" Carolyn cried. "It hates my father, and—"

Brother Paul squeezed her shoulders reassuringly. "It is a comprehensible, if not defensible syndrome. The Swami knows martial art and has very strong psychic force. Bigfoot may resent him, but be unable to overcome him directly, so it tries to hurt him through those close to him. His family."

Carolyn put her face against his chest and cried. "That's why I wanted to be with you," she sobbed. "I'm not close to my father, really; we're of different religions. I thought somehow—you're so strong and patient, you'd make such a good father—I thought we could just get on an airplane and go away somewhere where they never heard of Animation, where Bigfoot couldn't ever find me—oh, I'm *sorry!*"

"So it was *your* Animation, rather than mine," Brother Paul said, amazed. "I thought I had emerged from Animation—"

Carolyn tore herself away from him—but Jeanette caught her and held her instead. "Dear child! There's nothing wrong in wanting a real family. That's worth fighting for! That's what *I'm* fighting for. The only thing wrong is to give up your dream."

"But it didn't work!" Carolyn sobbed. "We had such a wonderful time for a while, visiting his old

school, but then I started being afraid *he* would
—would—something terrible would happen to him.
Because of me. And then it all went wrong, and we got
on the wrong plane and lost in the station, and it was all
my fault—"

"It *wasn't* your fault!" Brother Paul cried. "It
wasn't your Animation, either! You may have started it,
but I—"

"So I sneaked away, so as not to be a burden to him
anymore—"

"You nearly destroyed me!" Brother Paul cried. "I
was afraid you would get abducted or run over—"

"No, I just got in another Animation, like the other
one, when I played the Buddha—"

"*You* played Buddha?" Brother Paul demanded. Yet
her size and appearance jibed. Change the hair—easily
done in Animation!—and she could resemble a little
man, sitting under the Bo Tree. He had found her
without knowing it!

"Yes. I know about Indian history because of my
religion, so it was easy to—"

"What *is* your religion?"

"I worship the Nine Unknown Men. My mother
taught me. My father didn't like it too much, but since it
relates some to his religion, he let it be."

"I don't know that religion," Brother Paul said.
"Tell me about it."

Carolyn disengaged from Jeanette. "I'm okay now, I
think. It—I'll have to start at the beginning, if it doesn't
bother you. After what I did to you—"

Brother Paul looked her in the eyes. "One thing we
must get straight. You did nothing to me. Nothing bad,
I mean. You showed me something about myself I never
suspected before. I want a family too! I want a daughter
like you."

She brightened. "You do?"

"I was confused at first in that Animation. I thought
I was back in—in the mundane world, as I said. I knew I
didn't have a daughter, so it took me some time to ac-
climatize. But when I did—" He spread his hands. "I

took over that sequence and carried it forward the way I wanted it to go. Now I can't get used to the notion of *not* having a daughter like you.''

"Daughters are good too," Jeanette agreed. "Sons and daughters.''

"But you are the child of another man," Brother Paul said to Carolyn. "I am here for a few days; then I will be gone. I cannot take anyone with me; Earth spent more energy than it liked sending me here, and that's the limit. The Swami is your real father. I would not contribute to the alienation of—" He had to stop. *Why couldn't she have been his child?* He would so gladly have taken her away from all this, back to Earth and—

He came up abruptly against reality. And what? Even if Earth were to allow another person to mattermit, there was no life he could provide for her back on Earth! In the Animation he had been married with a home to take her back to. In real life his home was the Holy Order of Vision. A fine institution, but no substitute for a personal family. "Explain your religion," he concluded.

"Well, it started with Asoka," she said. "The Emperor Asoka of India who was born in 273 B.C. He was the grandson of Chandra-gupta who unified India. But there was still some land to add. So Asoka conquered Kalinga. His army killed a hundred thousand men in battle. When he saw all that gore he was horrified at such massacre. He renounced that kind of conquest and declared that the only true conquest was to win men's hearts. By being kind and dutiful and pious, and letting all creatures be free to live as they pleased. So he converted to Buddhism—"

"Beautiful!" Jeanette murmured.

"He was such a good Buddhist that a lot of other people joined too. Buddhism spread through India and Ceylon and Indon—Indon—"

"Indonesia," Brother Paul supplied.

"Yes. I can't remember all those otherworld names as well as my mother could. But Asoka respected all religions; he didn't *make* anybody turn Buddhist, and he didn't prosecute—is that right?"

"*Per*secute," Brother Paul said.

"You sure would make a good Daddy! He let each religion do its own thing, a little like the way it is here, only without all the screaming. He was a vegetarian, and he wouldn't touch alcohol. I think he was the best monarch ever!"

"History agrees," Brother Paul said. "Asoka was one of the finest."

"But he knew he wouldn't rule forever. He wanted to stop men from using their minds for evil. So he founded the wonderful secret society to do this. That's the Nine Unknown Men."

"But that was thousands of years ago," Jeanette protested. "What happened after they died?"

"They trained new men, each generation. So there have always been nine, right up till today, and each one is the wisest man there is. They have a secret language, and each one writes a book on his science. One knows psychology. Another knows fizz—"

"Physiology," Brother Paul said.

"Yes. He knows so much about it that he can kill a man just by touching him. Some of his secrets leaked once, and now they are used in judo."

"Judo!" Brother Paul exclaimed.

"That's a way of fighting," she said helpfully.

"Uh, yes, I understand. That strikes me as an excellent religion. But how do you know the identities of these Nine Men?"

"I *don't*. Nobody does. Except themselves. But I worship what they do because they are working to save us all. They are around somewhere, and—" She paused shyly. "Well, I think maybe—I don't know—my father the Swami Kundalini might be one. He knows so much—"

Brother Paul looked past her—and there stood the Reverend Siltz in the doorway. Brother Paul jumped up. "I didn't see you, Reverend!" he cried. "We were just—"

"I have been here for some time," Siltz said. "I did not wish to interrupt the child."

Jeanette turned. "Reverend, I came to—" She looked

at Carolyn, not wanting to bring up such a subject in the hearing of the child. "It doesn't matter now. I'll go."

Siltz pointed a finger at her. "The first grandson. Also the first granddaughter. Communist."

Jeanette's eyes widened. "You proffer compromise?"

"Granddaughters are good too," Siltz said defensively. "Sometimes even better than grandsons."

"I will not bargain for religion!" Jeanette said. "Anything else, not that. *All* will be Scientologist."

"*Now* who's the pighead?" Siltz demanded. "My son is outside."

"That's dirty fighting!" she cried.

"All's fair in love and war," Siltz said. "I am not certain which one this is or whether it is both. The first two children—even if both are female. My final offer!"

"I will not speak to you!" Jeanette flounced out. It was an impressive exit.

Siltz looked after her. He smiled grimly. "Two granddaughters like *her*. Church of Communism. They would convert the whole planet!"

"I did not realize your son was back," Brother Paul said. "I—"

"You want a daughter. So do I," Siltz said. "Do not be concerned. There is room. My son will not sleep here tonight."

"Oh, I would not think of—"

"I do not know where Ivan will sleep or what he will do," Siltz continued sternly. "But tomorrow—we shall see who is ready to compromise."

Brother Paul thought of Jeanette, vibrant in her ire, encountering the young man outside. The man she loved and wanted to marry. "She's right. You *are* fighting dirty."

Siltz nodded with deep satisfaction.

"It's like the Dozens," Carolyn said, smiling. "You have to turn the other person's thrust on himself."

"A dozen what?" Siltz asked.

"Never mind that!" Brother Paul snapped more to her than to him. From whose mind had come those sickening insults of the Dozens in that scene? He squeezed out that conjecture and oriented on Siltz. "I have a problem. As you may have overheard, we had considerable adventures in Animation—but I cannot say we found God. I am not sure it is *possible* to find God this way. Yet I hate to disappoint the colony."

Siltz considered. "I have only imperfect knowledge of your experience in Animation. But from what I overheard, you found the greatest meaning in the personal visions, not those of religion. Could it be you are looking in the wrong place?"

"But my mission is to find God, not to amuse myself!"

"You seemed closer to God when you put your arm about this child and comforted her, than when you talked religion." Siltz glanced at Carolyn who was in a chair. "She sleeps."

Just like that! One moment she was ready to discuss the Dozens; the next she had clicked out. Adults tended to lose that ability, which made them safer drivers but also less endearing. "She had a long, hard haul," Brother Paul agreed. "How can I find God by catering to my wish for a child?"

"You made the obvious plain to me, a better way to heat my house—by *not* heating it. Perhaps you could find God better—by finding yourself. You must believe you are worthy to judge God."

"I'll never believe that! I'm *not* worthy to judge God! I have seen depths of depravity in me that make me unfit to judge *anyone*! I—" Brother Paul stopped. "*That's* why I can't complete this mission. I know I'm not—"

"Then what are you worthy to find?"

"Satan," Brother Paul said morosely. "We had a small vision of Hell just before we emerged from Animation. I seek God—but I fear my affinities are closer to the Devil."

"Is not Satan also a God?"

Brother Paul stared at him. "You mean—I should search for Satan?"

"I cannot answer that. I only know that when I looked well at the little devil who pursued my son, I found a certain affinity for her. I saw how gentle she was with the child. So in examining the devil, I discovered instead an angel. I do not believe in your Satan—but is it possible he too would have merits? Perhaps he only seems evil because we do not understand him well enough.''

Brother Paul paced about the small room. "Somehow I am reminded of the Temperance card of Tarot. A woman pouring water from one jug into another, as if oxygenating it, renewing its life. Pouring a soul from one vessel to another, transferring the essence of a person from one life to another. Maybe from Earth to Hell. And you—you are transferring my thrust from one direction to another. Maybe, with precession, it would work.''

"We must all look where we must look," Siltz agreed, "and do what we must do. Some orient on gold, others on the Bible—but who is to say who is right and who wrong—or whether there *are* such things as right and wrong? It is obvious that Heaven has more merit than Hell—yet what is obvious is not necessarily true.''

Brother Paul nodded thoughtfully. He was thinking of the way huge Satan in Dante's Inferno had winked at him. Surely that was a shallow concept of Satan, one that could be laughed off—and indeed they had done just that. But what would happen if he now went to interview the *real* Satan? He had been more or less a spectator in a framework designed for Lee's torture. This time the torture would be attuned to Paul himself.

Yet as he pondered, it seemed increasingly necessary. He had tried to examine the Gods of others from an objective standpoint and failed because he did not know enough about them. He had tried to examine his own Christian religion and failed again. The answer, ultimately, had to lie within himself—and to know himself, he would have to put himself to the test. Only then would be able to prove his own fitness to judge God. As Lee had put himself to the test in his Hell—and found, after suffering and doubt, vindication.

The surest test of Brother Paul himself would be found in his own, personal Hell.

Appendix

ANIMATION TAROT

The Animation Tarot deck of concepts as recreated by Brother Paul of the Holy Order of Vision consists of thirty Triumphs roughly equivalent to the twenty-two Trumps of contemporary conventional Tarot decks, together with five variously titled suits roughly equivalent to the four conventional suits plus Aura. Each suit is numbered from one through ten, with the addition of four "Court" cards. The thirty Triumphs are represented by the table of contents of this novel, and keys to their complex meanings and derivations are to be found within the applicable chapters. For convenience the Triumphs are represented below, followed by a tabular representation of the suits, with their meanings or sets of meanings (for upright and reversed fall of the cards); the symbols are described by the italicized words. Since the suits are more than mere collections of concepts, five essays relating to their fundamental nature follow the chart.

No Animation Tarot deck exists in published form at present. Brother Paul used a pack of three-by-five-inch file cards to represent the one hundred concepts, simply writing the meanings on each card and sketching the symbols himself, together with any other notes he found pertinent. These were not as pretty or convenient as published cards, but were satisfactory for divination, study, entertainment, business and meditation as required. A full discussion of each card and the special conventions relating to the Animation deck would be too complicated to cover here, but those who wish to make up their own decks and use them should discover revelations of their own. According to Brother Paul's vision of the future, this deck will eventually be published, perhaps in both archaic (Waldens) and future (Cluster) forms, utilizing in the first case medieval images and in the second case images drawn from the myriad cultures of the Galactic Cluster, circa 4500 A.D. It hardly seems worthwhile for interested persons to wait for that.

SUIT CARDS

	NATURE	SCIENCE	FAITH	TRADE	ART
1	Do *Scepter*	Think *Sword*	Feel *Cup*	Have *Coin*	Be *Lemniscate*
2	Ambition Drive *Torch*	Health Sickness *Scalpel*	Quest Dream *Grail*	Inclusion Exclusion *Ring*	Soul Self *Aura*
3	Grow Shrink *Tree*	Intelligence Curiosity *Maze*	Bounty Windfall *Cornucopia*	Gain Loss *Wheel*	Perspective Experience *Holograph*
4	Leverage Travel *Lever*	Decision Commitment *Pen*	Joy Sorrow *Pandora's Box*	Investment Inheritance *Gears*	Information Literacy *Book*
5	Innovation Suspicion *Hand of Glory*	Equilibrium Stasis *Kite*	Security Confinement *Lock*	Permanence Evanescence *Pentacle*	Balance Judgment *Scales*
6	Advance Retreat *Bridge*	Freedom Restraint *Balloon*	Temptation Guilt *Bottle*	Gift Theft *Package*	Change Stagnation *Möbius Strip*
7	Effort Error *Ladder*	Peace War *Plow*	Promise Threat *Ship*	Defense Vulnerability *Shield*	Beauty Ugliness *Face*
8	Power Impotence *Rocket*	Victory Defeat *Flag*	Satisfaction Disappointment *Mirror*	Success Failure *Crown*	Conscience Ruthlessness *Yin-Yang*
9	Accomplishment Conservation *Trophy*	Truth Error *Key*	Love Hate *Klein Bottle*	Wealth Poverty *Money*	Light Dark *Lamp*

SUIT CARDS (Continued)

	NATURE	SCIENCE	FAITH	TRADE	ART
10	Hunger *Phallus*	Survival *Seed*	Reproduction *Womb*	Dignity *Egg*	Image *Compost*
	ENERGY	GAS	LIQUID	SOLID	PLASMA

COURT CARDS

	NATURE	SCIENCE	FAITH	TRADE	ART
PAGE	Child of Fire	Child of Air	Child of Water	Child of Earth	Child of Aura
KNIGHT	Youth of Work	Youth of Trouble	Youth of Love	Youth of Money	Youth of Spirit
QUEEN	Lady of Activity	Lady of Conflict	Lady of Emotion	Lady of Status	Lady of Expression
KING	Man of Nature	Man of Science	Man of Faith	Man of Trade	Man of Art
	ENERGY	GAS	LIQUID	SOLID	PLASMA

TRIUMPHS

0 Folly (Fool)
1 Skill (Magician)
2 Memory (High Priestess)
∞ Unknown (Ghost)
3 Action (Empress)
4 Power (Emperor)
5 Intuition (Hierophant)
6 Choice (Lovers)
7 Precession (Chariot)
8 Emotion (Desire)
9 Discipline (Strength)
10 Nature (Family)
11 Chance (Wheel of Fortune)
12 Time (Sphinx)
13 Reflection (Past)
14 Will (Future)
15 Honor (Justice)
16 Sacrifice (Hanged Man)
17 Change (Death)
18 Vision (Imagination)
19 Transfer (Temperence)
20 Violence (Devil)
21 Revelation (Lightning-Struck Tower)
22 Hope/Fear (Star)
23 Deception (Moon)
24 Triumph (Sun)
25 Reason (Thought)
26 Decision (Judgment)
27 Wisdom (Savant)
28 Completion (Universe)

NATURE

The Goddess of Fertility was popular in spring. Primitive peoples believed in sympathetic magic: that the examples of men affect the processes of nature— that human sexuality makes the plants more fruitful. To make sure nature got the message, they set up the Tree of Life, which was a giant phallus, twice the height of a man, pointing stiffly into the sky. Nubile young women capered about it, singing and wrapping it with bright ribbons. This celebration settled on the first day of May, and so was called May Day, and the phallus was called the Maypole. The modern promotion of May Day by Communist countries has led to its decline in the Western world, but its underlying principle remains strong. The Maypole is the same Tree of Life found in the Garden of Eden, and is represented in the Tarot deck of cards as the symbol for the Suit of Nature: an upright rod formed of living, often sprouting wood. This suit is variously titled Wands, Staffs, Scepters, Batons, or, in conventional cards, Clubs. Life permeates it; it is the male principle, always ready to grow and plant its seed. It also relates to the classic "element" of Fire, and associates with all manner of firearms, rockets, and explosives. In religion, this rod becomes the scepter or crozier, and it can also be considered the measuring rod of faith, the "canon."

FAITH

The true source of the mutliple legends of the Grail is
unknown. Perhaps this famous chalice was originally a
female symbol used in pagan fertility rites, a coun-
terpart to the phallic Maypole. But it is best known in
Christian mythology as the goblet formed from a single
large emerald, from which Jesus Christ drank at the
Last Supper. It was stolen by a servant of Pontius
Pilate, who washed his hands from it when the case of
the presumptuous King of the Jews came before him.
When Christ was crucified, a rich Jew, who had been
afraid before to confess his belief, used this cup to catch
some of the blood that flowed from Jesus's wounds.
This man Joseph deposited Jesus's body in his own
tomb, from which Jesus was resurrected a few days
later. But Joseph himself was punished; he was im-
prisoned for years without proper care. He received
food, drink and spiritual sustenance from the Grail,
which he retained, so that he survived. When he was
released, he took the Grail to England, where he settled
in 63 A.D. He began the conversion of that region to
Christianity. The Grail was handed to his successors
from generation to generation until it came at last to Sir
Galahad of King Arthur's Round Table. Only the chaste
were able even to perceive it. The Grail may also relate
to the Cornucopia, or Horn of Plenty, the ancient sym-

bol of the bounty of growing things. It is the cup of love and faith and fruitfulness, the container of the classic "element" of water, and the symbol of the essential female nature (i.e., the womb) represented in the Suit of Cups of the Tarot.

TRADE

It is intriguing to conjecture which of the human instincts is strongest. Many people assume it is sex, the reproductive urge—but an interesting experiment seems to refute that. A group of volunteers including several married couples was systematically starved. As hunger intensified, the pin-up pictures of girls were replaced by pictures of food. The sex impulse decreased, and some couples broke up. Food dominated the conversation. This suggests that hunger is stronger than sex. Similarly, survival—the instinct of self-preservation—seems stronger than hunger, for a starving person will not eat food he knows is poisoned, or drink salt water when dehydrating on a raft in the ocean. This hierarchy of instincts seems reasonable, for any species must secure its survival before it can successfully reproduce its kind. Yet there may be an even more fundamental instinct than these. When the Jews were confined brutally in Nazi concentration death-camps, they co-operated with each other as well as they could, sharing their belongings and scraps of food in a civilized manner. There, the last thing to go was personal dignity. The Nazis did their utmost to destroy the dignity of the captives, for people who retained their pride had not been truly conquered. Thus dignity, or status, or the perception of self-worth, may be the strongest human instinct. It is represented in the Tarot as the Suit of Disks, or Pentacles, or Coins, and associates with the "element" Earth, and with money (the ignorant person's status), and business or trade. Probably the original symbol was the blank disk of the Sun (gold) or Moon (silver).

MAGIC

In the Garden of Eden, Adam and Eve were tempted by the Serpent to eat of the fruit of the Tree of Knowledge of Good and Evil. The fruit is unidentified; popularly it is said to be the apple (i.e., breast), but was more probably the banana (i.e., phallus). Obviously the forbidden knowledge was sexual. There was a second special Tree in the Garden: the Tree of Life, which seems to have been related. Since the human couple's acquisition of sexual knowledge and shame caused them to be expelled from Eden and subject to the mortality of Earthly existence, they had to be provided an alternate means to preserve their kind. This was procreation—linked punitively to their sexual transgression. Thus the fruit of "knowledge" led to the fruit of "life," forever tainted by the Original Sin.

Naturally the couple would have escaped this fate if they could, by sneaking back into Eden. To prevent re-entry to the Garden, God set a flaming sword in the way. This was perhaps the origin of the symbol of the Suit of Swords of the Tarot, representing the "element" of air. The Sword associates with violence (war), and with science (scalpel) and intellect (intangible): God's manifest masculinity. Yet this vengeful if versatile weapon was transformed in Christian tradition into the symbol of Salvation: the Crucifix, in turn transformed by the bending of its extremities into the Nazi Swastica. And so as man proceeds from the ancient faith of Magic to the modern speculation of Science, the Sword proceeds inevitably from the Garden of Eden . . . to Hell.

ART

Man is frightened and fascinated by the unknown. He seeks in diverse ways to fathom what he does not comprehend, and when it is beyond his power to do this, he invents some rationale to serve in lieu of the truth. Perhaps the religious urge can be accounted for in this way, and also man's progress into civilization: man's insatiable curiosity driving him to the ultimate reaches of experience. Yet there remain secrets: the origin of the universe, the smallest unit of matter, the nature of God, and a number of odd phenomena. Do psychics really commune with the dead? How does water dowsing work? Is telepathy possible? What about faith healing? Casting out demons? Love at first contact? Divination? Ghosts?

Many of these inexplicable phenomena become explicable through the concept of aura. If the spirit or soul of man is a patterned force permiating the body and extending out from it with diminishing intensity, the proximity of two or more people would cause their surrounding auras to interpenetrate. They could thus become aware of each other on more than a physical basis. They might pick up each other's thoughts or feelings, much as an electronic receiver picks up broadcasts or the coil of a magnetic transformer picks up power. A dowser might feel his aura interacting with water deep in the ground, and so know the water's location. A person with a strong aura might touch one who was ill, and the strong aura could recharge the weak one and help the ill person recover the will to live. A man and a woman might find they had highly compatible auras, and be strongly attracted to each other. An evil aura might impinge on a person, and have to be exorcised. And after the physical death of the body, or host, an aura might float free, a spirit or ghost, able to communicate only with specially receptive individuals, or mediums.

In short, the concept of aura or spirit can make much of the supernatural become natural. It is represented in the Animation Tarot deck as the Suit of Aura, symbolized in medieval times by a lamp and in modern times by a lemniscate (infinity symbol: ∞), and embracing a fifth major human instinct or drive: art, or expression. Only man, of all the living creatures on Earth, cares about the esthetic nature of things. Only man appreciates painting, and sculpture, and music, and dancing, and literature, and mathematical harmonies, and ethical proprieties, and all the other forms and variants of artistic expression. Where man exists, these things exist—and when man passes on, these thing remain as evidence of his unique nature. Man's soul, symbolized as art, distinguishes him from the animals.